D0097897

BREATHING BOOKS

Cornelia Funke

RECKLESS

The Petrified Flesh

Book I

A MirrorWorld Novel

With Illustrations by the Author
Translated by Oliver Latsch

Breathing Books · Los Angeles

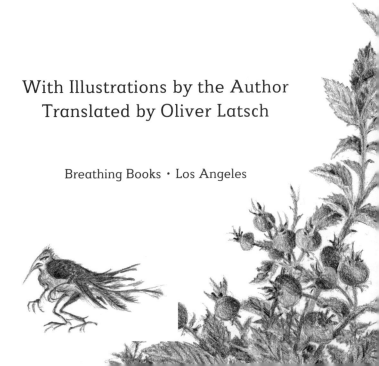

Inspired by a tale discovered and explored with Lionel Wigram.

Second Edition, Originally published under the title *Reckless*: September 2016

10 9 8 7 6 5 4 3 2 1

Book design by Mirada
Printed in Canada

For Lionel, who found the door to this story and who so often knew more about it than I did, friend and finder of ideas, indispensable on either side of the mirror.

And for Oliver, who again and again tailored English clothes for this story so that the Englishman and the German could tell it together.

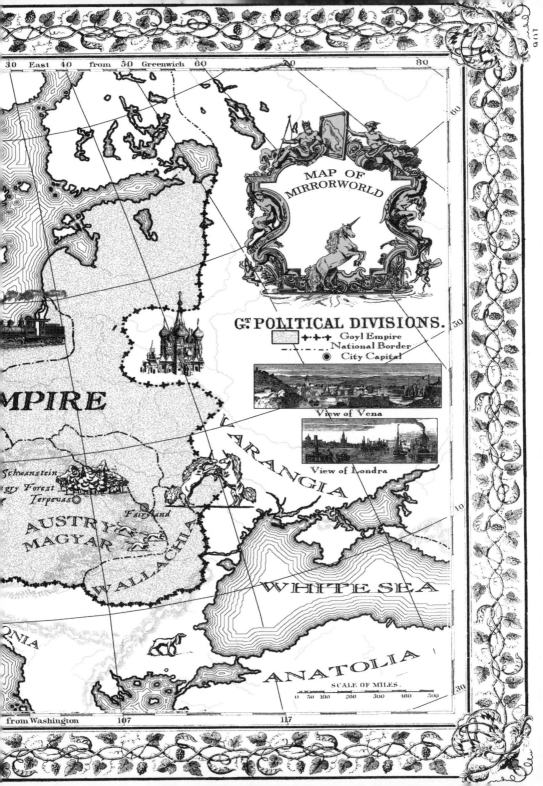

MAP OF
MIRRORWORLD

G.ᵗ POLITICAL DIVISIONS.

+ + + Goyl Empire
National Border
● City Capital

View of Vena

View of Londra

MPIRE

VARANGIA

Schwanstein
ngry Forest
Terpevas

Fairyland

AUSTRY
MAGYAR

WALLACHIA

WHITE SEA

ONIA

ANATOLIA

SCALE OF MILES.
0 50 100 200 300 400 500

1
ONCE UPON A TIME

The night breathed through the apartment like a dark animal. The ticking of a clock, the groan of a floorboard when Jacob slipped out of his room…everything drowned in its silence. But Jacob loved the night. It was like a black cloak woven from freedom and danger, its darkness filling the rooms with the whisper of forgotten stories, of people who had lived in them long before he and his brother had been born. The Kingdom…that's what Will had named the apartment they called home, probably inspired by their grandfather's yellow-paged fairy tale books, filled with German words, and images of castles and peasant houses that looked so different from the skyscrapers and apartment blocks outside. It had been easy to convince Will that the apartment was enchanted, with its seven rooms on the seventh floor. Two years ago, Jacob had even made him believe that the whole building

9

had been built by a giant who lived in the basement. He could make Will believe anything.

Outside, the stars were paled by the glaring lights of the city, and the large apartment was stale with their mother's sorrow. For Jacob, sadness smelled like his mother's perfume. Her sadness defined the vast rooms, as much as the faded photographs in the hallway and the old-fashioned furniture and wallpaper.

As usual, she did not wake when Jacob stole into her room. They had fought once again, and for a moment he yearned to caress her sleeping face. Sometimes he dreamt of finding something that would wipe all her sadness away — an enchanted handkerchief, or a glove enabling his fingers to paint a smile onto her lips. It wasn't just Will who had spent too many afternoons listening to their grandfather's tales.

Jacob opened the drawer of his mother's nightstand. The key he had come for lay next to the pills that let her sleep. *You again?* It seemed to mock him when he took it out. *Foolish boy. Do you nourish the hope that one day I'll unlock more than an empty room for you?*

Maybe. At the age of twelve, one could still imagine such miracles.

There was still a light burning in Will's room — his brother was afraid of the dark. Will was afraid of many things, in contrast to his older brother. Jacob made sure he was fast asleep before unlocking the door of their father's study. Their mother hadn't opened it since his disappearance, but Jacob couldn't count the times he had snuck into the empty room to search for the answers she didn't want to give.

It still looked as if John Reckless had last sat in his desk chair less than an hour ago, instead of more than a year. The sweater he had worn so often hung over the chair, and a used tea bag was desiccating on a plate next to his calendar, which still showed the weeks of a past year.

Come back! Jacob wrote it with his finger on the fogged-up window, on the dusty desk, and on the glass panels of the cabinet that still held the antique pistols his father had collected. But the room remained silent — and empty. He was twelve and no longer had a father.

Vanished.

As if he had never existed. As if their father had been nothing but one of the childish stories he and Will made up. Jacob kicked at the drawers he had searched in vain for so many nights, drowning in the helpless rage he felt each time he saw his father's empty chair in front of the desk. Gone. He yanked the books and magazines from their dusty shelves and tore down the model airplanes hanging above the desk, ashamed of how proudly he once painted them with red and white varnish.

Come back! He wanted to scream it through the streets that cut their gleaming paths through the city blocks seven stories below, scream it at the thousand windows that punched squares of light into the night. But instead he just stood between the shelves listening to his own heartbeat, so loud in the silent room.

A sheet of paper slipped out of a book on airplane propulsion. Jacob only picked it up because he thought he recognized his father's handwriting on it, though he quickly realized his error. Symbols and equations, a sketch of a peacock, a sun, two moons. None of it made any sense. Except for the one sentence he spotted on the reverse side:

11

The Mirror will open only for he who cannot see himself.

The mirror. Jacob turned around—and met the glance of his own reflection. He and his father had found it in one of the building's huge basement rooms, shrouded in a dusty sheet amid old-fashioned furniture and suitcases filled with the forgotten belongings of his mother's family. Once the whole building had belonged to them. One of his mother's ancestors had built it, *'manifesting a sinister imagination when designing it,'* his father would have added. The sculpted faces above the entrance still frightened Will, staring at every visitor with gold-encrusted eyes.

Jacob stepped closer to the mirror. It had been too heavy for the elevator. One could still see the scratches the frame had left on the walls when three men had carried it up to the seventh floor, swearing and cursing all the way. Jacob had always believed the mirror to be older than anything he had ever seen, despite his father's explanation that mirrors of that size could only be produced since the 16th century.

The glass was as dark as if the night had leaked into it, and so uneven one could barely recognize one's own reflection. Jacob touched the thorny rose stems winding across the silver frame, so real they seemed ready to wilt at any moment. In contrast to the rest of the room, the mirror seemed to never gather dust. It hung between the shelves like a shimmering eye, a glassy abyss that cast back a warped reflection of everything John Reckless had left behind: his desk, the antique pistols, his books—and his elder son.

12

The Mirror will open only for he who cannot see himself.

What was the meaning of that?

Jacob closed his eyes. He turned his back to the mirror. Felt behind the frame for some kind of lock or latch.

Nothing.

Only his reflection was looking him straight in the eye.

It took quite a while before he understood. His hand was barely large enough to cover the distorted reflection of his face. But the cool glass clung to his fingers as if it had been waiting for them, and suddenly the room the mirror showed him was no longer his father's study.

Jacob turned around.

Moonlight fell through a narrow glassless window onto walls built from grey stone, roughly cut. The room they enclosed was round and much bigger than his father's study. The dirty floorboards were covered with acorn shells and the gnawed bones of birds, and cobwebs hung like veils from the rafters of a pointed roof.

Where was he?

The moonlight painted patterns on Jacob's skin when he stepped toward the window. The bloody feathers of a bird stuck to its ledge, and far below he saw scorched walls and black hills with a few lost lights glimmering in the distance. Gone were the sea of houses, the bright streets—everything he knew was gone. And high among the stars were two moons, the smaller one as red as a rusty coin.

Jacob looked back at the mirror, the only thing that hadn't changed, and saw the fear on his face. But fear was an emotion

13

Jacob almost enjoyed. It lured him to dark places, through forbidden doors, and far away from himself. Even the yearning for his father could be drowned in it.

There was no door in the gray walls, just a trapdoor in the floor. When Jacob opened it, he saw the remains of a burnt staircase melting into the darkness below, and for a moment he thought he spotted a tiny figure climbing up the soot-covered remains. But before he could lean through the opening to have a closer look, a rasp made him wheel around.

Cobwebs fell down on him as something jumped onto his neck. Its hoarse growl sounded like an animal's, but the contorted face flashing its teeth at his throat looked as pale and wrinkled as an old man's. The creature was much smaller than Jacob, and as spindly as an insect, but terribly strong. Its clothes seemed to be made of cobwebs, its grey hair hung down to its hips, and, when Jacob grabbed its thin neck, it sank its yellow teeth deep into his hand. Screaming, he pushed the attacker off his shoulder and stumbled toward the mirror. The spidery creature came after him, licking his blood from its lips but, before it could reach Jacob, he pressed his unharmed hand against the mirror's glass.

Both the scrawny figure and the tower room disappeared, and behind him Jacob once again saw his father's desk.

"Jacob?"

Will's voice barely registered over the beating of his heart. Jacob gasped for air and backed away from the mirror.

"Jake? Are you in there?"

He pulled his sleeve over his mauled hand and opened the door.

Will's eyes were wide with fear. He'd had another bad dream. Little brother. Will followed him like a puppy, and Jacob protected

14

him in the schoolyard and in the park. Sometimes he even managed to forgive Will that their mother loved him more.

"Mom says we shouldn't go in there."

"Since when do I do what Mom says? If you tell on me, I won't take you to the park tomorrow."

Jacob thought he could feel the glass of the mirror like ice on the back of his neck. Will peered past him, but he quickly lowered his head as Jacob pulled the door shut behind them. Will. Careful where Jacob was rash, tender where he was short-tempered, and calm where he was restless. Jacob took his hand. Will noticed the blood on his fingers and gave him a quizzical look, but Jacob just quietly pulled him back to his room. What he had found behind the mirror was his.

His alone.

For twelve years that would be the truth. Until one day Jacob would wish he had warned his brother that night, of the mirror and of what its dark glass might hold. But the night passed and he kept his secret.

Once upon a time...that's how it always begins.

2
Twelve Years Later

The sun already hung low over the burnt walls of the ruin, but Will was still asleep, exhausted from the pain and the fear of what was growing in his flesh. *One mistake. After twelve years of caution.*

Jacob covered his brother with his cloak and looked up at the sky. The two moons were already visible, and the setting sun darkened the surrounding hills.

He had made this world his home. Twelve years was a long time. At fourteen, he already couldn't count the months he'd spent behind the mirror, despite his mother's tears, despite her helpless fear for him... *'Where have you been, Jacob? Please! Tell me!'* How? How could he have told her, without losing the precious freedom the mirror granted him, all the life he had found behind it, the feeling he could be so much more himself behind its glass.

'Where have you been, Jacob?' She never found out.

He had told Will of this world, convinced his brother would believe it all nothing but a fairy tale. He should have known him better. Why didn't he realize that his stories would fill Will with the same yearning that drove him through the mirror? *Be honest, Jacob, you didn't want to think about it.* No. He had longed to share what he had found with someone, but his father's study had kept the mirror's secret for so many years, and it had been far too easy to convince himself it would be safe there forever.

Maybe it would have been, if he hadn't been so eager to get back. He had forgotten to lock the door, and his hand had already pressed against the dark glass when Will walked in. It's so tempting to escape one's bad conscience by changing worlds. Everything in the apartment had reminded Jacob that he had been looking for a glass shoe while his mother was dying. *You have deserted her, Jacob,* her empty room had whispered. *Exactly like your father.*

In fairy tales, the heroes are punished when they run away from a task. The heroes, not their younger brothers…

The wounds at Will's neck healed well, but the stone already showed on his left arm. It was jade. That was unusual. Mostly it was carnelian, jasper, or moonstone…

"He already has the scent of a Goyl." The vixen stepped out of the shadows cast by the crumbling walls. Her fur was as red as if autumn itself had dyed it. At her hind leg, it was streaked with pale scars. It had been almost five years since Jacob had freed her from the iron teeth of a poacher's trap, and Fox had guarded his sleep ever since. She warned him of dangers that his dull human senses could not detect, and gave advice that was best followed.

"What are you waiting for? Wake him and take him back. We've been here for hours." The impatience in her voice was hard to miss. "That's what we came here for, didn't we?"

18

Jacob looked at his sleeping brother. Yes, that's why he had brought Will back to the tower: to take him back to their world. But how was he supposed to live there, growing a skin of jade? Jacob stepped under the arch which still held the scorched remnants of the castle's doors. A Heinzel scampered off as Jacob's shadow fell on him. They were barely bigger than a mouse, with red eyes above a pointy nose, pants and shirt sewn from stolen human clothes. The ruin was swarming with them.

"I changed my mind," he said. "There's nothing in the other world that can help him."

Jacob had told Fox years ago about the world he came from, but she didn't want to hear about it. What she knew was enough: that it was the place to which he disappeared far too often, bringing back memories that followed him like shadows.

"And? What do you think will happen to him here?"

In her world, fathers killed their own sons as soon as they discovered the stone in their skin. But Jacob was sure: if there was a cure, they would find it here.

At the foot of the hill, the red roofs of Schwanstein were fading into the twilight, and the first lights were coming on in the houses. In his first year behind the mirror, Jacob had worked in one of the town's stables. From a distance, it looked like one of the pictures printed on gingerbread tins. Only the tall smoke stacks of the factories, sending grey smoke into the evening sky, didn't fit into that image. *The New Magic*…that's what technology and science were called in this world. The Petrified Flesh, though, was not sown by mechanical looms or other modern achievements, but by the old magic that dwelled in its hills and valleys, its rivers, oceans, flowers, and trees—and in Seven Miles Boots, Witch

19

needles, and countless other magical objects that Jacob had made it his trade to find.

A Gold-Raven landed on the wall under which Will was sleeping. Jacob shooed it away before it could croak one of its sinister spells into his brother's ear.

Will groaned in his sleep. The human skin did not yield to the jade without a fight. Jacob felt the pain as his own and, for the first time in all the years, he caught himself cursing the mirror. He had only returned to the apartment for his brother, always at night to make sure his mother was sleeping. Her tears had made it too hard to leave again, but Will had just wrapped his arms around Jacob, asking what presents he had brought. The shoes of a Heinzel, the cap of a Thumbling, a button made of elven glass, a piece of scaly Waterman skin — Will had hidden Jacob's gifts behind his books, and then he had asked for more stories about the world where his brother found such treasure, until dawn cast its light onto the faded wallpaper and Jacob stole back to the mirror.

Now he knew how true they had all been.

Jacob pulled the coat over his brother's disfigured arm. The two moons were already in the sky.

He grabbed his rucksack. "I'll be back soon. If he wakes, tell him he has to wait for me. Don't allow him to go near the tower."

"And where are you going?" The vixen stepped into his path. "You can't help him, Jacob."

"I know. But I have to try."

Fox followed him with her eyes when he walked over to the broken stairs leading down the hill. The only footprints on the mossy steps were his own. The ruin was thought to be cursed. In Schwanstein, people told hundreds of stories about its demise, but after all these years Jacob still didn't know who had left the mirror in its tower. Or where his father had vanished to.

3

GOYL

The barren field still reeked of blood, the scent of all battlefields. Hentzau's horse was used to it, as were his soldiers. The rain had filled the trenches with a muddy sludge and, behind the walls both sides had built, the ground was covered with rifles and bullet-riddled helmets. Kami'en had ordered the horse cadavers and human corpses to be burnt before the air filled with the scent of their decay. His own dead soldiers, though, the king left where they had fallen, as was Goyl custom. In just a few days, they would be all but indistinguishable from the rocks protruding from the trampled earth, and the heads of those who had fought valiantly had already been sent to the Royal Fortress to line the underground Avenues of the Dead.

Another battle. Hentzau was tired of them, but he hoped that this would be the last one for a while. The Empress was finally ready to negotiate, and even Kami'en wanted peace. Hentzau covered his mouth as the wind blew ash down from the hill where they had burnt their fallen enemies. Six years above ground, six years without the protecting shield of the earth between him and the sun. His eyes ached from all the light, and the air made his skin as brittle as chalk. Hentzau's skin resembled brown jasper—not the finest color for a Goyl. Hentzau was the first jasper Goyl to have risen to the highest military ranks. But then again, before Kami'en, the Goyl had never had a king, and Hentzau liked his skin. Jasper provided far better camouflage than onyx or moonstone.

Kami'en had set up camp not far from the battlefield, in the hunting lodge of one of the Empress's generals who, along with most of his officers, had died in the battle.

Two Goyl sentries were guarding the gate. They saluted as Hentzau rode past them. The king's bloodhound...that's what they called him. His jasper shadow. Hentzau had served under Kami'en since they had first challenged the other chiefs. It had taken two years for them to kill them all, and for the Goyl to crown their first king.

The drive leading up to the lodge was lined with statues. It always amused Hentzau that humans immortalized their gods and heroes with stone effigies while they loathed his kind. Even the Doughskins had to admit it: in this world, only stone could claim to last.

They had bricked up the windows of the lodge, as they did in all buildings they occupied, but Hentzau didn't feel at ease until he descended the steps to the cellars and finally felt the soothing darkness one could only find below ground. The vaults, once stacked with supplies and dusty trophies, housed Kami'en's general staff, and no Goyl needed lamps or candles to see in the dark.

24

Kami'en. In their language, it meant nothing more than "stone." His father had governed one of the lower cities, but fathers did not count among the Goyl. It was the mothers who raised them, and by the age of nine Goyl were considered grown up and had to fend for themselves. At that age, most of them went to explore the Lower World, with its crystal caves, black lakes, and petrified forests, proving their courage by advancing deeper, to the Lost Palaces with their mirrors and silver columns, until the heat became unbearable even for Goyl skin. Kami'en, however, had never been interested in exploring the deep. All he cared for was the world above. He had lived for a while in one of the cave cities they had built above ground when the copper-plague raged in their lower cities. When a human attack killed one of his sisters, he had begun to study their weapons and strategies. At nineteen, he had conquered one of their cities. The first of many to come.

When the guards waved Hentzau into Kami'en's quarters, he was standing at the table where the positions of his enemies were staged each morning. He had ordered the figurines crafted after he had won his first battle: soldiers, snipers, gunners, cavalry…the Goyl were carved from carnelian, the Empress's troops marched in ivory, Lotharaine wore gold, and Albion was cast in copper. Kami'en eyed the figurines as if he were searching for a way to beat them all at once. He was wearing black, as he always did when out of uniform. It made his pale red skin look like petrified fire. Never before had carnelian been the color of a Goyl leader. For centuries, onyx had been the color of their nobility.

Kami'en's mistress was wearing green, as usual, layers of emerald velvet enveloping her like the petals of a flower. The most beautiful Goyl women paled next to her, like pebbles next to polished moonstone, but Hentzau had ordered his soldiers not to look at her. The old jasper Goyl was long past the age where he'd believed in fairy tales, but he believed all the stories told about Fairies and the lovelorn idiots whom they turned with a glance into thistles or helplessly wriggling fish. Their beauty was more lethal than spiders' venom. The water had given birth to them all. Hentzau feared them as much as he feared the oceans that gnawed at the rocks of his world. He hated them especially for that fear.

The Dark Fairy smiled as if she had read his mind. Many believed she could, but Hentzau didn't. She would have long killed him for what he thought about her. She was the most powerful of them all.

He turned his back on her and bowed his head to his king.

"I was told you need me to find someone."

Kami'en took one of the ivory figurines and set it aside. Each one represented a hundred soldiers.

"Yes. A human growing the Petrified Flesh."

Hentzau cast a quick glance at the Fairy.

"And how am I supposed to do that? There are thousands of them by now!"

Man-Goyl. Nobody fought humans with less mercy, but Hentzau despised them just as much as he despised the Fairy who had created them. The Goyl had always used their claws to kill, but now her spell had turned them into tools of sorcery. Like all Fairies, the Dark One couldn't bear children, so she gave Kami'en sons by sowing stone into his enemies' flesh with every strike of his soldiers' claws.

"Don't worry. It won't be difficult to find this one." Kami'en removed another two ivory figurines from the map. "He grows a skin of jade."

The guards exchanged a quick look, but Hentzau frowned with mocking disbelief. Lava-Men who boil the blood of the earth, the eyeless bird that sees everything under and above the ground, and the Goyl with jade skin who grants invincibility to the king he serves...these were stories told to children to paint images into the darkness underground.

"I'll have the scout executed who told you that." Hentzau rubbed his aching skin. The damn cold would soon make him look like a cracked jar. "The Jade Goyl is a fairy tale! Since when do you confuse those with reality?"

The guards nervously ducked their heads. Any other Goyl would have paid for that remark with his life, but Hentzau knew that Kami'en loved him for his honesty. And for the fact that he still wasn't afraid of him.

"You have your orders," he said as casually as if he hadn't noticed Hentzau's mockery. "Find him. She saw him in her dreams."

Ah, there was the source.

The Fairy smoothed the velvet of her dress. Six fingers on each hand, each one for a different curse. Hentzau felt the rage they all bore in their flesh rise in him. He would die for his king if necessary, but to search for his mistress's daydreams was an entirely different matter.

"The King of the Goyl doesn't need a Jade Goyl to be invincible!"

King. Still an unfamiliar word for Goyl tongues. But by now even Hentzau hesitated to address Kami'en by only his name. And yes, he held his jasper dog in high esteem for not being as docile as most of his officers, but to disrespect his mistress was something he didn't forgive that lightly.

"Find him!" he repeated, eyeing Hentzau like a stranger. "She says it is important, and so far she's always been right."

The Fairy stepped to Kami'en's side. Hentzau pictured himself breaking her pale neck, but not even that gave him comfort. She was immortal, and one day she would watch him die. Him and the king. And Kami'en's children and his children's children. They all were nothing but her mortal toys. But Kami'en loved her. More than his two Goyl wives, who had given him three daughters and two sons.

Because she had hexed him!

"I saw him in the Hungry Forest." Even her voice sounded like water.

"That forest covers more than sixty square miles!"

She once again smiled. She probably imagined him as a fish twisting breathlessly at her feet. Hentzau almost choked on his hatred.

"That sounds as if you're asking for some help." She clearly enjoyed his alarm, and raised her hand to open the pearl clasps holding her hair. It reached down to her hips when they fell open. Most people compared it to finely spun copper or red gold, but to Hentzau its color resembled dried blood. Black moths fluttered out from under her fingers when she drove her hand through it. The pale spots on their wings were shaped like skulls.

The guards quickly opened the doors as the moths swarmed toward them. Hentzau's soldiers, who had been waiting outside, recoiled with equal haste. It was well known that Fairy moths even penetrated Goyl skin with their sting—and that their victims rarely survived.

"Once they find the Jade Goyl—" their mistress said, pushing the clasps back into her hair, "They'll let you know. And you will bring him to me."

His men stared at her through the open door.

Fairy.

Damn her and the night she had appeared among their tents. The third battle, and their third victory. She had appeared between the tents as if the groans of their wounded had summoned her. Hentzau had stepped into her path, but she had just walked through him, like liquid through porous stone, and then she had stolen Kami'en's heart to fill her own heartless bosom with it. True, their best weapons combined did not spread half as much terror amongst their enemies as her curse. Yet he was certain they would have still won the war without her, and that victory would have tasted so much sweeter.

Kami'en was watching him. No, the Fairy couldn't read his thoughts, but his king did it with ease. "I will find the Man-Goyl," he said, pressing his fist against his heart, their oldest gesture of respect. "If he really is more than just a dream."

He still felt the Fairy's gaze when he stepped out into the daylight that clouded his eyes and cracked his skin.

He couldn't remember ever having hated like this.

4

CLARA

Will's voice had sounded so different, Clara barely recognized it. No call or message for weeks, and then this stranger on the phone who wouldn't really say why he was calling. Fear. That's what Clara had heard in his voice. Worse than the fear she knew from the hospital corridors, where she tried to learn how to daily face sickness and death.

She had to see him. That was all she knew. Find out what had happened and why he had disappeared for weeks.

The streets were even more congested than usual, and it seemed to take her half a lifetime to reach the old apartment building where Will had grown up. Chiseled faces stared down from the gray facade, their contorted features eroded by exhaust fumes. Their eyes were gilded, Clara noticed for the first time. The doorman in the hall was as bad-tempered as usual—Tomkins, yes, that was his name. He reminded Clara of a cat in his uniform, a fat grey tom cat, who licked his lips each time he saw her.

"Nobody at home up there, Miss," he said while he openly scrutinized her from head to toe.

Clara realized she was still wearing the pale green hospital gown under her coat. She had been in such a hurry she hadn't taken the time to change. Will had sounded so lost. Like someone who was drowning.

The grilled doors of the elevator were stuck, as usual. Will called it the Hänsel-cage. Tomkins didn't come to her aid and Clara was relieved when the elevator finally moved. *'Don't take him serious,'* Will had advised when she had complained about the doorman's rudeness. *'He's known me and Jacob since we were born and treats everyone this way. Sometimes he even tells people we're not at home, because he doesn't like them.'* And then he had kissed her.

Will.

The old elevator took so long that Clara always felt she had reached the top of the world when she stepped out on the seventh floor. She first tried the bell, but there was no answer. The copper nameplate next to the door was so tarnished that she was always tempted to wipe it with her sleeve. RECKLESS. Will often made fun of how that name did not suit him at all. When Clara finally used the key he had given her, she stumbled into a pile of unopened mail behind the door. Had Will called her from somewhere else?

She walked into the kitchen. A dirty coffee mug on the table. A book he had been reading.

"Will?" His mother's room was still unchanged, although she had died four months ago. Clara hesitated before she opened the door of his brother's room. *Jacob.* She still hadn't met him. *'Jacob*

32

is traveling.' Jacob was always traveling. Sometimes she wasn't sure whether he actually existed.

Will's room was empty too. Just the usual mess. His clothes on the floor. A bowl of half-eaten cereal. Judging from the mold, it had been sitting there for weeks.

Where was he?

She noticed the open door to his father's study only when she stepped back into the corridor. Will never entered that room. He ignored anything that had to do with his father. *'He's gone. Left us without a word and broke my mother's heart,'* was all he ever told her about him.

Clara stepped through the open door. A desk, bookshelves, a glass cabinet filled with old-fashioned pistols. Above the desk, a few model planes were gathering dust on their wings like dirty snow.

Between the bookshelves, a huge mirror leaned against the wall. Dozens of roses opened their blossoms on the silver frame. The thorns almost pricked Clara's finger when she touched one of the flowers. Each was shaped so perfectly that their scent seemed to linger in the dusty air. The glass they framed was as dark as if it had caught the night, and so clear Clara wondered who had polished it...but right where she saw the reflection of her face was the imprint of a hand.

5

SCHWANSTEIN

The light of the lanterns filled Schwanstein's streets like spilled milk. Gaslight, wooden wheels bumping over cobblestones, women in long skirts, their hems soaked from the rain...Jacob couldn't recall when he had begun to perceive all this as normal and the world he came from as a sometimes-more-bewildering reality. At fourteen? Sixteen? No, probably much sooner. One could often get along with a slightly old-fashioned English behind the mirror, and Jacob used it with Fox; her mother tongue resembled the French of his world. In Schwanstein, though, it had proved to be helpful that his mother's father had talked German with them, as it made him speak Austrish quite well. Nevertheless...it hadn't been easy to keep himself from starving or ending up in a workhouse. That neither had happened to him, Jacob owed to two people. One of them was a Witch, a white one. Alma Spitzweg practiced as a healer in a village on the other side of the castle hill and had saved him many times, but this time even her magic wouldn't help. As for the other one — well, if anyone in this world knew of a way to save his brother, it would be Albert Chanute.

The church bells were ringing in the evening as Jacob walked down the street that led to Schwanstein's market square. A Dwarf woman was selling roasted chestnuts in front of a bakery. Their sweet aroma mixed with the smell of the horse manure scattered all over the cobblestones. The idea of the combustion engine had not yet made it through the mirror. The monument at the center of the square showed Karolus, the Goyl Burner, an ancestor of the reigning Empress Therese of Austry, who had not only made necklaces for his mistress from moonstone Goyl skin, but had also been a tireless hunter of Giants in the surrounding hills. It was one of Jacob's greatest regrets that both Giants and Dragons were by now extinct behind the mirror. He had to admit that he wouldn't have missed the Stilt who almost had torn out his throat at his first visit. But what about Grass Elves, Heinzel, Thumblings, Nymphs, or Witches? Would they be next to disappear? Schwanstein had changed since Jacob had stepped through the mirror for the first time. The damp autumn air smelled of smoke, and soot blackened the laundry that hung between the pointy gables. There was a railway station opposite the old coach station, a telegraph office, and a photographer who fixed stiff hats and ruffled skirts onto silver plates. Bicycles leaned against walls on which posters warned of Gold-Ravens and Watermen. Sometimes Jacob wondered whether Schwanstein embraced the modern times even more eagerly than the rest of this world, and how much of that could be blamed on the mirror in his father's study.

36

Grass Elves, Heinzel, Thumblings, Nymphs, Witches...what about the Goyl, Jacob? Every human citizen of this world would have celebrated their extinction.

The paperboy standing next to the Goyl Burner's monument, shouting the latest news into the gathering dusk, had surely never seen more than the footprint of a Giant or the faded scorch marks of Dragon-fire on the town walls. But the Goyl were part of his reality as much as the Dwarf woman selling roasted chestnuts, or the Heinzels assisting the bakers to roll out the dough.

Decisive battle, terrible losses...secret negotiations with the Goyl...

The MirrorWorld was at war, and it was not being won by humans. Four days had passed since he and Will had run into one of their patrols, but Jacob could still see them coming out of the forest: three soldiers and an officer, their stone faces wet from the rain — golden eyes, black claws tearing open his brother's neck — Goyl.

'Look after Will, Jacob. He's so different from you.'

He put three copper coins into the paperboy's grubby hand. The Heinzel sitting on his shoulder eyed them suspiciously. Many of them chose human companions who fed and clothed them — though that did little to improve their crabby dispositions.

"How far away are the Goyl?" Jacob took a newspaper.

"Less than five miles from here, sir." The boy pointed southeast. "With the wind right, we could hear their cannons. But it's been quiet since yesterday." He sounded almost disappointed. At his age, even war sounded like an adventure. The imperial soldiers filing out of Albert Chanute's tavern knew better. THE OGRE. Jacob had met the man-eater who had given the tavern its name and cost its owner his right arm.

37

Albert Chanute was standing behind the counter, wearing a grim expression as Jacob entered the dingy taproom. Chanute was such a gross hulk of a man that people suspected him of having Troll blood running through his veins, not a compliment in the world behind the mirror. But until the Ogre had chopped off his arm, Albert Chanute had been the best treasure hunter in all of Austry, and for many years Jacob had been his apprentice. Chanute had shown him how to gather fame and fortune behind the mirror, and in return Jacob had prevented the Ogre from also hacking off Chanute's head.

The mementos of his glory days covered the walls of the taproom: the head of a Brown Wolf, the oven door from a gingerbread house, a Cudgel-in-the-Sack that jumped off the wall whenever a guest misbehaved, and, right above the bar hanging from the chains with which he'd used to bind his victims, the right arm of the Ogre who had ended Chanute's treasure-hunting days. The bluish skin still shimmered like a lizard's hide.

"Look who's here!" Chanute's grouchy mouth actually stretched into a smile. "I thought you were in Lotharaine, looking for an Hourglass."

Chanute had been a legendary treasure hunter, but Jacob had by now gained an equally famous reputation in that line of work, and the three men sitting at one of the stained tables curiously lifted their heads.

"Get rid of them!" Jacob whispered across the counter. "I have to talk to you."

Then he climbed up the worn stairs to Chanute's guest rooms. Jacob had rented one, years ago, to keep some things safe when he was travelling. There was no place he called home, either in this world or in the other. He always yearned for unknown places,

38

secrets revealed, treasures found…there was so much he still hadn't seen. But it felt like home to travel with Fox by his side.

A Wishing Table, a Glass Slipper, the Golden Ball of a princess — most of the treasures Jacob had found in this world he had sold to kings and queens, or rich men and women, whose wishes only magic could fulfill. Some, though, he had kept for himself. The chest Jacob kept them in, hidden under the bed in the small room he rented from Albert Chanute, had been built by a Troll whose talents as a carpenter were legend. The objects guarded by his masterly carvings were the tools of Jacob's trade. Now they would have to help him save his brother.

The first item he took out of the chest was a handkerchief made of simple linen. When rubbed between two fingers, it reliably produced one or two gold sovereigns. Jacob had received it years ago from a dark Witch in exchange for a kiss that had burned his lips for weeks. The other items he packed into his knapsack looked just as innocuous: a silver snuffbox, a brass key, a tin plate, and a small bottle made of green glass. Each of these items had saved his life on more than one occasion.

When Jacob came back down the stairs, he found the taproom empty. Chanute was sitting at one of the tables. He pushed a mug of wine toward Jacob as he joined him.

"So? What kind of trouble are you in this time?" Chanute looked longingly at Jacob's wine; he only had a glass of water in front of him. In the past, Chanute had often been so drunk that Jacob started hiding the bottles, though he'd often paid for that with bruises or a split lip. Chanute had often beaten him, even when he'd been sober — until Jacob had one day pointed his mentor's own pistol at him. He had also been drunk in the Ogre's cave. He would have probably kept his arm had he been able to see straight, but after that he had quit drinking. Albert Chanute had been a miserable replacement father, but a very good teacher on most days, even friend, and Jacob had countless times asked for his advice, although never before with his brother's life at stake.

"What would you do if a friend of yours had been clawed by the Goyl?"

Chanute choked on his water and eyed him closely, as if to make sure Jacob was not talking about himself.

"Who is it?" he grunted. "The guy you went hunting the Bluebeard with? Or the one with the rattail, up in Albion?"

Jacob shook his head. "You don't know him."

"Of course. Jacob Reckless likes it mysterious. How could I forget?" Chanute mocked, but he sounded slightly injured. Jacob sometimes suspected that he considered Jacob the son he'd never had. "When did they get him?"

"Four days ago."

The Goyl had attacked them not far from a village where Jacob had been looking for the Hourglass. He had underestimated how far their patrols were already venturing into imperial territory and, after Will had been clawed, he'd been in such pain that the journey back took them days. *Back where?* There was no "back" anymore, but Jacob hadn't had the courage yet to tell Will.

Chanute brushed his hand through his spiky grey hair. "Four days? Forget it. He's already half one of them. You remember the time when the Empress was collecting them in all their skin colors? And that farmer tried to peddle us a dead moonstone as onyx, after he covered the corpse in lamp soot?"

Yes, Jacob remembered. The stone faces. That's what they were called back then, and children were told stories about Goyl to prevent them from stealing out of the house at night. During

40

his travels with Chanute, he had often witnessed humans going on the hunt for Goyl. Now their king had made the prey the hunters.

There was a rustling near the back door, and Chanute drew his knife. He threw it so quickly that it nailed the rat in mid-jump against the wall.

"This world is going down the toilet," he growled, pushing back his chair. "Rats as big as dogs. The air on the street stinks like a Troll's cave from all the factories, and the Goyl are standing just a couple of miles from here."

He picked up the dead rat and threw it onto the table.

"There's nothing that helps against the Petrified Flesh. But if they'd gotten me, I'd ride to a gingerbread house and look in the garden for a bush with black berries. It's got to be the garden of a child-eater, though."

"I thought the child-eaters all moved to Lotharaine since the other Witches started hunting them."

Chanute wiped the bloody knife on his sleeve.

"Their houses are still here. The bush grows where they buried their leftovers. Those berries are the strongest antidote to curses I know of."

Witch-berries. Jacob looked at the oven door on the wall. "The Witch in the Hungry Forest was a child-eater."

"One of the worst. I once looked in her house for one of those combs that you put in your hair and they turn you into a crow."

"I know. You sent me in there first."

"Really?" Chanute rubbed his fleshy nose. He'd convinced Jacob that the Witch had flown out.

"You poured liquor on my wounds." The imprints of her fingers were still visible on his neck. It had taken weeks for the burns to heal.

41

Jacob threw the knapsack over his shoulder. "I need a packhorse, some provisions, two rifles, and ammunition."

Chanute didn't seem to have heard him. He was staring at his trophies. "Good old days," he mumbled. "The Empress received me three times. Personally! How many audiences have you racked up?"

Jacob closed his hand around the handkerchief in his pocket until he felt two gold sovereigns between his fingers.

"Two," he said, tossing the coins onto the table. He'd had six audiences with the Empress, but the lie made Chanute very happy.

"Put that gold away!" he growled. "I don't take money from you."

"Here," he said handing his knife to Jacob. "There's nothing this blade won't cut. I have a feeling you'll need it more than I will."

6

TRUTH OR LIE

Provisions for two weeks, a packhorse, and two horses for him and Will...although Jacob wasn't sure the pain would allow his brother to ride. Ammunition. Yes, he had brought plenty of that, and an additional rifle. *What do you think will happen to him here?* From now on, everyone they met, be it man or Goyl, would be their enemy. Man-Goyl had no friends and that's what his brother would be called.

Jacob had bought a hooded cloak for Will to hide his face in case the jade began to show there. *In case?* The Petrified Flesh grew fast.

All the way back to the ruin, Jacob tried to come up with the right words to break the news to Will that he couldn't go home. For Will, there had never been a doubt where that was. As far as Jacob knew, his younger brother had never longed for other places, to leave the all-too-familiar behind...*should he tell Will*

43

about the gingerbread house? Or finally explain to him what was happening? No. He simply couldn't bear to tell him. Truth or lie...he had always chosen the lie, to spare his little brother any unpleasant truth. His mother had done the same. *Don't tell Will!* But it had been Will who had watched her die.

What will you do Jacob?

Lies.

Yes. For now he would lie.

But when he led the horses through the ruin's withered gates, Will was gone.

"I tried to stop him, but he is as stubborn as you." The vixen appeared as usual without a sound between the charred walls. The night dyed her fur black.

Curse you, Jacob. He should have taken Will with him to Schwanstein.

He tied the horses to the trees and hastened toward the tower.

Ivy grew so densely on its walls that the evergreen vines covered the entrance like a curtain. The tower and a chapel further down the hill were the only parts of the castle that had survived the fire nearly unscathed.

"Will?"

There was no answer. Only a few bats were startled by his voice. The rope ladder Jacob had installed to replace the burned staircase shimmered like silver. The Grass Elves liked to leave their dust on it.

The tower room was filled with the light of the red moon when Jacob pushed himself through the trap door. It reflected on the mirror's glass and drew his brother's silhouette into the night.

Will was not alone.

The girl stepped out of his embrace when she heard Jacob behind her. She was even prettier than the photos Will had shown him.

"Have you lost your mind?" Jacob felt his own anger like frost on his skin. "You told her?"

In all the years Jacob had often considered moving the mirror from his father's study to a place only he knew, he had always decided against it, worried it would lose its magic. Fear was never a good reason.

"Clara." Will said her name as if he had pearls on his tongue. He had always taken love too seriously. "This is my brother, Jacob."

Jacob brushed the elven dust from his hands. It granted sweet dreams when inhaled.

"Send her back. Now."

What did you expect, Jacob? Will had talked about her all the time. Her name had been the first thing that came over his lips after the Goyl had injured him. But Jacob wished for one of those sacks the King of Lotharaine used to make his enemies disappear.

She was afraid, but she tried her best to hide it. Afraid of the place that could not be, the red moonlight—*and of you, Jacob.* She seemed surprised he actually existed. Will's older brother. He probably appeared as unreal to her as the world she had stepped into.

"What is that on your skin?" She pointed at Will's arm. *Ah, she came straight to the point.* "I've never seen a rash like this."

Of course. Student of medicine. *You don't want to know the answer,* Jacob thought. *And neither does Will.* How she looked at his brother. She was just as lovesick as Will. So lovesick that she had followed him into another world.

Why didn't he just send them both back? Who could say? Maybe Fairy curses didn't work on the other side. After all...any magical object Jacob had brought through the mirror had lost its magic on the other side. But he knew it wasn't true with this. Will would take the Petrified Flesh with him.

From the rafters above came a scraping sound, and a scrawny face peered down at them from one of the beams. The Stilt's teeth were still as sharp and yellow as when it had dug them into Jacob's hand. He had tried quite a few times to get rid of it, but so far in vain. Its ugly face quickly disappeared behind the cobwebs when Jacob drew his pistol. It was a weapon from his father's collection, but he'd had a gunsmith in New York put the workings of a modern pistol inside.

Clara stared in disbelief up at the Stilt and then at the revolver.

"Send her back, Will." Jacob pushed the pistol back into his belt. "I won't tell you again."

"Can I go with her? We came here to go back, didn't we?"

"Not yet. We have to find something."

Will returned his gaze with the same silent persistence he had used to hold up against Jacob as a child. He knew all too well how much his older brother loved him. Even when he was that angry. But finally he turned to Clara.

"He's right," Jacob heard him whisper. "I'll be with you soon. It will disappear. You'll see. Jacob will find a way. He always does."

Nothing had ever been able to shake Will's trust in him, not even all the years during which Will had barely seen him. There had been too many times Jacob had protected him on school yards and playgrounds, Will and the injured birds and stray dogs he found everywhere. And all his friends who, equally gentle and wide eyed, were so easily pushed around by bullies. *'I get my brother. He is not afraid. Of anything.'*

Everybody is afraid of something. But that wasn't a truth to reveal to one's little brother. And neither was the truth that he had stumbled into the wrong world and would soon have a skin of stone. Or that this time his older brother might not be able to protect him.

"Let's go." Jacob turned around and went toward the hatch.

"Go back, Clara. Please," he heard Will say.

He had already reached the bottom of the tower by the time Will finally grabbed the rope ladder. He climbed down as slowly as if he wished to never reach the bottom. When he finally stood by Jacob's side, he stared first at the elven dust on his hands and then up to the still open trap door.

"I had to call her. That's the only reason why I went back. She hadn't heard from me for weeks! I didn't expect she would come after me!"

That was a lie. Will had always been a bad liar. Jacob was sure that he had waited for her, staring into the mirror. Had he searched for the first traces of jade in his face?

Fox was waiting where Jacob had left the horses. She didn't like that he came back with Will.

No one can help him, her eyes still said.

We shall see Fox.

The horses were restless. They sensed the stone and backed away from Will. A new experience for him. Will usually made friends with every creature. As a child, he had cried bitter tears over poisoned rats in the park.

"Where are we riding to?"

He looked up at the tower.

47

Jacob gave him one of the rifles. "To the Hungry Forest."

Fox lifted her head.

Yes, Fox, I know. Not one of our favorite places.

Jacob's mare didn't like the sound of it either. She shoved her head into his back. He had paid Chanute a whole year's earnings for her, and she was worth every farthing.

"The Hungry Forest?" Fox sat down by his side. "With your milk-face of a brother? Did Chanute come up with that idea?"

Jacob didn't get a chance to answer. The vixen uttered a growl.

The ivy covering the tower's entrance moved. Clara pushed through the vines and looked in disbelief at the scorched walls, the horses, the fox...

No.

Will's face lit up, but then he looked at Jacob. No, Will wasn't sure he wanted her here either. Will knew too well by now how dangerous a place this was.

Clara looked at Jacob. She knew whom she'd need to convince she could stay.

"I won't go back."

She took a deep breath when a wolf howled in the distance. But she didn't move.

"Please!" She still looked at Jacob, not at Will. "He needs me. And I need to know what happened."

Fox eyed her like a strange animal. The women in her world wore long dresses and kept their hair pinned up or plaited, like peasant girls. This one's hair was almost as short as a boy's.

Will pulled Clara away with him. For a moment, her face reminded Jacob of their mother's. *Why had he never told her about the mirror?* Lies, there as well. It had always been too easy for him to come up with them. Sometimes the truth was the only thing that frightened him. To tell it. Or to face it. Maybe this world could have wiped at least some of the sadness off his mother's face.

Too late, Jacob. Much too late.

A second wolf howled. They were usually quite peaceful, but lately there had been a few Brown ones further down the hill, and those did like the taste of human flesh.

Will was still pleading with Clara.

Fox lifted her muzzle. "We should leave," she whispered to Jacob.

"Not before he sends her back."

Fox looked at him. Eyes of pure amber. "Take her along."

"What? She'll only slow us down!" And he didn't have to tell Fox that his brother was running out of time. Although he still would have to explain that to Will.

Fox turned.

"Take her along!" she repeated. "Your brother will need her. Or don't you trust my nose anymore?"

7

THE HOUSE OF THE WITCH

At some point, all fairy tales lead into the woods. And their heroes first have to get lost to come back with what they have set out to find—if they find it at all. The Hungry Forest had swallowed many men who went in to hunt treasure among its trees. Treasure, healing, or a darker kind of magic—to win love or to curse a neighbor. The Hungry Forest was old. Very old. A thicket of roots, thorns, and leaves of ancient trees covered in moss gave way to saplings shooting up between their roots, ferns so high a man could get lost underneath their fronds, swarms of will-o'-the-wisps above ponds filled with rotting leaves, and clearings where toadstools were drawing their red-capped circles…

Jacob had last been in the Hungry Forest four months earlier, to find a Man-Swan wearing a shirt of nettles over his feathers. But the sting of a fever-thistle had forced him to abandon the search.

51

It took them until midday to reach the forest because Will had been in pain again. The jade had spread all over his neck, though Clara pretended not to see it. *Love makes you blind*—she seemed intent on proving that proverb. She never left Will's side. She wrapped her arms around him whenever the stone grew a little further and he doubled over in the saddle with pain. Only when she felt unobserved, Jacob saw his own fear on her face. He gave her the same lies he had given his brother: that only Will's skin was changing, and that there was plenty of magic in this world that could heal the jade-colored rash. She hadn't taken much convincing. Both she and Will were only too happy to believe whatever comforting lies Jacob told them.

Clara rode better than he'd expected. Jacob had bought her a dress at a market they had passed along the way, but she made him swap it for men's clothes after trying in vain to mount the packhorse in the wide skirt. A girl in men's clothes, and the jade in Will's skin—Jacob was glad when they could finally ride under the trees, even though he knew what would be awaiting there.

Barkbiters, Mushroom-Wights, Trappers, Crow-Men. The Hungry Forest had many unpleasant inhabitants, though the Empress had been trying for years to clear it of its terrors. Despite the dangers, there was a lively trade in horns, teeth, skins, and other body parts of the forest's creatures. Jacob had never earned his money that way, but there were many who made quite a decent living of it: fifteen silver dollars for a Mushroom-Wight (a two-dollar bonus if it spat real fly-agaric poison), thirty for a Barkbiter (not a lot, considering the hunt could easily leave the hunter dead), and forty for a Crow-Man (who at least only went for the eyes).

Many trees were already shedding their leaves, but the canopy above them was still so dense that the day beneath it dissolved into a checkered autumnal twilight. They soon had to start leading the horses on foot to keep them from getting caught in the thorny undergrowth. Jacob had instructed Will and Clara not to touch the trees. However, the shimmering pearls that a Barkbiter had left sprouting as bait on an oak limb made Clara forget his warnings. Jacob barely managed to pluck the foul creature from her wrist before it could crawl up her sleeve.

"Look at him," he said, holding the Barkbiter close enough to show Clara the sharp teeth above its scabbed lips, "His first bite will make you drowsy. A second one, and you'll be paralyzed, but still fully conscious while its entire clan feasts on your blood. Trust me, it's not a pleasant way to die."

From then on, she was careful. It was she who noticed the glistening net of a Trapper stretched across their path and pulled Will back in time. She even shooed away the Gold-Ravens trying to squawk dark curses into their ears.

The forest tried hard to make them lose their way. Fox wouldn't play that game. The will-o'-the-wisps, drifting in thick iridescent swarms among the trees, had often led even Jacob astray with their alluring hum, but the vixen just shook them from her fur like troublesome flies and led their small band on unwaveringly.

After three hours, the first Witch-tree appeared between the oak and ash trees. Jacob was just about to warn Will and Clara about their branches, and how they loved to poke at human eyes, when Fox suddenly stopped.

The faint noise was nearly drowned out by the hum of the will-o'-the-wisps. It sounded like the snip-snap of a pair of scissors. Not a terribly threatening sound. Will and Clara didn't even notice it.

53

But the vixen's fur bristled, and Jacob put his hand on his saber. Only one creature in the Hungry Forest made such a sound, and it was the only one whose path he definitely didn't want to cross.

"How much farther is it to the house?" he whispered to Fox.

Snip-snap. It was coming closer.

"We have to move faster," Fox whispered back.

The snipping stopped, but the sudden silence was equally ominous. No bird sang. Even the will-o'-the-wisps had vanished. Fox cast a worried glance at the trees before she scampered ahead again, so briskly that the horses barely managed to keep up with her through the dense undergrowth.

The forest was growing darker, and Jacob pulled a flashlight from his saddlebag, although he mostly tried to avoid using objects from the other world. More and more often they now had to skirt around Witch-trees; hawthorn took the place of ash and oak, and pines sucked up the scant light with their black-green needles. Then they saw the house behind the trees.

The horses shied at the sight. They could barely make the animals move on. When Jacob had come here with Chanute, the red roof tiles had shone through the undergrowth as brightly as if the Witch had painted them with cherry juice. Now they were covered in moss, and the paint was peeling off the window frames. But there were still a few pieces of gingerbread stuck to the walls and the steep roof. Sugary icicles hung from the gutters and the windowsills, and the whole house smelled of honey and cinnamon—as befitted a trap for children. The Witches had tried many times to banish the child-eaters from their clans, and two years ago they had finally declared war on them. The Witch who had plagued the Hungry Forest had been sentenced by her sisters to spend the rest of her long life as a warty toad in a silty pond. Jacob considered that a very modest punishment. He still felt her hot fingers around his neck sometimes, but the comb he had stolen from her, at Chanute's request, had paid for his first decent horse.

There were still a few colorful remains of candy on the wrought-iron fence that surrounded the house. Jacob's mare trembled as he led her through the gate. The fence of a gingerbread house would admit anyone, but it was not that easy to get out again. During their visit, Chanute had taken care to leave the gate wide open. Now, Jacob was more worried about what was following them than about the deserted house. As he closed the gate behind Clara, the snipping could again be heard clearly, and this time it sounded almost angry. But at least it didn't come any closer. Fox shot Jacob a relieved glance. It was just as they had hoped: their pursuer had been no friend of the Witch.

"What if he waits for us?" As happened so often, Fox put Jacob's own thoughts into words.

Yes, what then, Jacob? He didn't care, as long as they found the bush Chanute had described in the Witch's overgrown garden — and a few berries on its branches.

Will led the horses to the well. They had grown accustomed to the Goyl scent. Maybe they still sensed Will's gentleness underneath. Or the threat of the gingerbread house made them forget the jade. Will eyed the house as if it were a poisonous plant. Clara, however, touched the icing as if she could not believe that what she saw was real.

Nibble, nibble, little mouse, who's been nibbling at my house?

Which version of the story had Clara heard?

Then she took hold of Hansel with her bony hand, carried him away to a little hutch with a barred door, and shut him up there. He could shout all he liked, but it did him no good.

"Take care she doesn't eat any of the cakes," Jacob said to Fox. Then he set off in search of the berries.

Behind the house, the nettles were growing so high it looked as if they were standing guard over the Witch's garden. They burnt Jacob's skin when he beat a path through their poisonous leaves, but the reward was growing right behind them, between hemlock and deadly nightshade: a nondescript bush with feathered leaves. Jacob was filling his hand with its black berries when he heard footsteps.

Clara stood between the overgrown plots.

"Monkshood, May lilies, hemlock...so the Witches do indeed use all the plants associated with them."

Jacob wondered whether she had learned about Witch plants as a student of medicine, or from her childhood's fairy tale books. Will had told him the story of how he met her at the hospital where their mother had been treated. *When you were not there, Jacob.* He wasn't sure what he was searching for when she first fell sick. A princess' Golden Ball, as far as he recalled.

He got to his feet. "These are mostly plants you'll find in the child-eaters' gardens. The healing Witches grow many others, and if they use these they know ways to make them heal."

Out in the forest, the sound of snipping could again be heard.

Jacob filled Clara's hands with the shiny black fruit they had come for. "I doubt you've ever learned about these berries. Will must eat at least a dozen of them. They should have done their

56

work by the time the sun rises. Persuade him to lie down in the house; he hasn't slept in days."

Goyl didn't need much sleep. One of the many advantages they had over humans.

Clara looked at the berries in her hand. She had a thousand questions on her tongue, but she didn't ask them. The stories Will had told her about Jacob were mostly the memories of a boy who adored his older brother without really knowing much about him. They were so different that it was hard to believe they had the same mother. And father. Maybe she dreamt them both. Maybe she had fallen asleep over one of her old fairy tale books. As a child, she had despised and loved them, as they were so strange and so different from her other books. *Clara, wake up!* she told herself, but the hand that used to wake her from bad dreams was long gone. The gingerbread house was still there, right in front of her, surrounded by hemlock and monkshood, and so was Will's brother, so much darker, as wild as the fox who followed him...

Clara turned around and listened.

This time she had heard the snipping as well.

"What's that?" she asked.

"They call him the Tailor. He doesn't dare to cross the Witch's fence, but we cannot leave as long as he's there. I'll try to drive him off." Jacob pulled the key from his pocket that he had taken from the Troll's chest. "The fence won't let you leave. But this key opens every door. I'll throw it over the gate once I'm out, just in case I don't come back. Fox will lead you back to the ruin. But don't unlock the gate before dawn."

Clara had another thousand questions. But she knew Jacob still wouldn't answer any of them.

57

"Don't let Will sleep in the room with the oven," he told her. "The air there gives bleak dreams. And make sure he doesn't try to follow me."

"I promise," she said. *If you promise to come back,* she added in her mind.

Brothers. She didn't have any siblings. But she remembered all the stories Will had told her about how Jacob had protected him as a child, and that his brother wasn't afraid of anything. Or anyone. But Jacob was afraid of the creature hiding between the trees. Clara saw it in his face, although he was very good at hiding what went on inside.

Will was still standing by the well. He stumbled with fatigue as he walked toward her. And he ate the berries without hesitation. The magic that would heal everything. Even as a child he had believed in such things much more readily than Jacob. It was obvious how tired he was, and he didn't protest when Clara led him toward the gingerbread house.

Jacob waited until they had both disappeared behind the sugar-coated door. The sun was setting behind the trees, and the red moon hung above the Witch's roof like a bloody fingerprint. When the sun returned, the jade in his brother's skin would be nothing but a bad dream. *If the berries worked.*

If.

Jacob went to the fence and stared out into the forest.

Snip-snap.

Their pursuer was still there. Of course. He had a reputation of being a tireless hunter.

Fox's eyes followed Jacob as he walked toward the mare and pulled Chanute's knife from the saddlebag. Bullets were useless against the enemy waiting for him. Rumors said they even made the Tailor stronger.

The gathering night filled the forest with a thousand shadows, and Jacob believed he could see a dark figure standing among the trees. He didn't look as tall as the stories about him claimed. *At least he'll help pass the time until sunrise, Jacob.* He pushed the knife into his belt and once again took the flashlight from his knapsack. Fox followed him when he walked towards the fence.

"You can't go out there. It's getting dark. Wait at least until morning."

"And then?"

"Maybe he'll be gone by then!"

"Why should he?"

The gate sprang open as soon as Jacob pushed the key into the rusty lock. Surely many desperate children had rattled that gate in vain.

"You stay here," he said. "The vixen can't fight the Tailor and, if he is as good as they say, you will be Will's only chance to get out of this forest."

"So? He is your brother, not mine," Fox replied and slipped out of the gate. Jacob knew her too well to fight her. He closed the Witch's gate behind him and cast one more glance at the house where his brother slept. Then he followed Fox into the forest.

8
UNDER THE WITCH'S ROOF

The first room was the one with the oven. It smelled of cake and roasted almonds, and Clara pulled Will along when he looked through the door. In the next room, a shawl was draped over the back of a tattered armchair, its red silk embroidered with a pattern of ravens. The bed was in the last room. It was barely big enough for both of them, and the blankets were moth-eaten, but Will was already fast asleep by the time Jacob pulled the gate shut outside.

The jade traced patterns on Will's neck, resembling the shadows in the forest. Clara gently touched the pale green stone. So cool and smooth. So terrible and yet so beautiful.

What would happen if the berries didn't work? She felt that Jacob knew the answer, and that it frightened him even more than the creature he had set out to fight.

The bedroom of a Witch. Clara looked at the dust-covered lamp above her. The white porcelain looked so normal. Its ordinariness made the terror of the house even more palpable for Clara. She could barely breathe, though Will was sleeping so peacefully. He didn't wake up when she freed herself from his embrace. A moth had landed on his shoulder, black winged, like an imprint of the night. Clara chased it away. She couldn't say why. It frightened her as much as the house. Everything in this world frightened her. How could Jacob prefer it to the one they came from? So much danger, so much darkness. All the magic, she didn't want it. She preferred clarity, order, safety...

Even the night seemed to smell of cinnamon and cloves when she stepped out of the house. The vixen was nowhere to be seen. Of course. She had gone with Jacob. The house covered in cakes, the red moon above the trees—everything seemed so unreal that Clara felt like a sleepwalker. Will was the only familiar thing, but the strangeness was already growing in his skin.

The key was lying right behind the gate, as Jacob had promised. Clara picked it up and ran her fingers over the engraved metal. Will-o'-the-wisp voices filled the air. A raven cawed somewhere in the trees. But Clara was listening for another sound: the sharp snipping that had darkened Jacob's face with worry. What creature could be so terrible that it turned even the house of a child-eater into a safe haven? Clara was not sure she wanted to learn the answer.

Snip-snap. There it was again. Like the snapping of metallic teeth. Clara backed away from the fence. Long shadows were growing toward the house, and she felt the same fear she'd felt as a child when she was alone and heard steps in the hallway.

She should have told Will what his brother was planning. He would never forgive her if Jacob didn't come back.

He would come back.

He had to come back.

They would never find their way home without him.

9
The Tailor

Was he coming after them? Jacob walked slowly, so the hunter he was trying to lure could follow. But all he heard was his own steps, rotting twigs snapping under his boots, leaves rustling as he pushed through the undergrowth. *Where was he?* Jacob was beginning to fear that their pursuer had forgotten his wariness of the Witch and was sneaking through the gate behind his back, when suddenly he heard the snipping again, coming through the forest to his left. It was just as everybody said: the Tailor loved to play a little cat-and-mouse with his victims before commencing his bloody work.

Nobody could say who or what exactly the Tailor was. The stories about him were almost as old as the Hungry Forest itself. There was only one thing everybody knew for certain: the Tailor had earned his name by tailoring his clothes from human skin.

65

Snip-snap, clip-clip. The trees opened into a clearing. Fox gave Jacob a warning look as a murder of crows fluttered up from the branches of an oak. The *snip-snap* grew so loud that it drowned out their squawks, and under an oak the beam of Jacob's flashlight found the outline of a man.

The Tailor did not like the probing finger of light. He uttered an angry grunt and swatted at it as if it were an annoying bug. But Jacob let the light explore further, over the bearded, dirt-caked face, the gruesome clothes, which at first sight simply looked like poorly tanned leather, and on to the gross hands with which the Tailor plied his bloody trade. The fingers on his left hand ended in broad blades, each as long as a dagger. The blades on the right were just as long and lethal, though these were slender and pointed, like giant sewing needles. Both hands were missing a finger—obviously other victims had tried to defend their skins—though the Tailor did not seem to miss them much. He let his murderous fingernails slice through the air as if he were cutting a pattern from the shadows of the trees, taking measurements for the clothes he would soon fashion from Jacob's skin.

Fox bared her teeth and retreated with a bark to Jacob's side. He drew his saber with his left hand and Chanute's knife with his right. *There is nothing this blade won't cut.* Jacob could only hope that wasn't one of Chanute's boastful lies, which he turned for himself so easily into undoubted truth.

Their opponent moved clumsily, like a bear, while his hands cut a path through bramble and thistles with terrifying zeal. His eyes were as blank as a dead man's, but the bearded face was contorted into a mask of bloodlust, and he bared his yellow teeth as if he wanted to use them to peel off Jacob's skin.

Don't run, Jacob.

The Tailor raised his terrible hands. One more step. The stench rising from his foul clothes made Jacob choke. At first, the Tailor hacked at him with the broad blades. Jacob blocked them with his saber while he slashed at the needle hand with his knife. He'd fought a half dozen drunken soldiers, the guards of enchanted castles, highwaymen, and even a pack of trained wolves, but this was far worse. The Tailor's hacking and stabbing was so relentless, Jacob felt as if he were caught in a threshing machine.

His foe wasn't very tall, and Jacob was more nimble, yet soon he felt the first cuts on his arms and shoulders. *Come on, Jacob. Look at his clothes. Do you want to end up like that?* He hacked off one of the needle fingers with his knife, used the ensuing howls of rage to catch his breath—and barely managed to yank up his saber before the blades could slash his face. Two of the needles cut his cheek like the claws of a cat. A third neatly pierced his arm. Jacob retreated between the trees, letting the blades cut into the bark and not his skin, but the Tailor freed himself again and again and didn't seem to tire, while Jacob's arms grew ever heavier.

He cut off another finger as one of the blades hacked into the bark right next to him. The Tailor howled like a wolf, yet he slashed with even greater rage—and there was no blood running from his wounds.

You will end up as a pair of pants, Jacob! His breathing grew labored. His heart was racing. He stumbled over a root and, before Jacob could catch himself, the Tailor stabbed one of his needles deep into his shoulder. The pain buckled his knees, and he had no breath left to call Fox back as she jumped at the Tailor and sunk her teeth deep into his leg. She had so often saved Jacob's skin, but never quite so literally. The Tailor tried to shake her off. He had forgotten about Jacob, and as he angrily struck out to hack

67

his blades into the vixen's red fur, Jacob slashed off his left arm with Chanute's knife.

The Tailor's scream echoed through the Hungry Forest. He stared at the useless stump of his arm and at the bladed hand lying on the moss in front of him. Then he spun around, wheezing, to face Jacob. The remaining hand came down on him with deadly force. Three steel needles, murderous daggers. Jacob thought he could already feel their metal inside him, but before they could pierce his flesh, he rammed his knife deep in the Tailor's chest.

His enemy grunted, pressing his fingers to his terrible shirt. Then his knees buckled.

Jacob staggered to the nearest tree, fighting for breath while the Tailor thrashed in pain on the wet moss. One final gasp and then silence. Jacob did not drop his knife, even though the glazed eyes in the grimy face stared emptily skyward. He wasn't convinced there was such a thing as death for the Tailor. He let himself drop to his knees, and stared at the lifeless body. He had no idea how long he remained crouched there. His skin was burning as if he'd been rolling around in broken glass. His shoulder was numb with pain, and in front of his eyes the blades were still performing their murderous dance.

"Jacob!" Fox's voice seemed to come to him from afar. She was shivering as if hounds had been after her. "Get up. It's safer at the house!"

He barely got to his feet.

The Tailor still wasn't moving.

It seemed a very long way back to the gingerbread house, and when it finally appeared between the trees, Jacob saw Clara waiting behind the fence.

"Oh, God!" was all she murmured when she saw the blood on his shirt. She fetched water from the well and washed the cuts. Jacob flinched as her fingers probed his shoulder.

"This one is deep," she said as Fox anxiously crouched by his side. "I wish it would bleed more freely."

"There's iodine and some bandages in my saddlebag." Jacob was grateful that she was used to the sight of bloody wounds. "What about Will? Is he asleep?"

"Yes." And the jade was still there. She didn't have to say it.

Of course she wanted to know what had happened in the forest, but that was the last thing Jacob wanted to remember.

Clara fetched the iodine from his saddlebag and dripped the tincture on his wound, but she still looked worried.

"Fox, what plants do you usually roll in when you're wounded?" she asked.

The vixen found the herbs in the Witch's garden. They gave off a bittersweet aroma as Clara plucked them apart and pressed them against Jacob's pierced skin.

"Like a born Witch," he said. "Didn't Will meet you in a hospital?"

"Have you forgotten?" she replied. "In our world, the Witches work in hospitals."

She noticed the scars on his back when she pulled the shirt over his bandaged shoulder. "Those must have been terrible injuries."

Fox shot him a knowing look, but Jacob just buttoned his shirt with a shrug.

"I survived."

Another event he didn't want to remember.

Clara handed him the key that opened every gate. Magical tools. Without Chanute's knife he probably wouldn't have come back.

"Thank you," Clara said. "I really don't know what I would have done, if..." She didn't say it. As if it could still come true in a world where so many things proved to be real, and on the other side filled books and nightmares.

Then she got up and went back into the house where Will was still sleeping.

10
Fur and Skin

Jacob knew too much about gingerbread houses to sleep under the sugar-icing roof. He took the tin plate from his saddlebag and sat down with it in front of the well, polishing it until it filled with bread and cheese. It wasn't a five-course dinner, like the one provided by the Wishing Table he had found for Therese of Austry, but at least the plate fit into a saddlebag.

The red moon splashed rust into the night, and dawn was still hours away, but Jacob didn't dare to go find out whether the jade in Will's skin had vanished. The vixen was licking her fur. The Tailor had kicked her, and she had several cuts on her body, but she would be fine. Human skin was so much more fragile than fur—or Goyl skin.

"You should try to sleep," she said.

"I can't sleep."

71

His shoulder ached, and he imagined the Witch's black magic battling the Dark Fairy's spell.

"What are you going to do if the berries do work? Take them back?"

Fox tried hard to sound unconcerned, but Jacob heard the unspoken question behind her words. *Will you go with them?* No matter how often he told her that he considered this world his true home, she still feared that one day he would climb up the tower to never return.

"First of all: no. I won't go with them," he said. "But yes: I'll bring them back to the ruin. And then, hopefully…happily ever after."

It is not easy to read a vixen's face, but Jacob knew her well enough to feel her relief.

"So once they're gone…" she nestled close to his side when he shuddered in the cold night air, "What about us? Winter's coming. We could head south, to Granady or Lombardia, and look for the Hourglass."

The Hourglass that stops time. Just a few weeks back, it had been all Jacob could think about. The Talking Mirror. The Glass Slipper. The Spinning Wheel that spun gold. There was always something to hunt for in this world. The fact that he did it so successfully made him most times even forget that he still hadn't found any trace of his father.

He took a piece of bread from the plate and offered it to the vixen. "When did you last shift?"

She backed away.

"Fox!"

She gave a sharp bark of disapproval, but then her shadow, cast by the moonlight, began to change its shape.

72

Fox. The girl rising to her feet just a few steps away from him had hair as red as the pelt she so much preferred to her human skin. It fell down her back as though she were still wearing her fur. Even the russet dress she wore over her freckled skin shimmered in the moonlight as if it had been woven from the silky coat of the vixen.

She had changed in these past months, nearly as suddenly as a fox cub becomes a vixen. But Jacob still saw the ten-year-old girl he had found one night crying at the bottom of the tower because he had stayed much longer in the world he had come from than he had promised. The vixen had been following him for nearly a year by then, without ever showing Jacob her human form. He often reminded her that she would one day lose it if she kept wearing her fur too often, although he knew she would always choose the fur, should anything force her to decide. She had been seven years old when she had saved a vixen's cubs from the sticks of her elder brothers. The next day, she'd found the furry dress on her bed. It had given Fox the body she had come to regard as her true self, and her greatest fear was that, someday, someone might steal the dress and take the fur away from her.

Jacob leaned back against the well. *The berries will work, Jacob.* But the night seemed endless and finally he fell asleep, next to the girl who did not want the skin that his brother had to fight for. His sleep was troubled. Even his dreams were made from stone. Chanute, the paperboy on the square in Schwanstein, his mother, his father...they all froze into statues standing among the trees next to the dead Tailor.

"Jacob! Wake up!"

The vixen was standing beside him as if he had dreamed her human form as well. The first light of dawn was seeping through

73

the pine trees and his shoulder ached so much that he barely managed to get to his feet. *Everything will be fine, Jacob. Chanute knows this world like no one else. Remember how he exorcised the Gold-Raven's spell from you? You were already half-dead.*

Nevertheless, his heart beat faster with every step he took toward the gingerbread house.

The sweet smell inside nearly choked him. It was probably the reason that Will and Clara were still fast asleep. She had her arms wrapped around Will, whose face was so peaceful, as if he were sleeping in the bed of a prince, not a child-eater. But his left cheek was speckled with jade, as if it had spilled onto his skin, and the nails on his left hand were nearly as black as the claws that had sown the Petrified Flesh into his neck.

How loud a heart can beat.

The berries will work.

Jacob was still staring at the jade when Will finally stirred. Jacob's eyes told him everything. Will put his hand to his neck and traced the stone up to his cheek.

Think, Jacob. But his mind drowned in the fear flooding his brother's face.

They let Clara sleep. Will followed Jacob outside like a sleepwalker caught in a nightmare.

Fox backed away from him. The look she gave Jacob said only one thing.

Lost.

And that was how Will stood there. Lost. He touched his face, and for the first time Jacob could no longer find the trust his brother had always granted him so freely. Instead, Jacob believed he saw all the blame he put on himself. All the, *If only you'd been more careful, Jacob...if you only hadn't taken him so far east...if only...*

74

Will stepped to the window behind which the oven stood, and he stared at the image the dark panes threw back at him. Above him, the sugared roof was lined with soot-blackened cobwebs. Jacob couldn't take his eyes off them. They reminded him of other webs, just as dark, spun to catch the night.

What an idiot he was. *What was he doing at a Witch's house?* This was the curse of a Fairy. *A Fairy!*

Fox was watching him.

"No!" she barked. "Forget it!"

Sometimes she knew what he was thinking even before he himself could give words to his thoughts.

"She'll definitely be able to help him. After all, she is her sister."

"You can't go back to her! Ever."

Will turned around. "Go back to whom?"

Jacob didn't answer. He reached for the medallion beneath his shirt. His fingers still remembered picking the petal that he kept inside it. Just as his heart remembered the one from whom the leaf protected him.

"Go and wake Clara," he said to Will. "We're leaving."

It was a long way—four days, maybe more—and they had to be faster than the jade.

Fox was still looking at him.

No, Jacob! No! her eyes pleaded with him.

Of course she remembered it all as well as he did, if not better. *Must have been terrible injuries.* Yes. He had almost died.

But this was the only way, if he wanted to save his brother.

11
HENTZAU

The Man-Goyl they found in a deserted coach station was growing a skin of malachite. Half of his face was already grained with the dark green stone. Hentzau had let him go, like all the others they had found, with the advice to seek refuge in the nearest Goyl camp—before his own kind would murder him. But there was no gold yet in his eyes, and he still missed his human skin, so he ran away as if there was still a chance to return to his older life. Hentzau shuddered watching him stumble away over the barren fields. *What if the Fairy one day decided to sow human flesh into his jasper skin?*

Malachite, bloodstone, carnelian...they found the king's color quite often. The Fairy seemed to have made sure that many of the sons she gave to Kami'en resembled him. So far, there'd been no trace of the stone they were looking for, though.

Jade. The sacred stone of the Goyl.

Their old women wore it as talismans around their necks and knelt before idols carved from the stone. Mothers sewed jade into their children's clothes so the stone would grant them protection and make them fearless. But there had never been a Goyl with jade skin.

How long would the Dark Fairy have him search? How long would he have to act like a fool in front of his soldiers and his king? What if she had invented the dream to separate him from Kami'en? *Yes, that's what she was after.* She despised his devotion and his influence on the king. And instead of saying *No*, he'd run off, ever loyal and obedient, like a dog.

Hentzau eyed the trees lining the deserted road. His soldiers were growing nervous. The Goyl avoided the Hungry Forest as much as the humans did. The Fairy knew that very well. This was a game — her game. He was so tired of dancing like a puppet when she pulled the strings. And watching Kami'en getting caught in them too, more and more with every day.

The moth settled on Hentzau's chest just as he was about to give the order to mount up. It clawed itself to his gray uniform, right above his heart, and Hentzau saw the Jade Goyl just as clearly as the Fairy had in her dreams.

The pale green stone ran through his human skin like a promise. *It could not be.*

But then the deep brought forth a King, and when there came a time of great peril for him, the Jade Goyl was summoned to come to his aid, born from glass and silver and a Fairy's magic, and he protected the King from his enemies and made him invincible, even to death.

78

Old wives' tales. As a child, Hentzau had loved nothing more than listening to them because they gave the world meaning and a happy ending. A world that was clearly divided into above and below, and was ruled by soft-fleshed gods. But since then Hentzau had sliced their soft flesh and he had learned that they weren't gods, just as he had learned that the world made no sense and there were no happy endings.

The images the moth made him see told another story. They claimed that the fairy tales were telling the truth. The Jade Goyl... Hentzau saw him as clearly as if he could reach out and touch the pale green stone in his skin. A Fairy's curse had brought the oldest myth of the Goyl to life. Had this been her plan all along? Had she sown all that petrified flesh only to reap him?

What do you care, Hentzau? Find him!

The moth spread its wings one more time, and he saw the fields he had fought on just a few months earlier. Fields that bordered the eastern boundary of the Hungry Forest. He was searching on the wrong side.

Hentzau suppressed a curse and swatted the moth dead.

His soldiers mounted their horses reluctantly when he gave the order to ride east, as that meant they would have to continue through the Forest. Hentzau wiped the crushed moth from his uniform as he swung himself into the saddle. None of his men had seen the moth. They would all confirm he had found the Jade Goyl without the Fairy's help—just as he kept telling everyone that it was Kami'en who was winning the war, and not the curse of his immortal beloved.

The Jade Goyl.

She had indeed dreamed the truth.

Or spun the truth from a dream.

79

12
His Own Kind

It was early afternoon by the time they finally left the Hungry Forest behind. Dark clouds hung above fields and meadows, patches of green, yellow, and brown that stretched to the horizon. Elderberry bushes bore heavy clusters of black berries, and Grass Elves, their wings wet with rain, fluttered among the wildflowers by the roadside. One of them landed on Clara's shoulder, and for the first time she felt the enchantment that had been drawing Jacob through the mirror for all these years. However, the farms they passed were deserted, and on the fields cannons were rusting among the unharvested wheat.

Jacob was grateful for the abandoned farms. Not even the hooded cloak could hide the jade any longer, and the dense rain pouring down from the sky made it shimmer on Will's face like the glaze of a sinister potter.

Jacob still hadn't told Will where he was leading him, and he was grateful Will didn't insist on knowing. Fox punished him with a frosty silence for his decision to seek help at the only place in this world to which he had sworn never to return.

The rain was falling by now so mercilessly that even the vixen's fur no longer gave her any protection. Jacob's wound throbbed as if the Tailor was once again jabbing his needles into his shoulder, but every glance at Will's face made him push away any thought of rest. They were running out of time. Sometimes the transformation took less than week, but some bodies could resist longer. Jacob still hoped that his brother got some kind of protection from the fact that he hadn't been born in this world, but it was just a feeble hope. After all, it hadn't protected Will from being changed by the Fairy's curse.

Maybe it was the wound that made him careless. He had developed a fever and the pain numbed all his senses. Jacob barely noticed the abandoned farm when it appeared by the side of the road. They had passed so many, and Fox only caught the men's scent when it was already too late. There were eight of them, ragged but armed. They emerged so suddenly from the ruined barn and aimed their rifles at them before Jacob could draw his pistol. Two of them were wearing the long coats of the imperial troops, and a third the gray jacket of a Goyl soldier. Plunderers and deserters. The human debris of war. One of them had the trophies hanging from his belt that many imperial soldiers liked to display: the fingers of their stone-skinned enemies, in all the colors they could find.

For one brief moment, Jacob nursed the foolish hope that they wouldn't notice the jade. Will had drawn the hood of his cloak down over his face. However, one of them, a scrawny weasel of a man, noticed the stone on Will's hand as he dragged him from his horse.

The man yanked the hood off his head.

Clara attempted to shield Will, but the one with the Goyl jacket slapped her and pushed her roughly out of the way. Will's face turned into that of a stranger. It was the first time Jacob saw such a powerful desire to hurt someone in his brother's gentle features. Will freed himself and drove his elbow so violently into the man's face that blood poured out of his nose. Jacob wanted to come to Will's aid, but before he could pull his pistol, the gang's leader put the muzzle of his rifle to his chest.

He was a heavyset fellow with only three fingers on his left hand. His threadbare coat was covered with the semi-precious stones Goyl officers wore on their collars to denote rank. There was a lot of booty to be grabbed on the battlefields once the living left the dead behind.

"Why haven't you shot that Man-Goyl yet?" the leader asked while he searched Jacob's pockets. "Haven't you heard? There are no more rewards to be had for them, now that our Empress started negotiating with their King."

"Really?" Jacob said. "I heard in Terpevas the Dwarfs still pay very well for them."

Threefingers pulled out the gold handkerchief. Luckily he shoved it back heedlessly before it dropped coins into his calloused hand.

Distract him, Jacob. Talk.

Behind them, the vixen scurried into one of the ruined stables. Jacob could feel Clara looking at him pleadingly, but what did she expect? That he could take on eight men at once?

"Terpevas?" Threefingers poured out the contents of Jacob's purse and gave a disappointed grunt when all he found were a few copper coins. "That's where you were heading? Bad luck. No Goyl gets past us alive, even if those damned Dwarfs pay their weight in gold."

The others were still staring at Will as if they had caught a rabid dog. They were going to kill him. Out of hatred or just for the fun of it. They would adorn their belts with his brother's fingers.

Do something, Jacob! But what?

"Okay, I lied. We are not heading for Terpevas." The rain was running down his face, and the weasel was jabbing his rifle under Will's chin.

Talk, Jacob.

"He's my brother. I am taking him to someone who will give him back his human skin. Let us go, and in a week's time I'll be back with a sack of gold."

"Sure!" Threefingers nodded to the others. "Take them behind the barn. Burn the Goyl. The girl is mine. And this one — " he pointed at Jacob, " — shoot him in the head. I like his clothes."

Jacob pushed away the two men who reached out to grab him, but a third put a knife to his throat. He was wearing the clothes of a peasant. Most of them hadn't always been robbers.

"What are you talking about?" he hissed into Jacob's ear. "Nothing can give them their skin back. I shot my own son when the moonstone started growing on his forehead!"

The blade pushed against his throat with such ferocity that Jacob could barely breathe.

"It's the curse of the Dark Fairy!" he croaked. "So I'm taking him to her red sister. She'll break it."

How they all backed away. *Fairy.* Five letters, melting all the magic and all the terror of this world into one word. And surely they had all heard about the Dark Fairy's red sister, although she rarely showed herself amongst mortals.

The pressure of the knife eased, but the man's face was still contorted with rage and helpless grief. Jacob was tempted to ask him how old his son had been.

"You're lying! Nobody just goes to see a Fairy." The boy who stammered these words was fifteen at the most. "They come and get you."

"I know a way." *Keep talking, Jacob.* "I've visited the Red One before."

"Really? So why aren't you dead, then?" The knife was breaking his skin. "Or crazy, like the ones who come back and then drown themselves in the nearest pond?"

Jacob felt Will staring at him. What was he thinking? That his older brother was telling fairy tales, just as he had done when they were young and Will couldn't sleep?

"They say the Red Fairy is not as powerful as her dark sister," said one of the others.

"She's powerful enough, and she will get rid of the stone," Jacob said, hoarse from the pressure of the knife. *But before that, you'll kill us. And it still won't bring back your son.*

The weasel pushed the muzzle of his rifle into Will's jade speckled cheek. "Going to see the Fairies? Can't you see he's making fun of you? Come on. I want to see the Goyl burn!"

He shoved Will in the direction of the barn. Two of the others grabbed Clara. *Now, Jacob. What have you go to lose?*

But Threefingers suddenly spun around and stared past the stable to the south. Through the rain came the snorting of horses.

85

Riders.

They came over the fallow fields on horses as gray as their uniforms, and Will's face said very clearly who they were, even before the weasel yelled it to the others.

"Goyl!"

The peasant pointed his rifle at Will, as if only he could have called them, but Jacob shot him before he could pull the trigger. Three of the Goyl drew their sabers. They still preferred fighting with their swords, though they won their battles by now with guns and cannons.

Clara stared, dumbfounded, at the stone faces. Then she looked at Jacob. *Yes, that's what he's becoming. You still love him?*

The bandits sought cover behind a toppled cart. They had clearly forgotten about their prisoners, and Jacob quickly pushed Will and Clara toward the horses.

"Fox!" he yelled, grabbing the mare's reins. *Where was she?*

Two of the Goyl fell off their horses; the others took cover behind the barn. Threefingers was a good shot.

Clara was already sitting on her horse, but Will was just standing there, staring across the yard at the Goyl.

"Get on your horse, Will!" Jacob screamed as he swung himself onto his mare.

But his brother didn't stir.

Jacob was about to drive his horse toward Will when he saw Fox scamper out of the barn. She was limping, and the weasel was aiming his rifle at her. Jacob shot him down, but just as he reined in the mare and leaned forward to grab the vixen, he was hit on his injured shoulder by the butt of a rifle. The boy. He was standing there, holding his empty weapon by the barrel. He was

86

already striking out again as if, by killing Jacob, he could slay his own fear.

The pain made everything swim in front of Jacob's eyes. He managed to draw his pistol, but the Goyl were quicker. They swarmed out from behind the barn, and one of their bullets struck the boy in the back.

Jacob managed to grab Fox and lifted her into the saddle. Will had also swung himself back onto his horse, though he was still staring at the Goyl.

"Will!" Jacob yelled again. "Ride, dammit!"

His brother didn't even look at him.

"Will!" Clara screamed, glancing desperately at the fighting men.

But Will only came to his senses when Jacob snatched his reins.

"Ride!" he yelled at Will once more. "Ride, and don't look back."

And at last his brother turned his horse.

13
OF THE USE OF DAUGHTERS

Defeated. Therese of Austry was standing by the window, staring down at the palace guards. They were patrolling in their white uniforms as if nothing had happened. All of Vena lay below her as if nothing had happened, with its cupolas and towers, its pride and bombast of a triumphant past. But she had lost a war. For the first time. And every night she dreamed she was drowning in bloody water, which invariably turned into the pale red carnelian skin of her foe.

For the past hour, her ministers and generals had been explaining to her why she couldn't blame them for the defeat. They were all gathered in her audience chamber, decorated with the medals she'd given them, and they tried to put the blame on her. "We warned you, Your Majesty! The Goyl have better rifles." "Our troops' weapons are obsolete." "Their trains are faster. Their roads are better..." But the King with the carnelian skin was winning this war because he had a better grasp of strategy than all of them together. And because he had a mistress who, for the first time in more than three hundred years, had put the magic of the Fairies in the service of a mortal King.

A carriage drew up to the gate.

There they were. Her enemies. Three Goyl officers. They acted so civilized. They weren't even in uniform. How she would have loved to order her guards to drag them through the courtyard and club them to death, as her grandfather would have done. But these were different times. Now it was the Goyl who did the clubbing. So her counselors would sit down with them, offer them food they despised, and negotiate terms of surrender.

The servants opened the coach's doors, and the Empress turned her back to the window as the Goyl climbed the steps of the palace.

They were still talking—all her useless, medaled generals—while her ancestors stared down at her from the golden, silk-draped walls. Right next to the door was a portrait of her father, gaunt and upright like a stork, continuously at war with his royal brother from Lotharaine, just as she had been fighting his son, the Crookback, for years. Next to her father was his father who, like the Goyl King, had once had an affair with a Fairy. His yearning for her had finally driven him to drown himself in the lily pond behind the palace. He'd had himself portrayed as a knight who had caught one of the Fairies' Unicorns. His favorite horse had played the Unicorn, with a narwhal horn attached to its head. The portrait looked as ludicrous as the one that showed another ancestor of hers standing next to a slain Giant's head. Therese had always preferred the painting at the very end of the illustrious row. It showed her great-grandfather with his elder brother, who had been disinherited because he had taken his alchemical experiments too seriously. Her father had always been outraged that the painter had shown his great-uncle's blind eyes so realistically. Therese, though, would push a chair under the picture as a child, to get a closer look at the scars around those empty eyes. He'd supposedly been blinded by an experiment in which he had tried to turn his own heart into gold, and yet, of all her ancestors, he was the only one on all the portraits who was smiling—which had always made her think that his experiment must have been successful and that he indeed had a golden heart beating in his chest.

Men. All of them. Crazy or sane. Always just men.

For centuries they had claimed the exclusive right to ascend to the throne of Austry. That had changed only because her father had sired four daughters but not a single son.

Therese, too, had no son, just a daughter. But she had never intended to turn Amalie into a bargaining chip, as her father had done with her younger sisters. One for the Crookback, in his sinister castle in Lotharaine; one for her cousin in Albion, who paid far more attention to his dogs and the hunting season than to his wife; and the youngest had been bartered away to one of the eastern Wolf Lords who had already buried two wives.

No. Therese had wanted to put her daughter on the throne, to see her portrait on that wall, framed in gold, between all those men. Amalie of Austry, daughter of Therese, who had once dreamed of being called The Great, as she had defeated so many men. But not the one with the carnelian skin. And now she would have to give him her daughter or they would both drown in that bloody water—she, her daughter, her people, her throne, this city, and the whole country—together with those idiots who were still holding

91

forth about why they hadn't been able to win this war. Therese's father would have had them all executed. But then what? The next lot wouldn't be any better, and their blood would not bring back all the soldiers she had lost, the provinces that now belonged to the Goyl, or her pride, which in the past six months had been choked in the mud of four battlefields.

"Enough!"

One word, and the room where her great-grandfather used to sign death warrants fell silent. Power. It still intoxicated Therese like a good wine.

Look at them, Therese. How they drew their vain heads between their shoulders. *Wouldn't it be nice to have them all chopped off after all?*

The Empress adjusted the tiara of elven glass that her great-grandmother had worn before her and waved one of the court Dwarfs to her desk. They were the only Dwarfs in Austry who still wore beards. Servants, bodyguards, confidants. Generations of service to her family, and still in the same livery they had worn for over two hundred years. Lace collars over black velvet, and then those ridiculously wide breeches. Tasteless and completely unfashionable, but you couldn't argue with Dwarfs about tradition any more than you could argue with priests about religion.

"Write," she ordered.

The Dwarf climbed onto her chair. He had to kneel on the pale golden cushion. Auberon. Her favorite and the smartest of them all. The hand that reached for the quill was as small as a child's, but those hands would break iron chains as easily as her cook's hands cracked an egg.

"We, Therese of Austry—" Her ancestors stared down at her disapprovingly. What did they know of kings brought forth from the bowels of the earth, and a Fairy who turned human skin to stone to make it resemble the skin of her lover? "—herewith offer to Kami'en, King of the Goyl, our daughter Amalie's hand in marriage, to bring an end to the war and to bring peace to our two great nations."

How the silence erupted. As if her words had shattered the glass house in which they had all been sitting. It wasn't she, but the Goyl who had struck the blow, and now she had to give him her daughter.

The Empress turned her back on them, silencing their angered voices. Only the rustle of her dress followed her as she stepped toward the doors, so high that they seemed to be built not for humans but for the Giants who, thanks to her great-grandfather's efforts, had been driven to extinction fifty years ago.

Power. *Intoxicating like wine when one possessed it. Like poison when it was lost.* Therese already felt it eating away at her.

Defeated.

94

14

THE CASTLE OF THORNS AND ROSES

"But it's been too long. He just won't wake up!" The voice sounded worried. And familiar. Fox.

"That's all I can do. Please don't worry. I think he's just sleeping." That voice he recognized as well. Clara.

Wake up, Jacob. Fingers touched his searing shoulder. He opened his eyes and saw the silver moon drifting behind a cloud, as if trying to hide from its red twin. Its rusty light shone down into the dark courtyard of a castle, reflecting on countless high windows. They were all dark. No lanterns cast their light above the stucco-framed doors or under the overgrown archways. No servant hurried across the yard where the layer of wet leaves was so thick that clearly no one had raked it in years

"Finally! I thought you'd never wake up."

Jacob groaned as the vixen nudged her nose into his shoulder.

Clara helped him sit up. There was a fresh dressing on his shoulder, but the wound hurt more than ever. The bandits, the Goyl...the pain brought it all back, but Jacob couldn't remember when he had lost consciousness.

"That wound doesn't look good." Clara got up. "I wish I had some pills from the hospital."

Jacob wished for those too, but he had given the last ones to Will.

"Where are we?" he asked her.

"At the only hiding place I could find. The castle is deserted. At least by the living." Fox pushed aside the leaves, revealing a shoe.

Jacob looked around. In many places the leaves lay suspiciously deep, as if covering outstretched bodies.

Which castle was this?

He sought support from a wall to pull himself to his feet, and immediately drew back his hands, cursing. The stones were covered in thorny vines. They were everywhere, as if the entire castle had grown a hide of thorns.

"Roses," he muttered, picking one of the rosehips that grew from the twisted branches. "I've been searching for this castle for years! Sleeping Beauty's bed. The Empress would pay a fortune for it."

Clara stared incredulously across the silent courtyard.

"It's said that anyone who sleeps in her bed will find true love. But it seems—" Jacob gazed at the dark windows, "the prince never came."

Or he had perished on the thorns like a skewered bird. A mummified hand stuck out from between the roses. Jacob covered its stiff fingers with leaves before Clara noticed them.

96

A mouse scampered across the courtyard. The vixen jumped after it, but she stopped with a whimper.

"What is it?" Clara asked.

"Nothing." Fox licked her side. "Threefingers kicked me."

"Let me have a look." Clara leaned over her and carefully prodded her silky fur.

"Come on. Lose the fur, Fox," Jacob said. "Clara knows more about humans than foxes."

Fox hesitated. She didn't like to share her secret. The only other person she'd told was Chanute. But finally she shifted shape and Clara stared incredulously at the girl who suddenly stood a few steps away from her.

What kind of world is this? her face asked as she turned to Jacob. *If fur turns to skin, and skin to stone, what remains?* Fear. Bewilderment. And enchantment. All of that was in her eyes. She touched her own arms as if she felt the fur spreading there too. Then she stepped toward Fox and examined the body which had, just a moment ago, been the body of a vixen.

"Where's Will?" Jacob asked, looking for him in vain in the silent courtyard.

Clara pointed to one of the castle towers. "He's been up there for hours. He hasn't said a word since he saw them."

They all knew who she was talking about. The Goyl had saved their lives, but Jacob doubted they had come for that.

❊ ❊ ❊

The roses covering the tower's walls were a red so dark that the night almost dyed them black, and the scent they wove into the cold air was as heavy and sweet as if they didn't sense the autumn yet.

Jacob already guessed what he would find under the tower's pointed roof before he started climbing its steep spiral stairs. The rose tendrils clung to his clothes and he had to keep freeing his boots from their thorny stems, but finally he reached the room where, two hundred years earlier, a Fairy had delivered her birthday present.

The spinning wheel stood next to a narrow bed that had never been meant for a princess. She was still sleeping in it, rose petals covering her body. The Fairy's curse had kept her from aging, but her pale skin was like parchment and nearly as yellowed as the dress she'd been wearing for two centuries. The pearls it was embroidered with had kept their lustrous white, but the lace at the hem had turned as brown as the petals covering the dress.

Will was standing by one of the windows, as if the prince had finally arrived after all. Jacob's steps made him spin around. The jade now also tainted his forehead, and the blue of his eyes was drowning in gold. The bandits had robbed them of their most precious possession—time.

"This doesn't look like 'happily ever after'," Will said, looking over at the princess. "And as far as I remember, it was also a Fairy's curse that did this to her." He leaned his back against the rough wall. "Are you feeling better?"

"Yes," Jacob lied. "What about you?"

Will didn't answer right away. And when he did, his voice sounded as cool and smooth as his new skin.

"My face feels like polished stone. The night grows brighter with every passing day, and I could hear you long before you reached the stairs. I don't just feel it on my skin now. It's inside me as well."

He approached the bed and stared down at the mummified body. "I'd forgotten everything. You. Clara. Myself. All I knew was I wanted to join them."

Jacob searched for words, but he found none.

"Is that what's happening? Tell me the truth." Will looked at him. "I won't just look like them; I'll be like them. Won't I?"

Jacob had the lies ready on the tip of his tongue, all the *'Nonsense! Everything will be fine! I'll make sure it will.'* But he couldn't say them. His brother's gaze wouldn't allow it.

"Do you want to know what they're like?" Will plucked a rose leaf from the dead princess's straw-like hair. "They're angry. Their rage bursts inside you like a flame. But they are also as calm and strong as the stone. It speaks to them, in many voices. They miss the caves it forms for them and they yearn for the warmth underground. I always thought stone to be cold, but they hate the cold."

He eyed the black nails on his hand.

"They are darkness," he said quietly. "And heat. And the red moon is their sun."

Jacob shuddered when he heard the stone in Will's voice.

Say something, Jacob. Anything.

"But you are not one of them. And you never will be." His own voice sounded like a stranger's, so hoarse with fear. "Because I won't allow it."

"How?" There it was again, the glance that held none of the trust Will had once granted his older brother without question. "Is it true, what you told those bandits? You're taking me to another Fairy?"

"Yes."

99

Will touched the dead princess's parchment face. "One as dangerous as the one who did this? Look out the window. There are corpses hanging in the thorns. You think I want you to end up like that for my sake?"

His eyes belied his words. *Help me,* they said, even though they were drowning in gold.

Jacob gently pulled him away from the bed and the mummified body.

"The Fairy I'm taking you to is different." *Is she, Jacob?* He heard a whisper inside him, but he ignored it. He put all the hope he possessed into his voice. And all the confidence his brother yearned to hear. "She'll help us, Will, I promise!"

15

Soft Flesh

Threefingers with the butcher's face was the first to speak. Humans so liked to choose the wrong men as their leaders. Every Goyl could see his cowardice as clearly as the watery blue of his eyes. But at least he had told them a few interesting details Hentzau hadn't learned from the moth.

The Jade Goyl was not alone. He was with a girl and—far more importantly—he had a brother who was determined to rid him of the jade. If Threefingers was telling the truth, that brother was planning to take the Jade Goyl to the Red Fairy. Desperate, but probably the right idea. The Red One despised her sister as much as did the other Fairies. Still, Hentzau was sure she wouldn't be able to break the curse. The Dark Fairy's magic was much more powerful than her sisters.

No Goyl had ever seen the island where they dwelled, let alone set foot on it. The Dark Fairy guarded their secrets, even though they had cast her out, and every fool knew you could only reach the Fairies' island if they wanted you to.

"How is he going to find her?"

"He didn't say!" Threefingers stammered. "I swear!"

Hentzau nodded to the only She-Goyl he had included in his search squad. He himself didn't enjoy striking human flesh. He could kill them, yes, but he avoided touching them. Nesser had no such qualms.

She kicked Threefingers in the face with such force that Hentzau gave her a look of warning. For a brief moment, Nesser held his gaze. She could be quite stubborn, but then she lowered her head. Her sister had been killed by humans; that's why she tended to overdo it. Hatred covered them all like slime by now.

"He didn't say," Threefingers stammered again, blood pouring out of his broken nose. "I promise. Not a word!"

His flesh was as pale and soft as a snail's. Hentzau turned away in disgust. He was certain they had told him all they knew, but thanks to them the Jade Goyl had gotten away.

"Shoot them!" he ordered, and went outside.

The shots sounded strange in the silence, like something that didn't belong in this world. Guns, steam engines, trains — to Hentzau, all of it still felt unnatural. He was getting old, that was the trouble. The sunlight had clouded his eyes, and his hearing had been so damaged by all the battle noise that Nesser had to raise her voice whenever she addressed him. Kami'en pretended to not notice. He hadn't forgotten that Hentzau had grown old in his service. But the Dark Fairy would make sure everybody else saw it, as soon as she found out that he had allowed a bunch of plunderers to stand in his way when the Jade Goyl had been so close that even his clouded eyes couldn't overlook him.

102

Hentzau still saw him, standing behind the fighting men, staring at the Goyl, his human skin suffused with the most sacred of stones. No. His own eyes must have betrayed him. It was impossible. He must be as fake as one of those wooden fetishes, swindlers covered with gold leaf to sell them as solid gold. *'Behold, the Jade Goyl has come to make our King invincible. But don't cut too deep, or you will find human flesh.'* Yes, that's what it was. Nothing but another attempt by the Fairy to make herself indispensable.

Hentzau squinted into the gathering night, but all he saw was the boy with the skin of jade.

What if you're wrong, Hentzau? What if he is the real thing? What if your King's destiny depends on him?

And he had let him get away.

When the scout finally returned, Hentzau read from his face that he had lost the trail, even before he stammered his excuses Once he would have killed the Goyl on the spot, but he'd learned to control the rage that lurked in all of them, although not half as well as his King.

That meant all he had to go on was what Threefingers had told them about the brother and the Red Fairy. *May all the Lava Devils underground come to his aid!* He would have to swallow his pride once more and ask the Dark Fairy for help to find her red sister.

"How could you lose their tracks?" he barked at the scout. "Three horses and a fox. Even my horse would be able to find those tracks!"

How he squirmed in his moonstone skin. All moonstones were idiots.

Hentzau was considering several punishments when Nesser approached him. She was a jasper Goyl, like him, but her skin was darker and, as was the skin of all Goyl women, veined with amethyst. Nesser had only just turned thirteen. At that age Goyl were considered adults, but most of them didn't join the army until they were at least fourteen. Nesser was neither very good with the saber nor a particularly good shot, but her courage more than made up for those shortcomings. At her age, fear was an unfamiliar concept; at thirteen you didn't have to be a Fairy to consider yourself immortal. Hentzau remembered the feeling all too well.

"Commander?"

He loved the reverence in her young voice. It was still the best antidote for the doubts the Dark Fairy sowed in him.

"What?"

"I know how to get to the Fairies. Not to the island...but to the valley from which it can be reached."

"Is that so?" Hentzau's heartbeat quickened, but he didn't show his relief. He had a soft spot for the She-Goyl and that made him even more strict with her.

"I was part of the escort the King sends with the Dark Fairy when she goes traveling. I accompanied her on her last visit to her sisters. She left us to wait for her in the ravine through which you reach the valley. I am sure I'll remember the way..."

This was too good to be true. He would not have to beg the Fairy for help. He might even be able to make sure she'd never learn of the Jade Goyl's escape. Next time, he wouldn't let him get away. No, he wouldn't.

"All right," he said, his tone studiously uninterested when he met Nesser's eager gaze. "Tell the scout you'll be leading the way from now on. But you'd better not get us lost."

"I won't, Commander!" Nesser's golden eyes glistened with confidence as she quickly walked away.

104

Hentzau stared down the unpaved road on which the Jade Goyl had escaped. One of the looters had claimed that the brother was injured, and at some point they would need to rest and sleep, whereas Hentzau and his men could go for days without it. They would soon catch up with them and, this time, that gentle-faced boy with the jade in his skin would not escape.

He had to be fake.

Hentzau couldn't wait to be the one to prove it.

16

Not Ever

It was still dark when Jacob made them set off again. He desperately needed rest, but not even Fox could convince him to stay longer, and Clara had to admit that she was glad to get away from the rose covered castle and all its sleeping dead.

It was a clear night and the stars were pearls stitched by an embroiderer onto the black velvet of the sky. The trees and hills were the cut silhouettes she remembered from her childhood's fairy tale books, and Will was riding by her side, so distant even though he was so close. Clara could feel him drifting away from her, from his brother. He smiled at her when he felt her gaze, but it was a mere shadow of the smile she knew. It had always been so easy to get a smile from Will. He gave love so freely; at least, that's what she had come to believe. And it was so easy to love him back. Nothing had ever been that easy. She didn't want to lose him, but the world that had lured them through the mirror weaved its net around him and Clara heard it whisper: *'He belongs to me.'* All she wished for was to ride back to the ruin and press her hand against the dark glass that had brought them here. Instead they left it further behind with every day, riding on as if they needed to find the very heart of this world to free Will from its sinister spell.

Let him go! Clara begged with every mile enveloping her in its frightening beauty. *Please. Let him go!*

But the strange night whispered: *'Which skin shall I give you, Clara Ferber? Do you want fur? Do you want stone?'*

"No," she whispered back. "All I want is that you give me back what's mine."

Yet she already felt her new skin growing. So soft. Far too soft. She was so afraid.

17
A Guide to the Fairies

It was true what they said about the Fairies. You could only find their realm if one of them showed you the way. Jacob had faced that problem before—when he'd set out three years ago to steal a Fairy lily for the Empress from their enchanted lake. There was one solution for the problem: you had to bribe the right Dwarf. There were many Dwarfs who bragged about trading with the Fairies and proudly displayed lilies in their family crests.

Therese of Austry, who was known for her beauty, hadn't passed it on to her daughter. Rumors said she blamed her husband for Amalie's ugliness. When he died in a suspicious hunting accident shortly after Amalie's twelfth birthday, Therese of Austry had offered a fortune in gold for whoever brought her a lily. Fairy lilies had the reputation for turning even the ugliest girl into a beauty. So Jacob, who at that time was already treasure hunting without Chanute, had set off to find a Dwarf. Most of them usually revealed, after telling a few dusty tales, that a great-grandfather entering the Fairy realm had been the last family member who had actually seen a Fairy. It had been one of Therese's court Dwarfs, Auberon, the Empress's favorite, who mentioned the name Evenaugh Valiant to Jacob.

Valiant resided in Terpevas, the biggest Dwarf city in Austry, and for a sizable amount of gold he had actually led Jacob to the valley from which one could reach the Fairies' realm. Valiant hadn't mentioned its guardians though; Jacob had nearly died while the Dwarf had sold the lily to the Empress, which had turned Amalie into an even more celebrated beauty than her mother, and Evenaugh Valiant into a purveyor to the court.

Jacob had often dreamt of paying the Dwarf back for his betrayal but, after his return from the Fairies, he had lost his taste for revenge. In the end, he had erased Evenaugh Valiant as thoroughly from his mind as he suppressed the memory of the island where he had been so happy that he had forgotten himself. Now this renounced revenge might save his brother.

So what does that teach you, Jacob Reckless? he wondered as the first Dwarf dwellings appeared among the fields and hedgerows. *That, on the whole, revenge is not such a great idea.* Nevertheless. He still longed to break Valiant's greedy neck.

By now there was no way to conceal the jade, so Jacob decided to leave Will and Clara behind with Fox while he rode into Terpevas (which, in the language of its inhabitants, meant simply 'Dwarf City'). In a stretch of woodland, Fox found a cave the local shepherds used as a shelter. Will followed her into its shade as if he couldn't wait to get out of the daylight. There was only a small patch of human skin left on his right cheek. He looked like his own sculpture, chiseled from jade. His eyes were

110

both drowning in gold, and Jacob found it harder and harder to convince himself that he hadn't already lost the fight.

Clara didn't follow Will into the cave. When Jacob walked to the horses, she was standing among the trees looking so lost that, in her men's clothes, Jacob almost mistook her for one of the homeless boys one found everywhere in this world, orphaned and looking for work. Her hair was the same color as the autumn grass growing between the trees, and by now one could barely see that she was a stranger to this world. The city they all had grown up in, its lights and noise, and the girl she had been there—all but faded, far away. The present so swiftly becomes the past.

"Will doesn't have much time left, right?"

She faced things, even if they scared her. Jacob liked that about her, even though she approached life too pragmatically for his taste. Clara wanted to understand, while Jacob mostly took things the way they were. He liked to be enchanted, seduced, bewitched, and usually he found the questions more enticing than the answers, which he mostly didn't trust anyway. Clara, on the contrary, loved answers. She found secrets and magic to be exhausting, as far as he could see, and what was happening to Will would certainly not change that.

"It will be time enough," he replied, although he was more and more convinced that might be a lie.

He barely made it into the saddle. The flowers, leaves, and roots Fox continued to show Clara to treat his wound calmed the infection, but he could barely move his left arm and the fever weakened him more than he would admit.

"You should see a doctor in Terpevas," Fox said when he flinched with pain picking up the reins. "You know the Dwarfs have better doctors than the Empress."

111

"Yes, if you're a Dwarf. Their only ambition with human patients is to make them pay and then send them to an early grave. Dwarfs don't think very highly of us," he added when he saw Clara's puzzled look. "We give them plenty of reason, one has to admit."

"But you still know one you can trust?"

"Trust? On the contrary." The vixen bared her teeth. "The Dwarf he's going to see is less trustworthy than a viper. Ask him where he got the scars on his back."

"That's a long time ago." Jacob turned the mare. "And this time I know who I'm dealing with."

The vixen answered that with a contemptuous purr and Clara grabbed his reins.

"Why don't you at least take Fox with you?"

The vixen cast her an affectionate glance. She had grown fond of Clara. She even shifted into her human form more often, as if Clara was proof that being a woman might not be such an unattractive existence after all.

"You and Will can't stay here alone," Jacob said while he once again turned his horse. "You still don't know this world."

Clara didn't protest. She knew he was right, and so did Fox. And luckily Fox did care for both of them, more than at the beginning of their journey.

Will was still in the cave. He didn't come out when Jacob rode away. He hadn't even asked where Jacob was going. His brother was learning to fear the sun.

18

WHISPERING STONE

Will could hear the stone. He heard it as clearly as his own
breathing. In the cave walls, the jagged ground beneath his feet,
the rocky ceiling above...vibrations to which his body responded
as if it were made of them. He no longer had a name, only the new
skin that cocooned him, cool and protective, the new strength in
his muscles, and the pain in his eyes when he looked at the sun.

He ran his hands over the rock, reading its age with his fingers.
It whispered to him about what was hidden beneath the innocuous
gray surface: striped agate, pale white moonstone, golden citrine,
black onyx. It made him see images of underground cities, petrified
water, dim light reflecting in windows of malachite...

"Will?"

He turned around, and the rock fell silent.

Clara was standing in the cave's entrance, the sunlight clinging
to her hair as if she were made of it. Her face brought the other

world back, where stone had meant nothing more than walls and dead streets.

"Are you hungry? Fox caught a rabbit, and she showed me how to make a fire."

She approached him and took his face between her hands, such soft hands, so colorless against the green that was spreading through his own skin. Will tried to hide that her touch made him shudder. If only her skin weren't so soft and pale.

"Can you hear anything?" he asked.

She looked at him, puzzled.

"Nevermind," he said, and kissed her to make himself forget that he suddenly longed to find amethyst in her skin. Her lips brought back more memories: the old apartment house as high as a tower, nights lit by artificial light. Light his golden eyes didn't need anymore...

"I love you." Clara whispered the words as if she wanted to banish the jade with them. But the stone whispered louder.

I love you, too. He wanted to say it with as much conviction as he'd said and meant it so many times before. But everything felt so different with a heart turning into jade.

"You'll be fine," Clara whispered. She caressed his face, as if she were trying to find his old flesh under the new skin. "Jacob will be back soon."

Jacob. Even his brother's name sounded different. How was it possible that he had never noticed how much pain clung to it. Had he forgotten how often he had called that name without receiving an answer? Empty rooms, empty days. He had left them alone, him and their mother, like the man who called himself their father. All those years in that vast empty apartment. Waiting for his brother, who came and left as he pleased, until more and

114

more often he had wondered lying in his bed whether he had just dreamt him up. His fearless older brother, who would come and protect him from the bad dreams that kept him awake so many nights. But he hadn't come and sometimes Will had lain awake all night waiting for him.

Yes. *Why not forget it all?* All the loneliness. All the longing. All that anger he had never shown. *Why not forget that whole world and become somebody else? Who exactly had he been before he had grown jade in his skin?* The younger brother. So gentle. So calm.

He grabbed Clara's hand when she caressed his cheek.

"Please," he said. "Don't."

She backed away from him, her face showing all the emotions Will knew from his mother's face. Pain. Love. Blame. He didn't want all that anymore. He wanted the jade, cool and firm. As a child he had sometimes felt like a mussel that had lost its shell. A snail without its house. So soft. So terribly soft.

Yes, maybe he had called the jade himself. *Wasn't that what this world was about?* All those magical things that made the most secret wishes come true?

"Go." He turned his back on Clara. "Please go. I want to be alone."

With the rocks. And the images they painted. And with the jade that would turn all that terrible softness in him into stone.

19

VALIANT

If its archives could be trusted, Terpevas was the oldest Dwarf settlement behind the mirror. The city walls were roughly five hundred years old but the large posters covering most of it, advertising anything from beer and eyeglasses to patented gas lamps, made it clear to all visitors that its citizens welcomed progress with a passionate embrace. Like most Dwarfs, they honored their traditions but never allowed them to stand in the way of a new idea that could improve their lives and, equally important, fill their wallets. Dwarf trading posts could be found in every corner of this world, despite the fact that they were nearly half the size of their human customers. Each Dwarf was very proud of that fact, and their talents as spies, acrobats, and professional thieves were unsurpassed.

The traffic in front of the city gates was nearly as congested as on the bridges and crossroads of Jacob's world, though here the noise came from carriages and carts competing with riders and pedestrians for space on the gray cobblestones. They came from everywhere to Terpevas. The war had increased business for the Dwarfs. Their merchants had been trading with the Goyl for ages, and to show his gratitude Kami'en had made many of them his chief purveyors. Evenaugh Valiant, whom Jacob had come to see, had been trading with the Goyl for years, true to his motto of always getting on the winning side in time.

Let's just hope the devious little bastard is still alive! Jacob thought as he steered his mare past coaches and chaises toward the city's southern gate. After all, it was quite possible that another cheated customer had ended Valiant's life by now.

Even three Dwarfs standing on each other's shoulders wouldn't have matched the height of the sentries who channeled the torrent of visitors through Terpevas' gates. Many cities behind the mirror hired Giantlings, men who claimed their direct descent from the extinct Giants, as guards. Terpevas was no exception. Giantlings were also vastly popular as mercenaries, despite their reputation for being rather dimwitted. The Dwarfs obviously paid them very well, as the two guarding the gates had even squeezed themselves into the old-fashioned uniforms used by their employers' army. Not even the Empress's cavalry wore helmets plumed with swan feathers anymore, but the Dwarfs liked to enjoy the modern era in the reassuring decor of more traditional times.

When Jacob rode past the Giantlings, he fell in behind two Goyl. One had a skin of moonstone; the other one was an onyx. Their attire was not any different than that of the human factory owners whose carriage the Giantlings waved through the gates, but their tailcoats bulged over pistol handles. Their wide lapels were embroidered with jade, and the dark glasses shielding their

118

shade-loving eyes were made of obsidian, cut thinner than any human stonecutter could have ever achieved.

Both Goyl ignored the disgust their presence clearly evoked in all the human visitors. Their faces said it quite clearly: this world belonged to them now. Their King had plucked it like a ripe fruit, and its crowned leaders who had once allowed raiding parties and lynching crowds to hunt them were now burying soldiers in mass graves and begging Kami'en to make peace.

Will's face resembled the Goyl's so much by now that Jacob reined in his horse and stared after them until the angry shouts of a Dwarf woman, who couldn't get past his horse with her two tiny children, brought him back to his senses.

Dwarf city. Shrunken world.

Jacob left the mare in one of the stables by the city wall. The main roads in Terpevas were as wide as the streets in human settlements, but beyond those the city made no attempt to conceal that it had been built for inhabitants who were barely larger than a six-year-old human child. Some of the alleys were so narrow that Jacob could barely pass through them, even on foot. Like all cities behind the mirror, Terpevas was growing so rapidly that it nearly choked on its own growth. Smoke from too many coal furnaces blackened the windows and walls, and the cold autumn air did not smell of damp leaves, even though the Dwarfs' sewer system was vastly superior to that of the Empress. The world behind the mirror seemed determined not to leave out one mistake made on the other side.

Jacob didn't know the Dwarf alphabet well enough to decipher the street signs and, as he didn't remember much from his last visit, he had soon managed to get hopelessly lost in the maze of narrow alleyways. After he hit his head for the third time on the

119

same barber's sign, he stopped a messenger boy and asked him whether he knew the way to the house of Evenaugh Valiant, Trader in Rarities of Any Kind. The boy barely reached Jacob's knee and eyed him with the suspicious air most Dwarfs demonstrate towards humans. His demeanor didn't improve when Jacob counted two copper coins into his tiny hand, but he accepted them with a nod and darted ahead so quickly that Jacob had trouble keeping up with him. He was just wondering whether his guide tried to shake him off, when the boy, slightly breathless, but clearly proud of his navigating skills, came to a halt in front of the house Jacob had been looking for.

Valiant's name was etched in golden letters on the entrance door's glass and, like all human clients, Jacob had to bend his knees to fit through the doorframe. The reception room, though, was tall enough for him to stand upright, and Jacob spotted some illustrious clients in the photographs on the walls. By now, even this world's rulers went to a photographer for a portrait instead of spending weeks sitting for a painter, although the photos still showed them only in sepia or greyish black. The portrait of the Empress was hanging right next to that of a Goyl officer, of course. Valiant was still serving both sides. The photos were framed with moon-silver, a very rare metal that owed its name to the rich luster it showed even in the dark. The chandelier hanging from the ceiling was inlaid with the glass hairs of a Djinn, an even more expensive material. Clearly business was going well.

Jacob was the only customer present. Last time one secretary had greeted him, but now there were two, equally unwelcoming. The younger one eyed Jacob with the same disdain the messenger boy had demonstrated, while the older Dwarf didn't even lift his head when Jacob approached his barely knee-high desk.

Dwarfs did not even pretend to like humans when they were doing business with them.

Nevertheless, Jacob gave both of them his friendliest smile.

"I take it Mr. Valiant still does trade with the Fairies?"

"Indeed," the older one replied without looking up. "But we don't currently have any moth cocoons in stock." His voice, like that of most Dwarfs, was surprisingly deep. "New supplies are expected to come in at the end of the year."

Jacob had to admit that he was looking forward to what would follow.

Both Dwarf heads shot up when he cocked his pistol with a soft click.

"I'm actually not here for moth cocoons. Would you both do me the favor of stepping into that wardrobe over there?"

Dwarfs were known for their enormous strength, but Valiant obviously didn't pay his secretaries well enough to risk being shot. Both climbed into the wardrobe without any resistance, and the lock looked solid enough to ensure they wouldn't call Terpevas' vastly efficient Dwarf police system while Jacob had a conversation with their employer.

The crest proudly displayed on Valiant's office door showed, above the Fairy lily, a badger sitting on a mound of gold coins, a heraldic animal Jacob suspected Valiant had himself come up with. The door was made of rosewood, a material known for its superior soundproofing qualities, evidence that Valiant was still doing the kind of business that was best discussed behind such doors. It also meant that he probably wasn't aware of Jacob's arrival and the events that just transpired in his front office.

The Dwarf was sitting behind a human-sized desk, its legs adjusted to his height, puffing on a cigar that would have looked huge even in a Giantling's mouth. Valiant's eyes were closed, and there was a very self-satisfied smile on his lips. His beard was gone, as was now the fashion among Dwarfs; his eyebrows, usually as bushy as most Dwarfs', had been carefully trimmed; and his tailored suit was made of velvet, a fabric rich Dwarfs held in high esteem. Jacob would have loved to toss his old enemy through the window behind him, along with his wolf-leather chair. The pain and terror he owed Valiant came back even more sharply than he had anticipated. And the shame about his own naivety.

"Hadn't I told you to disturb me under no circumstances, Banster?" Valiant sighed without opening his eyes. "Don't tell me it's about that stuffed Waterman again."

He'd grown fat. And older. His curly red hair was turning gray, early for a Dwarf. Most of them lived to be at least a hundred and fifty, and Valiant was barely sixty—unless he'd also lied about his age.

"No, a stuffed Waterman isn't quite what I came to complain about," Jacob said, pointing his pistol at the curly head. Yes, this felt good. So good. "Three years ago, I paid for services I never received."

Valiant opened his eyes and nearly choked on his cigar. He stared at Jacob as incredulously as expected for one who had left someone to the mercy of a stampeding herd of Unicorns.

"Jacob Reckless!" he exclaimed.

"Oh, you actually remember my name."

Valiant dropped his cigar to reach under the desk, but he pulled his hand back hastily when Jacob's bullet nearly took one of his fingers off. Rosewood reduced even a shot to the sound of a whisper.

"You should consider your actions carefully!" Jacob said. "You won't need both your arms to take me to the Fairies, and neither will you need your ears or nose. Hands behind your head. Now!"

Valiant raised his hands, forcing his lips into far too broad a smile.

"Jacob!" he purred. "What is this? Of course I knew you weren't dead. After all, everybody's heard your story. Jacob Reckless, the fortunate mortal whom the Red Fairy kept as her lover for twelve blissful months. Every man, be he Dwarf, human, or Goyl, turns green with envy at the mere thought of it. Go on—admit it. Whom do you have to thank for that? Evenaugh Valiant! Had I warned you about the Unicorns, you would've been turned into a thistle or a fish, like any other uninvited visitor. But not even the Red Fairy can resist a man who's lying, helpless, in his own blood."

Even Jacob had to admire the brazenness of that argument.

"Tell me!" Valiant whispered across his oversized desk without even a hint of remorse. "How was she? And how did you manage to get away?"

Jacob grabbed the Dwarf by his well-tailored collar and pulled him out from behind his desk. "This is my onetime offer: I won't shoot you, and in return you'll take me to their valley once again, but this time you show me how to get past the Unicorns."

"What?" Valiant tried to wriggle free, but Jacob's pistol quickly changed his mind. "It's a two-day ride, at least!" he whined. "I can't just leave the business!"

No, he hadn't changed. Jacob shoved him toward the door.

The two secretaries kept so silent in the wardrobe that Valiant only cast a questioning glance at their empty desks.

123

"My prices have increased considerably in the past three years," he said. plucking his hat from the coatrack by the door. "Don't forget, you are dealing with a purveyor of the Empress by now."

"I'll let you live. That's a lavish payment considering the debts you have with me."

Valiant adjusted his hat in the glass of his front door. Like most Dwarfs, he had a weakness for top hats, as they added a fair number of inches to his stature. "You seem to be quite desperate to get back to your Fairy lover," he purred, "And the price rises with the desperation of the customer."

"Not just the price, but the risk as well," Jacob replied, waving him to the door. "Trust me. This customer is desperate enough to shoot you at a moment's notice."

20

Too Much

Fox smelled golden revulsion, petrified love. The scent came from the cave, and her fur bristled when she found Clara's tracks leading away from it. She had stumbled, more than walked, towards the trees facing the cave's entrance. Fox had heard Jacob warn Clara about those trees, but she'd rushed toward them as if their shadows were exactly what she was looking for.

Clara's scent was familiar. It reminded Fox of the scent she wore when she let go of the vixen's fur. Girl. Woman. So much more vulnerable than the vixen. Or men. Strength and weakness side by side, and a heart that knew no armor. Clara's scent told Fox about all the things she feared and from which the fur protected her. Clara's hasty steps wrote them into the dark forest soil. The vixen didn't need her nose to know why she was running. She had tried to run away from pain herself. The shadows of hazel and wild apple trees darkened her fur. They both easily befriended

125

other creatures, be they bird, human, or fox. Each forest contains friends and foes. But Clara couldn't distinguish between them. Every child behind the mirror stayed far away from the trees whose bark was as spiny as the shell of a chestnut. *Bird-trees*. Under their branches the sunlight dissolved into a gloomy brown. Each squirrel knew how to read that warning, but Clara had stumbled right into it, and the tree had grabbed her with its wooden claws. She screamed for Jacob, but he was far away. Roots were curled around her arms and ankles, and the tree's feathery servants already descended on her body, their plumage as white as virgin snow, birds with pointed beaks and eyes like red berries.

The vixen jumped among them, her teeth bared, deaf to their angry cries, and snapped one of them before it could escape into the tree's branches. Fox felt the bird's heart racing between her jaws, but she did not bite; she just held on firmly, very firmly, until the tree let go of its human prey with an angry groan. Its roots slid off Clara's trembling limbs like snakes and, when she struggled back to her feet, they were already slipping back under the autumn-brown leaves, where they would lie in wait for their next victim. The tree's birds chattered angrily from the branches, but the vixen only let go of her feathered captive when Clara staggered to her side. She was as white as the feathers that stuck to her dress, but Fox did not just smell the fear of death. There was another scent—of a heart raw with pain, freshly wounded.

They barely spoke a word on their way back to the cave. Clara stopped several times as if she could not go on, but then she did, wordlessly. When they reached the cave, she looked at the dark entrance as if she hoped to see Will there. But then she just crouched down in the grass next to the horses, with her back to the cave. She was unharmed, apart from a few small grazes on her throat and ankles, but Fox saw how ashamed she was of her aching heart and of having run away, despite Jacob's warnings.

For a moment the vixen intended to leave her alone, but then she shifted shape and sat down next to her.

"Will doesn't love me anymore, Fox." Even her voice was soaked with tears.

"He is changing," Fox plucked a white feather from Clara's hair. "He doesn't understand himself anymore. He's not sure who he is. And who he wants to be. It's not easy to love when you don't know yourself."

She knew how it felt: another skin, another self. But the vixen's fur was soft and warm. How did it feel to grow a skin of stone?

Clara looked toward the cave.

"Jacob will help him!" Fox said. "You'll see. He loves his brother very much."

Too much, her heart whispered. *He will go back to her to save Will. And she will kill him and you will die too, Fox. How could you live without him?*

21
HIS BROTHER'S KEEPER

The vixen was waiting in front of the cave when Jacob returned. Will and Clara were nowhere to be seen.

"Will you look at that! That mangy fox is still following you around?" Valiant jeered as Jacob lifted him from the horse. He had tied the Dwarf up with a silver chain, the only metal they couldn't tear apart like thread.

Jacob had expected Fox to welcome Valiant with a growl and a bite, as she had urged him for a long time to take revenge on the Dwarf. Instead she ignored his prisoner, as if Valiant was just an additional sack of provisions brought back from Terpevas. Something had happened in his absence and it had upset her. Which didn't happen easily.

"You have to talk to your brother," she said, plucking a feather from her fur. It was as white as snow. Jacob knew those feathers.

"What happened?" He tied the Dwarf to a tree and cast a worried glance at the cave where Will was hiding.

"Not him." The vixen pointed her nose toward an oak tree. Clara was sleeping underneath it. The shirt he had bought her was torn, and there was blood on her throat.

"A Bird-tree," Fox explained. "She ran into the woods, after they had a fight."

'I won't just look like them; I'll be like them. Won't I?'

❊ ❊ ❊

Jacob found Will in the darkest corner of the cave. He was sitting on the ground, his back against the rock. They had switched roles. It had always been him who was hiding in the darkness, in his bedroom, in the laundry chamber, in his father's study. *'Jacob? Where are you? What have you done now?'* Always Jacob, but not Will. Never Will.

His brother's eyes gleamed in the dark like gold coins.

"Fox says you and Clara had a fight?"

Will looked at his fingers. Jade fingers. "Not really. I just told her I need to be alone."

"You're the one who wanted to bring her along!"

Jacob, stop it. But his shoulder was throbbing with pain, and the jade in Will's face frightened him so much more than he dared to admit.

"Fight it!" he said. "This time I can't do it for you."

Will got to his feet. His movements gave away his growing strength, and it was a long time ago that he had barely reached up to Jacob's shoulders.

"Do it for me?" he repeated. "When did that last happen? When I was seven? You still believe mom and I had a fairy tale time while you were hunting for glass shoes and Witch combs,

130

don't you? I guess I was quite good at making you believe we did. But what about her?"

There it was again. The anger. An anger Jacob didn't know in his brother. *Or had he just not seen it?*

"You know what I think? She sometimes hoped that you had gone to find our father. And that you would come back with him one day. Did you? Did you leave to look for him? Or was it just to get away?"

It felt as if they were back in the apartment, with all its empty rooms and the dark spot on the wallpaper where once the photo of their father had hung.

"I don't know," Jacob said. It was the truth.

"Come on! Take off that bloody chain, vixen!" Valiant's voice could be heard outside. "I won't be of much help if I fall off the horse because my limbs go all numb!"

Will walked to the cave entrance. He shielded his eyes with his hand when the daylight fell on his face.

"Is that the guide you were talking about?"

"Yes." Jacob couldn't take his eyes of him. A stranger and yet so much his brother.

"Why is he chained?"

"Because one can't trust him."

But you need to trust me, Jacob thought. *Or I won't be able to save you.* From what? His brother touched the jade in his skin almost tenderly by now.

"I am sorry for what I said to Clara," he said. "It won't happen again. I promise."

131

22

DREAMS

It was night and the Dark Fairy was heading East. She always travelled at night. It was too beautiful to sleep away. Black hills and forests drifted by the train's window under a star-studded sky, but from time to time the glass suddenly showed her a face. By now she saw him everywhere, whether she was awake or asleep. The boy made from sacred stone. Soon he would make all the stories come true, told long before he had been born. She saw it all so clearly. All Fairies knew about the fruit the future grew from the seeds of the past — even when time was still hiding it in its folds. Maybe it couldn't keep its secrets from them because past, present, and future don't mean anything to immortals.

The boy's face disappeared and the Dark Fairy saw only her own reflection drawn onto the night by the window glass: nothing but a pale phantom, behind which the world slipped past with frantic speed. Kami'en knew that she disliked trains almost as much as she disliked the depths of the earth, so he had asked his most gifted artists to cover the walls of her carriage with precious stone intarsia: jade hills were dreaming under an onyx sky studded with moonstone and, above the seats, ruby flowers blossomed amongst malachite leaves. The Dark Fairy ran her fingers over their red petals. *That was love, wasn't it?* And yet the noise of the train still hurt her ears, and all the metal made her shudder. She should have stayed in the castle with the bricked-up windows to wait for Hentzau, but Kami'en had wanted to get back to the mountains he called home and to his underground fortress. He longed for the deep as much as she longed for the night sky, and for white lilies floating on water—although she still tried to convince herself that all she needed was his love.

Outside, the two moons hung in the sky above a plain dyed raven black by the night, so calm and steady despite the haste of the train. The red moon always reminded her of Kami'en's skin.

Yes, she loved him. And he loved her. But he was still going to marry the human princess with the blank eyes and the beauty she owed to a Fairy lily. *Amalie.* The sound of her name was as bland as her face. How the Dark Fairy would have enjoyed killing her. A poisoned comb, a dress that would eat into her flesh when she put it on in front of her golden mirrors. How she would scream and scratch her skin, so much softer than that of her bridegroom. The Fairy pressed her forehead against the window's cool glass. Jealousy. She despised the feeling. She had never felt it before. *Why this time?* Kami'en had always taken other women besides her. No Goyl loved only once. Nobody loved only once...Fairies least of all.

Of course she had heard all the stories about her kind: that her sisters liked to turn their suitors into fish or reeds when they

134

grew tired of them; that they drove men mad with desire, until the men drowned themselves searching for their love even in death; that their moths were the souls of their dead lovers; and that they all had no hearts, just as they had neither fathers nor mothers. The stories were all true. The Dark Fairy touched her chest. No heart, like her sisters. *So where did the love come from?*

Outside, the moons were reflecting on the waters of a lake. They turned it into a mirror made from fire and silver. The Goyl were afraid of the water, even though the sound of its dripping was as natural a part of their underground cities as the sound of the wind was to cities above the ground. They feared the water so much that the oceans drew wet borders for Kami'en's conquests and made him dream of flying, but she couldn't give him wings any more than she could give him children. All the words that meant so much to both Goyl and men — brother, daughter, son — meant nothing to her, and the water he feared so much had given birth to her and her sisters.

It gave her a bittersweet satisfaction that his human princess couldn't give Kami'en children either, unless he wanted to sire one of those crippled monsters some mortal women had borne his soldiers. How often had he told her by now: *'I don't care for Amalie of Austry, but I need to make peace with her mother.'* He actually believed every one of his words, but she knew him better. Yes. He did want peace, but even more than that he yearned to caress human skin and to make one of them his wife. His fascination with all things human had for a while amused her, but by now she understood far too well that it worried not only his people, but even men as devoted to him as Hentzau.

Where did the love come from? What was it made of? Stone, like Kami'en? Water, like her and her sisters?

It had just been a game when she had first set out to find him. The lake that had given birth to all of them often showed them the faces of men. The ones they liked they lured to their island. But she hadn't seen Kami'en in the lake's water. She had seen him in her dreams: the Goyl who smashed the world to pieces and disregarded its rules, just as she did. And so she had sent out her moths to find him, despite her sisters' warnings. They didn't intervene with human or Goyl affairs. Her sisters stayed away from the world of mortals; the last one to break that rule wore a skin of bark and the leaves of a willow. But she had left them all behind, for him. The tent in which they first met smelled of blood and the death she didn't understand, and still she had thought of it all as a game. She had yearned to lay the world at his feet, sowing Petrified Flesh, giving his enemies a skin that resembled his. Too late had she realized what he was sowing in her. Love. The worst of all poisons.

"You should wear human dresses more often."

How was it possible that she believed she had always known his voice? There was no *always* for him. Maybe for her, but not for him.

Her dress rustled as if it were made from leaves when she turned. Human women dressed like flowers, layers of petals around a mortal, wilting core. Her seamstress had copied the dress from a painting at the dead general's castle. She had caught Kami'en a few times gazing at it, absentminded, as if it showed something he was yearning for. The green silk would have made ten dresses, but she loved its rustling and how smoothly it clung to her skin.

Kami'en didn't look tired, even though he had barely slept in days.

"Still no news from Hentzau?"

136

As if she didn't know the answer. The Jade Goyl...why hadn't her moths found him yet? She could see him so clearly.

"Hentzau will find him." Kami'en stepped behind her and kissed her neck. "If he exists."

He doubted her, but never his jasper shadow. Hentzau. Someone else she sometimes yearned to kill. But Kami'en would forgive his death even less than that of his future bride. He had killed his own brothers, as the Goyl often did, but Hentzau was closer to him than a brother. Maybe even closer than she was.

The train window melted their reflections into one. Her breath still quickened whenever he stood near her. *Where does love come from?*

"Forget the Jade Goyl. Forget your dreams," he whispered, undoing her hair. "I will give you new dreams. Just tell me what you want."

She had never told Kami'en that she had found him in her dreams. He wouldn't have liked it. Neither Goyl nor men lived long enough to understand that yesterday was born of tomorrow, just as tomorrow was born of yesterday.

23

TRAPPED

It felt like riding back into his own past. The creek running along the bottom, the spruces clawing into the steep slopes, the silence between the rocks...the gorge Jacob had passed three years ago to reach the Fairy valley hadn't changed, but the pain in his shoulder wouldn't allow him to forget how much had happened since. It was by now as fierce as if the Tailor were stitching seams through his skin.

Jacob was sharing the mare's back with Valiant. Having the Dwarf that close made it easier to watch him, but it had its disadvantages. Valiant had a close look at him as well, and the smile on his beardless face grew wider each time he turned around to cast a glance at Jacob's pain-ridden face.

Here we go. Another turn.

"Oh, you really look terrible, Jacob Reckless!" the Dwarf stated with undisguised glee. "And that poor girl...she is watching you. Do you see how worried she is? She's terrified that you'll fall off your horse before her beloved can get his skin back. But don't you worry. After you're dead and your brother has turned into a Goyl, Evenaugh Valiant will console her in person. I have a weakness for human women—did I ever tell you that?"

Jacob was too dazed by the fever to reply. He longed for the healing air of the Fairies almost as much for his own sake as for his brother's by now.

You just have to get through the gorge, Jacob. And then past the Unicorns. The Unicorns. His back hurt at the mere thought of them. What if the Dwarf betrayed him once again?

Will was riding next to Clara, trying to make her forget what he had said in the cave. But she couldn't forget. Jacob saw it in her face. She rarely looked at his brother. When she did, though, Jacob saw love, and fear.

The sun was already quite low, and the shadows in the ravine darkened the water of the foaming creek as if it were carrying the night into the gorge. They were halfway through it when Will suddenly reined in his horse.

"What is it?" Valiant asked anxiously.

"There are Goyl here." There was not a trace of doubt in Will's voice. "They are close."

"Goyl? Excellent!" Valiant cast them all a mocking glance. "I get on great with the Goyl. I guess that can't be said of the other members of this expedition?"

Jacob slowed the mare down and listened, but the rush of the water drowned out all other sounds.

"Pretend you're watering your horses," he whispered to Clara and Will while getting off his horse.

The vixen slipped to his side.

140

"Will is right," she hissed. "I smell them ahead of us."

Will shuddered, like a wolf catching the scent of its pack. "Why are they hiding?"

Valiant eyed him as if seeing him for the first time.

"You cunning dog!" he hissed at Jacob. "The stone in his skin...it's jade!"

"So what?"

"So what? Your brother. Right!" Valiant gave Jacob a conspiratorial wink. "The Goyl are offering two pounds of red moonstone for a Man-Goyl with jade skin. Well played. But why, in the name of all child-eating Witches, are you taking him to the Fairies?"

Two pounds of red moonstone...Jacob stared at Will's pale green skin. *Of course.* That's why the Goyl had shown up at the deserted farm. The wound did indeed fog his brain. The Jade Goyl who would make their King invincible. Chanute had once fantasized about finding him and selling him to the Empress. But nobody could seriously mistake his brother for the Jade Goyl, could they?

The travelers could already see the end of the gorge, and behind it the mist-shrouded valley. *So close.*

"Let's turn around and take him to one of their fortresses!" Valiant hissed. "The reward is lost if they capture him here themselves. Two pounds of moonstone! Come on!"

Will once again shuddered. He searched the steep slopes with his eyes. Golden eyes.

"Is there another way into the valley?" Jacob asked the Dwarf.

"Sure," Valiant replied with a smirk, "If you think your so-called brother has time to go the long way around...not to mention yourself. If you ask me, you look like you'll be dead in your boots by tomorrow."

Will looked around like a trapped animal.

Clara steered her horse next to Jacob's.

"Get him away from here!" she whispered. "Please! We have to turn around!"

And then what? The Fairy was Will's only hope.

A few yards to their left, a group of pine trees grew in front of the rocks. It was so dark under their branches that, even as close as this, Jacob couldn't see beneath them. He waved Will to his side.

"Follow me when I lead my horse to those pine trees," he whispered.

Will hesitated, but finally he did as he was told.

The shade under the pines was as black as soot. Jacob stepped close to the trees and grabbed Will's arm. "Remember how we fought when we were kids?"

"You always let me win."

"Exactly. That's what we'll do now."

"What's this?" The vixen had followed them. "We need to go back! Or do you want them to come and get him!"

"They won't, not if you do as I tell you." *Oh, she would be so angry once she realized what he was going to do.* Jacob tied his horse to one of the trees. "Whatever happens, Fox," he whispered, "I want you to stay with Will. Promise! If you don't, we'll all end up in a Goyl prison."

Will tied his horse to the trees. "I don't like this," he said under his breath. "I never liked our fights."

"Good," Jacob whispered back. "Show it. This one has to look real. And we need to end up under those trees."

Then he punched his brother in the face.

The gold in Will's eyes flared up.

142

He hit back so hard that Jacob fell to his knees. Skin of stone, and the rage of the Goyl.

Maybe it hadn't been such a good plan after all.

24

The Hunters

Hentzau had reached the ravine at daybreak. The Unicorns grazing in the misty valley beyond had left him with little doubt that Nesser had led them to the right place. However, when in the late afternoon they still hadn't spotted anything but wild boars and hares, Hentzau began to ask himself whether the Jade Goyl's brother had shot him after all.

He was just getting ready to order two men to the entrance of the gorge when Nesser alerted him to three riders, whose shadows the evening sun painted onto the rocks.

Yes, it was them. The two brothers, the girl, and the vixen Threefingers had driveled about. And they had caught themselves a Dwarf. Not a bad idea. Even Nesser didn't know how to get past the Unicorns, but Hentzau had heard rumors that some Dwarfs knew the secret. Be that as it may, he had no ambition to be the first Goyl to meet the Dark Fairy's sisters and set foot on their enchanted island. Hentzau would rather have ridden through a dozen Hungry Forests or slept with the Blind Snakes, who bred and killed in the deepest crevices of the earth. No. He would catch the Jade Goyl before he could hide behind the Unicorns.

"Commander! They're fighting." Nesser sounded surprised.

What did she expect? The rage came with the stone skin, just like the gold in the eyes, and who would feel the brunt of it first? The brother, of course.

Yes! Kill him! Hentzau thought, watching the two through his spyglass. *Maybe you wanted to do it before, but he was always the older, the stronger. You'll see: against the rage of the Goyl, all that doesn't count.*

His skin did look like jade. *Yes, it did...*

The older brother fought quite well, but he didn't stand a chance.

There. He fell to his knees. The girl pulled the Jade Goyl back, but he shook her off, and as his brother struggled to his feet, he kicked him in the chest so hard that he staggered back under the trees. The blackness beneath the branches swallowed them both, and Hentzau was just about to give the order to ride down, when the Jade Goyl reappeared from under the leaves.

He was already recoiling from the glare of the sun, pulling his hood down over his face before he untied his horse. The fight had made his step a little unsteady, but he would soon feel how much quicker his new flesh healed.

Hentzau signaled his men to mount up.

He was going to catch himself a fairy tale.

25

THE BAIT

Rocks. Shrubs. Where could they be hiding? *How would you know, Jacob? You're not a Goyl.*

Maybe he should have asked Will.

Jacob pulled the hood closer around his face and forced the horse into a slow gait. How could the Goyl have known they'd be coming through this gorge? *Not now, Jacob.*

He couldn't tell which hurt more, the shoulder or his face. Human flesh was so soft compared to jade knuckles. At some point, he had really thought Will would beat him to death, and he still wasn't sure how much of the rage he'd felt in those blows had been Goyl and how much had always been his younger brother's. Had he ever asked himself what it had meant for Will to be left alone with their mother and her sadness? No, he was very good at not asking such questions.

Will's gelding was still nervous about its new rider. Jacob could barely rule it in with one arm. He felt the splashes of water like ice on his feverish skin as he urged the horse through the lathering creek. But still nothing stirred on the gorge's slopes, and Jacob was beginning to wonder whether Will hadn't just sensed his own jade flesh when something moved on his left.

Now. He slackened the gelding's reins. It was not as fast as the mare but very hardy, and after all the years behind the mirror Jacob was an excellent rider.

The Goyl of course tried to cut him off, but their horses shied on the loose rocks, just as he had hoped, and the gelding dashed past them, galloping out into the misty valley. Memories...they made him choke as if the mist were made of them. Fear and bliss, love and death.

The Unicorns lifted their heads. Of course they weren't white. *Why were things in his world always whitewashed?* Their hides were brown and gray, mottled black, and pale yellow like the autumn sun drifting through the damp fog above. They were watching him, but so far none looked ready to attack.

Jacob looked around at his pursuers.

There were five of them. He immediately recognized the officer. It was the same one who had led the Goyl at the farm. His jasper-brown skin was cracked at the forehead, as if someone had tried to split it open, and one of his golden eyes was as cloudy as watery milk. So they really had been looking for Will when they showed up at the farm.

Jacob leaned down over the gelding's neck. Its hooves sank deep into the damp grass, but fortunately he hardly slowed down.

Ride, Jacob. He had to draw them away, to give Will a chance to get through the valley. Before he got it into his head to join them.

148

The Goyl were coming closer, but they didn't shoot. Of course not. If they believed Will to be the Jade Goyl, they'd want him alive.

One of the Unicorns whinnied.

No, Jacob. Forget about them.

Another glance over his shoulder. The Goyl had split up. They were trying to encircle him. The pain from the wound blurred his vision and made him remember the other pain, so vividly that he felt himself falling back through time, and was once again lying on the grass, his back pierced and torn open by the Unicorns' horns.

The gelding was panting heavily, and the Goyl no longer rode the half-blind horses they used to breed underground. One of them was getting very close. The officer. Jacob averted his face, but the hood slipped off his head just as he tried to reach for it. The surprise on the jasper face quickly turned into rage, the same rage Jacob had seen in his brother.

The game was up.

Where was Will? Jacob glanced desperately behind him. The Goyl officer was looking in the same direction.

Will did as Jacob had told him. He was galloping straight at the Unicorns with the Dwarf perched in front of him. Of course he had given Clara the faster mare. Will would have given it to a stranger. His unselfish brother. Still, despite the jade.

Fox was right behind the horses, almost invisible in the grass. It rippled where she ran as if the wind were blowing over it.

Jacob drew the pistol. His left hand no longer obeyed him, and he was a much worse shot with his right. Still, he managed to shoot two Goyl out of their saddles as they turned and headed toward Will. The Milk-Eye leveled his gun at Will, his jasper face stiff with rage. The anger had made him forget which brother he

149

was supposed to hunt, but his horse stumbled in the high grass, and his bullet missed its mark.

The gelding was still going, but Jacob barely managed to stay in the saddle. Will had nearly reached the Unicorns and Jacob prayed that the Dwarf had this time told them the truth. *Ride!* he thought desperately when Will suddenly slowed down, and did what Jacob had feared most: his brother brought his horse to a halt and stared at the Goyl, just as he had done at the deserted farm.

Milk-Eye cast Jacob a triumphant glance and turned his horse to go for his brother. Jacob took aim, but his shot just grazed the jasper skin.

Jacob yelled Will's name.

But he still didn't move.

One of the Goyl had nearly reached him. It was a female with amethyst and brown jasper skin. She drew her saber as Clara steered her horse protectively in front of Will's. But Jacob's bullet was faster. The Milk-Eye uttered a hoarse howl as the She-Goyl fell, and drove his horse even harder toward Will. Just a few more yards. The Dwarf was staring, wide-eyed, toward the Goyl. But Clara had gotten hold of Will's reins, and the horse she had ridden so many times yielded as she pulled it toward the Unicorns.

The herd had been as indifferent to the hunt as humans to squabbling sparrows, but they raised their heads when Clara rode toward them. Jacob forgot to breathe, but the Unicorns let her and Will pass. Valiant had told the truth. It was only when the Goyl rode toward them that the herd attacked.

The valley was filled with shrill whistles, beating hooves, and rearing bodies. Jacob heard shots. *Forget the Goyl, Jacob. Follow your brother!*

150

His heart pounding in his throat, he rode toward the agitated herd. He got ready to feel the horns once again pierce his back, his own warm blood running down his skin. *Not this time, Jacob. Do as the Dwarf told you. 'It's easy. You just close your eyes and keep them shut, or they will skewer you like windfalls.'*

Close your eyes...a horn brushed Jacob's thigh. Nostrils snorted in his ear and the cold autumn air carried the scent of horse and deer. The Unicorns surrounded him like a sea of shaggy bodies, swaying and shifting, pressing against him. But then, suddenly, he heard the wind in a thousand leaves, the lapping of water, and the rustling of reeds. He opened his eyes, and it was just as it had been back then.

Everything had vanished. The Goyl, the Unicorns, the misty valley. Instead, a lake glistened under the evening sky. On it floated the lilies for which he had come here three years ago. The leaves on the willows by the shore were as fresh and green as newly emerged shoots and, in the distance, drifting on the waves, lay the island from which there was no return unless the Fairies allowed it. He was the only one who had managed to steal away without permission.

The warm air caressed his skin, and the pain in his shoulder ebbed away like the water on the reed-lined shore.

He slid off the exhausted gelding.

Clara and Fox rushed toward him. Will, however, was standing by the shore, staring across at the island. He seemed unhurt, but when he turned to face Jacob, the jade was speckled with just a few last remnants of human skin.

"Here we are. Happy?" Valiant stood between the willows. He was plucking Unicorn hairs from his sleeve.

"Who took off your chain?" Jacob tried to grab the Dwarf, but Valiant dodged him nimbly.

"Luckily a female heart is much more compassionate than that piece of rock rumbling around in your chest," he purred while Clara sheepishly returned Jacob's glance. "And? What are you getting all huffy about? We're even! Except for the fact that the Unicorns trampled my hat!" Valiant accusingly patted his graying curls. "You could at least pay for that!"

"Us? Even? Shall I show you the scars on my back?" Jacob touched his shoulder. It felt as if he had never fought against the Tailor. "Just get out of here," he said to the Dwarf. "Before I shoot you after all."

"Really?" Valiant cast a contemptuous look at the island drifting in the distance. "I'm quite sure I'll live to see your name chiseled onto a gravestone long before mine. M'lady," he said, turning to Clara, "You should come with me. This will not end well. Have you ever heard of Snow-White, the human princess who lived with seven Dwarf brothers before falling for one of the Empress's ancestors? He made her dreadfully unhappy, and finally she ran away—with a Dwarf!"

"Really?" murmured Clara, but she didn't seem to have been listening. She stepped toward the shore of the blossom-covered lake as if she had forgotten everything around her, even Will, who was standing just a few yards away. Bluebells grew between the willows, their petals mirroring the dark blue of the evening sky. When Clara picked one, it chimed softly, wiping all the fear and sadness from her face.

Valiant uttered an exasperated groan.

"Fairy magic!" he muttered scornfully. "I think I'd better take my leave."

"Wait!" said Jacob. "There used to be a boat by the shore. Where is it?"

But when he turned around, the Dwarf had already disappeared between the trees.

Will was staring at his own reflection in the lake. Jacob skimmed a stone across the dark water, but his brother's reflection quickly returned. A face of jade.

"I nearly killed you when we fought." Will's voice was still not quite as hoarse as a Goyl's. "No matter what you're hoping to find here, it's too late."

Clara couldn't take her eyes off the flower in her hand. The Fairy magic clung to her like pollen. Only Will seemed immune to it.

"Let me join them. Please." He stepped away from Jacob as if he were afraid he might strike him again.

The sun was setting behind the trees, and its dying light spilled onto the lake like molten gold. The Fairy lilies opened their pale blossoms, welcoming the night. Jacob pulled Will away from the water.

"It's not too late," he said. "You didn't join them. You stayed with us! Wait here with Fox and Clara. I need to go to the island, but I'll be back soon. I promise."

The vixen stared at the island, her fur bristling. She had been standing at almost the same spot three years ago, when Jacob had made the same promise. He had kept her waiting for a year. This time, she expected him not to come back at all. Jacob saw it in her eyes.

26

THE RED FAIRY

They found the boat under one of the willows. It drifted on the water like an invitation. And a threat. *You won't return*, the water seemed to whisper, rocking it gently back and forth. *You should never have come back, Jacob Reckless.*

Fox didn't offer to come with him. She knew he had to go alone but, when Jacob climbed into the boat, she bit his hand so hard that the blood trickled down his fingers.

"As a reminder of the ones you leave behind!" she said while backing away from the water. But the fear in her eyes said: *you will forget us.* When Jacob pushed the boat away from the shore, she was gone. The Fairies had chased her away after they'd found him half-dead in their forest, and later on she had nearly drowned trying to follow them to the island. Still she had waited for him, spring, summer, autumn, and winter. But Jacob doubted that she would show such patience this time. He was never quite sure what Fox would do, whereas she could read him like a book. The vixen's fur made her so young and old at the same time, and so much a part of this world. More than he could ever be, in this world or the other.

Clara was standing among the willows when he rowed out onto the lake. Even Will watched him go this time.

It's too late... the waves lapping against the narrow boat seemed to echo Will's words, but Jacob was still sure that if there was a way to break the spell, the Dark Fairy's sister would know. He pulled out the medallion he wore under his shirt while he rowed the boat through the drifting lilies. The medallion contained one of their petals. He had picked it the day he'd left the island. The Red Fairy had told him that he could hide himself from her this way. When a Fairy loved a mortal man, she revealed all their secrets in her sleep; her lover just had to ask the right questions.

The island came closer so slowly that Jacob almost believed it sensed his betrayal. The other shore had disappeared in the mist, along with Clara and his brother. There seemed to be only the water, the sky studded with stars by now, and the island. Once again.

He saw four Fairies standing in the water when he finally reached the island's shore. Their long hair was drifting on the waves as if the night itself had spun it, but their red sister was not among them. One of them looked his way when Jacob hid the boat in the reeds, but she looked through him as if the petal had turned him into a ghost, and the thick carpet of flowers between the trees made his steps as silent as the vixen's paws. The flowers were blue, like the bluebell Clara had picked. The medallion didn't shield him from the memories their scent evoked,

156

and Jacob pressed his fingers firmly onto the bloody imprint the vixen's teeth had left on his hand.

Soon he saw the first of the dark nets spun by the Fairies' moths—tents as delicate as dragonfly skin, and so dark even in daytime that they appeared to have trapped the night in their mesh. The Fairies only slept there when the sun was in the sky, but Jacob could think of no better place to wait for the one he had come to find.

He had first heard about her at a tavern in Austry. The Red Fairy. A drunken mercenary had told him about a friend she had lured to the island and that he had drowned himself after his return, sick with yearning for her. One could hear those stories everywhere behind the mirror, though few men ever got to see a Fairy. Some thought their island to be the Realm of the Dead, but the Fairies knew nothing of human time or death. They had neither parents nor siblings, and the Red Fairy only called the Dark One her sister because they had both emerged from the lake on the same day. How could he hope she would understand the despair he felt about the jade in his brother's skin? *And how can you hope she is willing to forgive that you left her without warning?* something in him mocked. *Do you trust your charms to make her forget and forgive?*

Yes, maybe he did. Or maybe he just loved his brother that much.

The tent he had come for seemed darker than in his memories, when he finally spotted it between the oaks and beeches. Darker... and smaller. It didn't look like a place that for almost a year had been the beginning and the end of his world, and had held everything he ever dreamt of. The net clung to Jacob's clothes like spider webs as he felt his way through its gauzy walls. The

157

darkness between them was so deep, that his eyes took a while to find the moss-covered bed he had slept in so often. Jacob took a step back in surprise when he saw the sleeping figure on it.

She hadn't changed. Of course not. Fairies didn't age. Her skin was as white as the lilies drifting on the lake, and her hair as dark as the night she loved so much. So beautiful. Untouched by time and the decay it brought. But in the end he had longed to feel the mortality he sensed in his own flesh in the skin he caressed.

Jacob pulled the medallion from his shirt and unhooked it from the chain around his neck. Miranda stirred as soon as he placed it next to her. Yes, he knew her name, something Fairies don't forgive easily. Jacob stepped back from the bed when she whispered his name in her dream. It clearly wasn't a good dream, and finally she opened her eyes.

So beautiful.

Jacob's fingers sought the bite marks on his hand.

"Since when do you sleep away the night?"

For a moment she seemed to think he was still a dream. Then she noticed the medallion lying next to her. She opened it, let the petal drop into her six fingered hand.

"So that's how you hid yourself from me."

Jacob wasn't sure what he saw on her face. Anger. Love. Maybe both.

"Who told you about the petal?"

"You did." Her moths swarmed at his face when he took a step toward her. "I've come to ask for your help, Miranda. Against your sister."

She got up and brushed the moss from her dress. It was softer to the touch than the plume of a bird. Jacob's fingers remembered.

158

"I began to sleep away the nights after you left because they reminded me of you." She closed her hand over the petal. "By now it's just a bad habit."

Her moths tinged the night red with their wings.

"I see the vixen is still following you. And who is that girl? She looks as if she comes from far away. Very far away."

She crumbled the petal between her fingers.

"But you are not here about them, right? It is about the Goyl. Not even my sister dares to bring one of them to this realm."

"He's my brother. The Goyl invested him with your sister's curse. You can undo it, I know."

Miranda eyed him as if she searched for the love that had once kept him at her side. What if that was the prize she would ask for? Jacob tried to find it in his heart, but it was gone. All that was left were memories, wilted like the leaves of a past summer.

Of course she read that truth from his eyes.

"I can't help him. You've come to the wrong Fairy."

She seemed to be made of the shadows that surrounded her, of the moonlight and the night's dew. He had been so happy when his eyes had seen nothing but her. Until one day he had remembered that there was so much more. Unforgivable. They broke the spell, they alone. They asked for blindness in return for their love, oblivion…

"My sister isn't one of us anymore." Miranda turned her back to him. "She betrayed us for the Goyl."

"Doesn't that give you reason to help me?" Jacob reached for her arm.

"And reward you for betraying my love?" She freed her arm from his hand.

159

"I had to leave! I am mortal, have you forgotten? You could have come with me. For a while…"

"Fairies don't leave. Unless they forget who they are, like my sister."

That was not true. A few old stories described a past where they had all been involved with the mortal world, but none explained why they had withdrawn from it.

"I understand that you don't want to help me. But use me! To take revenge on your sister!"

She pressed her fingers on his lips and kissed him. Jacob returned the kiss, tasting what he had lost like ashes in his mouth. Maybe she would help them after all, if only he could make her believe he still loved her. Or make himself believe. He couldn't say who let go first. But when she stepped back he thought, for a brief moment, that he could see his death in her eyes.

The bark of a vixen echoed through the night.

Miranda lifted her hand. "There is only one way to break my sister's spell." One of her moths landed on her white fingers. So red, like freshly spilled blood. "You'll have to destroy her."

Jacob didn't easily admit he was afraid of someone. He was good at facing his fears, and at defeating them. But the Dark Fairy… *'She turns her enemies into the wine she drinks,'* even Chanute's voice sounded hoarse when he spoke of her, *'Or into the iron from which her lover builds his bridges and trains.'*

It was impossible to destroy her. She was immortal.

Miranda was watching him.

"I can tell you how."

For a moment, her beauty reminded Jacob of a poisonous flower. "How long does your brother have left?"

"I don't know. Not very long."

Voices pierced the dark. The other Fairies. Jacob had never found out how many there were of them.

Miranda gazed at the bed as if she remembered the times they had shared it. "My sister is staying with her Goyl lover, in his Royal Fortress."

That was a ride of at least six days.

"You can still get to her before it is too late."

The moth on Miranda's hand spread its wings and fluttered onto her shoulder.

"If I give your brother more time."

The vixen began to bark again. Miranda smiled. Maybe she remembered how she had chased Fox away, and how she had made Jacob forget her for a full year.

"I guess you know about the princess one of us cursed to die from a rose's sting on her fifteenth birthday. It never happened because we halted the curse. With a deep sleep."

"Yes," Jacob answered. "I saw her. She died anyway. Because nobody ever came to wake her."

Miranda shrugged. "To wake him is your responsibility. I'll just make him sleep. But make sure he doesn't wake before you have broken my sister's power."

The moth on her shoulder was preening its wings.

Jacob saw the dead body in the rose-covered tower before him. What did immortal Fairies care for the fate of a human princess? They had held up the curse because they had fought each other. And maybe Will could still be saved because Miranda despised her dark sister. To profit from their fights was probably all one could hope for when dealing with immortals. And to not get in their way. Jacob wondered whether there had ever been a Fairy as benevolent and helpful as the ones described in some fairy tales of his world. It would have been a comforting thought to trust in such help.

"The girl who is with you...she belongs to your brother?" Miranda brushed her naked foot over the ground, and the moonlight drew Clara's face on the dark earth.

"Yes. And she still loves him."

"Good. For should she not, he will sleep himself to death." Miranda wiped away the moonlight image. "Have you ever met my sister? She is the fairest of us all."

Yes. Jacob had seen blurry photographs, an etched portrait in a newspaper — Kami'en's demon lover, the Fairy Witch, who made stone grow in human flesh...so beautiful that it blinded men to look at her.

"Whatever she promises you — " Miranda caressed his face as if her fingers could still find the love they had once felt for each other, " — do not believe her. You have to do exactly as I say, or your brother is lost."

Again the vixen barked. *I'm fine, Fox,* thought Jacob. *All will be well.*

But would it?

Miranda took his hand. Six fingers, as white as the flowers on the lake. She kissed him once again.

"What if the price for my help is that you come back to me?" she whispered. "For all eternity? Death doesn't come to this island."

She had made the same promise three years ago. But Jacob didn't wish for immortality, something she would never understand. *Say yes,* his heart whispered, *why not? You escaped her once. You can do it again.* But before he could answer, Miranda once again covered his lips with her hand

162

"Don't worry. I'll get my revenge," she said. "And my price will be paid."

27
So Far Away

Will had not once taken his eyes off the island. It was painful for Clara to see the fear on his face. Was he worried for his brother? Was he afraid they had come here in vain?

"Jacob will be back soon," she said, stepping to his side. "I'm sure."

"Sure? With Jacob, you can never be sure," he replied.

He was both of them by now, the stranger from the cave and the other one, who had stood in the hospital corridor and smiled at her every time she walked past. Will. She missed him so much.

"He'll find a way," she said. "He will." She had to believe it or she'd lose her mind.

"Yes, he will try everything, I know…" Will stared at his reflection, jade green between the white petals of the lilies.

He still looked like the man she loved, despite the jade. And he was so alone. But when Clara reached for his arm he shuddered, as he had done in the cave.

It hurt so much. *What was she still doing here?*

He didn't want her. Not anymore. He wanted the jade. It was the truth none of them dared to look at and the fear on his face: that Jacob would find a way to drive the jade away.

It was too late.

Even if Jacob returned from the island.

Even if he learned there how to break the curse.

Will might not allow it.

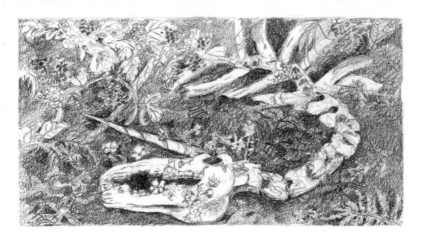

28
JUST A ROSE

Jacob stayed all night on the moss-covered bed, in the arms of the Fairy he didn't love anymore. He tried so hard to convince himself that he still did, to make sure Miranda would help his brother and to forget: the jade in Will's skin; the guilt about leaving him and their mother alone far too often, and for far too long; the sinister house of the Witch; the fight with the Tailor; the Goyl who might still be waiting for them in the valley of the Unicorns…so much to forget. Even the mirror and the good times it had granted him — this night he didn't want to remember any of it. And where else was that wish granted more easily than in a Fairy's arms? So he loosened Miranda's black hair in the darkness and kissed her white skin, pretending that everything was the way it used to be — that her kisses didn't taste like ashes and that her beauty still enchanted him.

When the first daylight stole through the net of her moths, the bite on Jacob's hand started to throb, and he was sure that Miranda knew it was all a lie, that their love was dead, and that it would be so easy to punish him by not helping his brother. But she kissed him again, despite the morning light, and made love to him, and when he finally told her he had to go, she didn't ask whether he would come back. She only made him repeat everything she'd taught him about her dark sister. Word for word.

The lilies were already closing their blossoms and Jacob saw none of Miranda's sisters on his way back to the boat. There was froth drifting on the water when he pushed the boat out of the reeds, heralding that the lake would soon give birth to another Fairy.

Will was nowhere to be seen when Jacob approached the shore, and neither was Fox. Only Clara was asleep under the willows. She woke with a start when he pushed the boat ashore. She didn't seem to notice the leaves in her hair, or her dirty clothes. All Jacob saw on her face was a hopelessness not even his return could change.

"Did they fight again?" he whispered to Fox when she appeared from under the willow branches.

"Some silences are worse than fighting," she replied. "You were gone for quite a while. I was just going to have a look at the fish to see whether any of them resembled you."

She knew. Of course she did.

"So how did you manage to get away this time?" she asked. "With the promise to come back?" Oh, she enjoyed this. Jacob believed he heard the vixen purr.

"She told me how to break the curse."

Clara got to her feet. But the vixen frowned. "Why?"

168

"Because she doesn't like her sister."

Fox stared across the lake, her eyes narrowed with suspicion. "So what did she suggest?"

Maybe Will had been listening the whole time. For an instant, Jacob was sure he had stayed too long in the Red Fairy's bed when he saw Will step out from under the willows. The jade had darkened and his brother's face merged with the green of the trees, as if he had become part of this world.

"We just have to find a rose," Jacob said.

"A rose?" Of course Clara thought of the roses growing on the walls of the silent castle, and of the dead princes entangled in their vines.

"Yes, but this one will deliver protection from a Fairy's spell."

That was only half the truth, but hopefully Will would trust him one more time and do exactly what he told him. Everything would depend on it.

Fox wouldn't take her eyes off him. *What are you trying to do, Jacob Reckless?* they asked. Jacob wished he could have told her. After all these years of hunting for treasure side by side, they were used to telling each other almost everything, and Jacob had never felt more in need for the vixen's advice. But the presence of Will and Clara didn't allow for the wordless understanding they usually shared. Jacob missed it, although he would never have said so. And neither would Fox.

I need to find the Dark Fairy, he wanted to tell her, *and I am not sure what frightens me more — the prospect of fighting her, or to fail and let my brother down.* Yes, all that he would have loved to say, but neither Clara nor Will could know what he had learned on the island, and Fox wouldn't like what he intended to do for his brother.

So all he said was, "The rose doesn't grow far from here."

169

Fox was still watching him.

Jacob was sure that she saw his fear, although she might not guess of what. His fear and his determination to protect his brother—at whatever price that protection came. Maybe not just because he loved him, but also to make up for all of those years when he had left Will alone. Guilt is a strong motivator, sometimes even stronger than love.

29

Through the Heart

Jacob led them northward along the lakeshore. The morning sun turned the water into liquid gold, and Clara caught herself thinking that everything might end well after all, although Will still avoided her eyes.

She couldn't tell for how long they had been riding. Time didn't exist in this realm. No seasons, no past or future, just the choir of a thousand scents, a thousand birdsongs, a thousand voices in the warm wind. When Jacob finally turned away from the lake, the horses soon sank deep into the vines of brambles, and above them the leaves lost the fresh green of the Fairies' eternal spring, spotting the moss at their feet with orange and yellow. When Jacob reined in his horse, they could already see the valley through the trees, and some of the Unicorns, but when they dismounted they were surrounded by bones. They were everywhere: Unicorn skeletons, moss and grass between their ribs, spiderwebs spanning their hollow eye sockets, the spiraled horns still on their bare-boned foreheads.

"They come here to die," Fox said. "And to receive their last farewell."

Vines covered the bones with white flowers, the Fairies' last gift to their guardians.

Jacob approached one of the skeletons.

A single red rose was growing out of its chest.

Will stepped to his brother's side, but he eyed the rose like a poisonous snake.

The vixen walked to the edge of the forest and peered toward the living Unicorns. "I smell Goyl."

Will cast Jacob an almost amused glance.

"I guess that's my fault, Fox."

There was a lightness in his voice, a freedom that was new, and Jacob caught himself hesitating. But they had come too far and there was so much fresh hope on Clara's face.

"You just have to pick it," he said, pointing at the rose. "But you have to do it yourself."

Will looked at his hand. It was solid jade by now, and disturbingly beautiful. Clara heard the stem snap when he finally leaned down and broke it. One of the thorns pricked his finger. The blood emerging from the tiny wound had the pale color of amber, proof of how profound the transformation was by now. Will stared at it incredulously. Then he dropped the rose. And swayed.

"What's going on? Jacob?" He looked in alarm at his brother.

Clara came to his aid, but Will once again flinched away from her. He stumbled into one of the skeletons, the bones breaking like rotten wood under his boots.

"Will, listen!" Jacob grabbed his arm. "I am sorry, but you have to sleep. I need more time. When you wake up, all this will be over. I promise."

Will pushed him away with such violence that Jacob staggered back, out from under the trees, into the open meadow. The Unicorns raised their heads.

"Jacob!" Fox barked. "Get back under the trees!"

But the shot was faster.

Such a sharp sound. Like splintering wood.

The bullet struck Jacob in the back.

The vixen's scream sounded almost human when he fell. Will ran to him before Clara could hold him back. He dropped to his knees next to his brother, calling his name, but Jacob didn't move. The bullet had torn open his chest, and blood soaked his shirt right above his heart.

The Goyl appeared from behind a tree, a safe distance from the Unicorns. He was still holding the rifle. One of his soldiers was by his side—Clara recognized her. It was the female Goyl Jacob had shot before she could kill Clara with her saber. Her uniform was soaked with the same pale blood that had seeped from Will's pierced finger.

The vixen attacked them both with bared fangs, but the Goyl with the rifle thrust the barrel of his gun between her ribs and Fox fell down with a gasp, changing shape as she collapsed in the yellow grass, the pain robbing her of her fur.

Will had gotten to his feet, his face ablaze with rage, while Fox crawled to Jacob's side. He reached for the rifle his brother had dropped, but he was still dazed from the rose's thorn, and the Goyl grabbed him before he could get hold of the weapon.

173

"Calm down!" he barked at Will while the She-Goyl pointed her pistol at Clara. "I had a score to settle with your brother, but we won't harm a hair on you. You have my word, and Hentzau's word—" he added with a satisfied glance at Jacob's outstretched body, "—is still as reliable as his shooting skills."

Fox pulled the pistol from Jacob's belt, but the She-Goyl kicked it out of her hand while Will just stood there, staring down at his brother.

"Look at him, Nesser," Hentzau said, forcing Will's face toward him. "The Jade Goyl...I admit I still had my doubts. But it looks like he is indeed not just a fairy tale."

Will tried to ram his head into the Goyl's face, but he could barely keep his eyes open, and Hentzau laughed.

"Yes, you're one of us!" he said. "Even though you may not admit it yet. Tie his hands!" he ordered the She-Goyl.

"Do we take him to the Fairy?" she asked while she grabbed Will. "Or to the King?"

"Is there still a difference?" Hentzau replied. He went over to Jacob's body and eyed him as a hunter would his prey.

"His face looks familiar. What's his name?" he asked Will.

Will didn't answer.

"Nevermind," the Goyl said, turning away. "You Doughskins all look the same, anyway. Round up the horses."

Nesser obeyed, but her eyes were still on Fox and Clara. Human women...so different and still so disturbingly similar when they cried.

"No!" Clara sobbed when Hentzau pushed Will toward Jacob's mare.

"Where are you taking him?"

174

"What does it matter to you?" The Goyl said over his shoulder. "Forget him! He will soon forget you."

30

A Shroud of Red Wings

The gunshot wound looked much less harmful than the wounds Jacob had suffered from the Unicorns. Back then, however, he had been breathing, and Fox had felt his faint pulse. Now he was just still.

So much pain. She wanted to dig the vixen's teeth into her human flesh just not to feel it anymore. But her fur wouldn't come back, and she felt as vulnerable and lost as an abandoned child.

Clara was cowering next to her, arms clasped around her knees. She had stopped crying. She just sat there, as if someone had cut out her heart. Clara was the first to see the Dwarf.

Valiant did his best to look as innocent as if they'd caught him picking mushrooms while he came closer. Who else but the Dwarf could have told the Goyl that the only way out of the Fairy realm was through the Unicorn graveyard?

Fox wiped the tears from her eyes and felt in the dewy grass for Jacob's pistol.

"Wait! Wait! What are you doing?" Valiant yelled as she pointed the muzzle at him, and he disappeared with surprising agility behind the nearest bush. "How could I know they'd shoot him right away? I thought they just wanted his brother."

Clara got to her feet.

"Shoot him, Fox," she said. "If you don't, I will."

"They caught me on my way back to the gorge!" Valiant clamored. "What was I supposed to do? Get myself killed as well?"

"And now? Why are you still here?" Fox yelled at him. "Come to plunder a corpse on your way back?"

"That's outrageous! I'm here to rescue you!" the Dwarf retorted with genuine indignation. "Two beautiful girls, all alone, lost and helpless..."

"....so helpless that we'd surely pay you to save us?"

The silence answering from the bush was very telling, and Fox lifted the pistol again. If only she could stop the tears. They blurred everything: the valley, the bush where the treacherous Dwarf was hiding, and Jacob's silent face.

"Fox!" Clara put a hand on her arm.

A red moth had landed on Jacob's blood soaked chest. Another spread her wings on his brow.

Fox dropped the pistol and chased them away.

"Go and tell your mistress he's never coming back!" she shouted, her voice drowning in tears. "Didn't I tell you," she whispered, leaning over Jacob, "Not to go back to the Fairies? That this time it would kill you?"

Another moth landed on the lifeless body. More and more of them fluttered out from under the trees. They settled on him in

178

such profusion that they looked like flowers sprouting from his shattered flesh.

Clara helped Fox to drive them away, but there were so many that finally they gave up and simply watched as the moths covered Jacob so thoroughly with their wings, as if the Red Fairy was claiming him even in death.

"We have to bury him, Fox," Clara whispered.

Fox pulled Jacob's coat over the terrible wound. *Bury him.* No. No, she couldn't.

"I'll do it." Valiant had actually dared to come closer. He picked up the rifle Jacob had dropped and slapped the barrel flat with his bare hand, as if the metal were as soft as clay.

"Bloody waste!" he muttered shaping the rifle into a spade. "Now none of us will get those two pounds of red moonstone! But no! Why listen to a Dwarf? We could have just shared the reward and the fool would still be alive!"

He dug the grave as effortlessly as if he'd dug many graves in his life, while Fox sat by Jacob's side holding his hand. So cold. So lifeless. The pain devoured her heart. It made her remember the other pain that had brought them together. She remembered the iron teeth in her flesh, the steps approaching, and then, for the first time, Jacob's face, and his hands when he had freed her leg. He couldn't be gone. He couldn't.

The moths were still covering him like a shroud when Valiant threw down the rifle-turned-shovel and brushed the soil off his hands.

"Right," he said. "Let's get him in there." He leaned over Jacob. "But first we should check his pockets. No point in letting perfectly good gold sovereigns rot in the ground."

That brought Fox's fur back in an instant.

179

"Don't touch him!" She bared her fangs. Oh, she wanted to tear him to shreds, the treacherous Dwarf. Why didn't she do it? *Bite him, Fox. Tear his flesh off his bones. Maybe that will ease the pain.*

Valiant tried to fend her off with the shovel-rifle, but the vixen tore into his coat and jumped at his throat. She already felt his skin under her teeth when Clara grabbed her by the fur and pulled her back.

"Fox, he's right!" she whispered while the vixen trembled with bloodlust. Yes, she wanted the Dwarf's blood in return for Jacob's. A river of his blood. But Clara still held her back.

"We may need the Dwarf alive, Fox. As a guide. And we'll need Jacob's money. His weapons. The compass...everything he had with him. To find Will. Jacob would have wanted us to find him, wouldn't he?"

Behind them, Valiant snorted in disbelief. "Will? Are you talking about the Jade Goyl?""

Clara bent over Jacob and put her hand in his coat pocket. Her fingers found the handkerchief and two gold coins dropped into the grass.

"They looked so different, didn't they?" Clara murmured. "Do you have siblings, Fox?"

The vixen pressed against the lifeless body.

"Yes, three brothers. But two of them are worthless."

The moths rose like red smoke, swirling above them. Then they fluttered toward the trees as if they had heard their mistress's voice. Or had done what they came for.

"Fox!" Clara whispered.

The vixen had seen it too. She backed away from Jacob.

His torn body shuddered. His lips gasped for air.

No. *The dead don't come back.*

Fox took another step back, her fur on end.

Even the Dwarf's face was grey with fear. Clara stared at Jacob as if it was his ghost she watched stirring in his blood-soaked clothes.

He slowly sat up and looked around, as disoriented as if someone had woken him too abruptly from a dream. Not a bad dream, it seemed. Just a dream. Then he noticed the blood on his shirt. He touched it as if it were another man's.

"What happened?"

His eyes were on Fox, as if she was the only thing he remembered. She shifted shape and knelt down by his side.

His hand was warm again when she grabbed it. He was not gone. He was still here. The joy cut into her heart as sharply as the pain.

"You were dead," she said.

It felt strange to say it while looking at him, so alive.

"The Goyl shot you." Clara's voice was barely a whisper. "It was a terrible wound."

Jacob looked at them both incredulously. His eyes were still dazed, his movements slow, as if he had to get used to his body again. He barely managed to unbutton the torn and bloody shreds of his shirt.

There was no wound. Not a trace of it. Instead, right above his heart, there was the imprint of a moth, as dark as a birth mark. Jacob ran his fingers over its wings. He was not fully back yet. Fox could see it in his eyes. *Where had he been?* She didn't ask. There would be time for it. But not now.

Jacob had noticed that someone was missing
"Where's Will?"

Yes, Fox had feared that question.

181

Jacob struggled to his feet. He had noticed the Dwarf, too. "What is he doing here?"

Valiant took a few steps back.

"I heard rumors that the Fairies sometimes bring their lovers back," he said, picking up the shovel-rifle, "But I wouldn't have thought it includes the ones who run out on them..."

"Where's my brother?" Jacob took an unsteady step toward the Dwarf, but Valiant managed to evade him with a quick leap across the empty grave.

"Easy, now!" he called, waving the mangled rifle at Jacob. "How am I supposed to tell you if you break my neck?"

Clara still held the handkerchief and the gold sovereigns in her hands. "I'm sorry," she said, holding both out to Jacob, "I took these to find Will."

Jacob didn't take his eyes off Valiant while he pushed the coins and the handkerchief back into his pockets. "So the Goyl took him. Do I get that right? And I guess the Dwarf told them where to find him?"

He reached for his pistol, but it was still lying in the grass where Fox had dropped it.

"Don't shoot him yet," she said, stepping to his side. "He probably knows where they took your brother."

"That's right. I do." Valiant snapped the bent barrel off the rifle as if it were a brittle twig. "And I had the muzzle of a Goyl rifle at my head when I told them where to find him. What would you have done? Well, probably you'd let them shoot you, as your old lover can bring you back from the dead. Most of us are not that fortunate."

"So where did they take him?" Clara asked.

182

"The Goyl's Royal Fortress." Valiant purred. "The last human who tried to sneak in there was an imperial spy. Kami'en had him cast in amber and put on display right next to the main gate. Terrible sight."

Jacob picked up his pistol. "But of course you know a way to get in."

Valiant's mouth stretched into such a smug grin that Fox was tempted to shoot him after all. "Of course."

"How much?" Jacob sounded as if he were still somewhere else.

Fox grabbed his arm when she felt him sway. He was back, as pale as a ghost, but back and breathing. She wanted to hold him and feel his heart beating against hers. The vixen didn't have wishes like that. It was the human skin. It made life complicated. Life, friendship, love...she loved him so much.

Valiant formed the metal of the broken rifle into a pistol.

"How much? That gold tree you sold to the Empress last year...word is she gave you a cutting."

Fox cast Jacob a glance that only he could read. There was indeed a cutting. He had planted it in the ruin's overgrown gardens. It had grown fast, but so far the only gold the young tree had yielded was its foul-smelling pollen.

Still, Jacob managed to produce an expression of honest indignation.

"That's an outrageous price!"

"On the contrary." Valiant's eyes glinted as if he could already feel the gold raining down on his shoulders. "It's a very modest demand, considering that we'll probably all end up cast in amber."

Fox would have loved to push him into the empty grave.

31
WHAT IF...

Without the horses, it took them hours to reach a road that led from the valley up into the mountains. Jacob missed the mare, and hoped the Goyl were as kind with their horses as rumors said. One's horse was, if well chosen, a treasured companion behind the mirror, and Jacob remembered them all, the ones he had lost, the ones that had run away…the two horses he finally bought from a farmer were no competition for any of them, but better than walking. The Dwarf protested elaborately when Jacob acquired a donkey for him, but he soon was so pleased with it that he filled their ears with musings about the advantages of a smaller body.

The paths leading north grew steeper, but Jacob only stopped when even the donkey stumbled in the dark. They found shelter beneath a ledge that shielded them from the wind, and soon Valiant was snoring as loudly as if he had crawled into one of the soft beds Dwarf inns were famous for. The vixen disappeared into

185

the night to go hunting, and Jacob advised Clara to sleep behind the horses so that they would keep her warm.

He lit a fire with some dry wood he'd found among the rocks and stared into the night, listening to his own heartbeat, as anyone likely would, having come back from the dead. He remembered darkness. And then light. The feeling to have left something important unfinished and the wish to forget about it and to get lost in the light. Peace. Yes, he remembered that feeling of peace very clearly. Of being everything and nothing. And then…he had heard the voice of the Fairy. Miranda's voice, calling him. And there had been wings. Red wings. And Fox. Yes, she was what he had come back for. Not the Fairy, not even Will—just the vixen.

But now everything was coming back, while the fire danced away the night: the Unicorn graveyard, the rose, and the way his brother had looked at him when he had felt its spell. *'When you wake up, all this will be over. I promise.'*

How, Jacob? Even if the Dwarf didn't double-cross him again. Even if he managed to find the Dark Fairy in the Goyl's Royal Fortress. How was he going to get close enough to her to use what her sister had revealed to him?

"Jacob?"

Clara was standing behind him, a horse blanket around her shoulders.

"You can't sleep?"

Jacob could still heard the disbelief in her voice that he was actually alive. And how much it frightened her. It frightened him too.

"Yes. That was to be expected, wasn't it?," he answered. "A few minutes in death make up for many hours of sleep, I guess."

186

An owl was screaming above them. In this world, owls were regarded as the souls of dead Witches. Clara knelt down next to him and held her hands above the warming flames.

"Please tell me. What did you learn on that island?"

She looked terribly tired.

"I can't tell you. I had to promise." Still only half the truth, but he wouldn't tell her what he hadn't told Fox. Although, at some point, he would need her help.

Her eyes were as blue as Will's. Before they had been drowned in gold.

"What if he likes the jade?" She spoke the words so softly that he could barely hear them. "Did you ever ask yourself that question?"

The flames striped her face with dancing shadows.

"What if…what if Will doesn't want us to help him?"

Yes, what if…

Of course, Jacob wanted to reply. *Of course I've asked myself that question.* But he couldn't offer Clara any answer. And certainly not this night, with a heart still beating in his chest as if it had forgotten how to do so.

32

THE RIVER

The Goyl's Royal Fortress lay deep under a mountain range that rose more than two hundred miles north of the Fairies' valley. It soon showed in the weather. Jacob was not the only one who wished for the warmth on the Fairy's island when their blankets were covered with frost in the mornings, and the rain fell so relentlessly from a grey sky that their clothes wouldn't dry.

"What's she still doing here?" Valiant asked when, after another cold night, Clara struggled to mount her horse. "Do all humans treat their women like this? She belongs in a house. Nice dresses, servants, cakes, a soft bed—that's what she needs."

"And a Dwarf for a husband, and a golden lock on her door to which only you have the key?" Fox snapped.

"Why not?" Valiant replied, giving Clara his most ravishing smile.

After a few days, she looked so pale with exhaustion that even Jacob started to worry, and he had them spend the night under the warming roof of an inn. Fox shared the bed with Clara while he put up with the Dwarf, but it was not Valiant's snoring that kept him awake. He still sometimes believed he could taste his own blood in his mouth, and there were times when he felt the gaping wound over his heart that the others had told him about.

On the evening of the fourth day, they reached one of the towers the Goyl built to guard their above ground borders, with walls bricked so seamlessly that most human buildings looked primitive in comparison. Behind its onyx windows, at least a dozen guards usually kept watch, but Valiant got them past it unseen. In these lands, the Goyl had been mentioned for centuries in the same breath as Ogres and Brown Wolves, but their worst crime had always been their resemblance to humans. They were the stone-skinned cousins who dwelled in the deep, mankind's reflection in a black mirror. Nowhere had they been hunted as mercilessly as in the mountains they came from, and the Goyl were paying it back by ruling their old homeland with less mercy than their other conquests.

Valiant avoided the highways used by their troops, but from time to time they couldn't avoid crossing paths with Goyl patrols. While the vixen slipped past them, Valiant introduced Jacob and Clara as rich clients who were planning to build a glass factory near the Royal Fortress. Jacob had bought Clara one of the gold-embroidered skirts worn by the rich women of the area, while he had swapped his clothes for those of a wealthy merchant, though he barely recognized himself in the fur-collared coat and soft gray trousers. Riding became even more cumbersome for

Clara in the wide skirt, but the Goyl waved them past each time Valiant told his story.

The air carried the scent of snow when, one evening, they finally reached the river beyond which the Royal Fortress lay. The ferry crossing was in Blenheim, a town the Goyl had captured many years before. Nearly half the houses had bricked-up windows; they had even canopied many roads to protect themselves from the sun and, behind the harbor wall, Jacob spotted a heavily guarded manhole, indicating one of the underground districts Kami'en had ordered built underneath many human cities.

While Fox disappeared between the houses to catch herself one of the pigeons pecking at the cobblestones, Jacob walked with Valiant and Clara toward the ferry landing. On the opposite shore, a wide stone gate stood out in the mountainside.

"Is that the entrance to the fortress?" Jacob asked the Dwarf.

Valiant shook his head. "No. No. That's just one of the cave cities they built above ground. The Royal Fortress is farther inland, so deep underground that you'll wish you could unlearn breathing."

The ferry that was anchored at the dock had clearly seen countless rough crossings. The metal plates covering its wooden hull had more dents than a battleship. The ferryman was already closing the landing with a rusty chain and, when Jacob asked whether he could take them across before nightfall, his lips bent into a scornful grin. He looked nearly as hideous as the infamous Wart Trolls, who were easily scared by their own reflections

"This river isn't a very hospitable place after dark." He spoke so loudly, as if he wanted to be heard on the other shore. "And tomorrow no one is allowed to cross the river because the crowned Goyl will emerge from his den to go to his wedding."

191

"Wedding?" Jacob looked at Valiant questioningly, but the Dwarf just shrugged his shoulders.

"Where have you been?" the ferryman sneered. "The Empress of Austry buys peace from the stone-faces by marrying her daughter to their King. Tomorrow they'll swarm out of their holes, and the Goyl will ride to Vena on his Devil-train to take the loveliest princess ever born down to his burrow. Curse him. Curse them all."

Jacob felt for once relieved that Will was not with him.

"Does the Dark Fairy accompany Kami'en to the wedding?"

Valiant cast Jacob a curious glance. It wouldn't take the Dwarf long to figure out that Jacob was not just looking for his brother, but the longer he could keep that a secret the better. Jacob was worried that not even a gold tree's sampling would keep Valiant by his side once he learned that Jacob planned to confront the Dark Fairy.

"Sure she does," the ferryman grunted. "Kami'en goes nowhere without the Fairy Witch. Not even when he marries another woman."

Jacob stared across the river. *Tomorrow.* Bad luck, once again. He would have even less time than expected to get to the Fairy. He put his hand in his pocket.

"Did you by any chance take a Goyl officer across today?"

"What?" The ferryman held a hand behind his ear.

"A Goyl officer. Jasper skin? Nearly blind in one eye. He had a female soldier with him. And a prisoner."

The ferryman's eyes narrowed with suspicion. "Why? Are you one of those who're still hunting them?" He was once again speaking so loudly that Jacob cast a worried glance at the Goyl sentries guarding the manhole entrance further up the shore. But, luckily, they had their backs turned.

"That prisoner he had with him would fetch you a fine price," the ferryman gave Jacob a conspiratorial wink. "His skin was jade! Their sacred stone. I've never seen one with that color."

Jacob had to resist the temptation of punching his ugly face. That's what his brother had become — a prey to be hunted for his skin. He rubbed the handkerchief until he felt metal between his fingers.

"This is for you," he said, dropping one of the coins into the ferryman's calloused hand. "You'll get another on the other side — if you take us across tonight."

The man eyed the coin greedily, but Valiant grabbed Jacob's arm and pulled him aside.

"Let's wait until tomorrow," he hissed. "It's getting dark, and this river is swarming with Lorelei."

Lorelei. Jacob's grandfather had sometimes sung them a song about those river nymphs. The words had made him shudder as a child, and behind the mirror the stories told about them were even more sinister. But tomorrow the Fairy would be gone and he would have to find her at a royal wedding.

"No worries!" The ferryman gave him a confident smile while he closed his fingers firmly around the golden coin. "I'll make sure we won't wake them."

He reached into his baggy pockets and handed Jacob and Valiant each a pair of wax earplugs, which looked as if they had been used in countless ears.

"Just to be on the safe side," he said. "You never know. She doesn't need them," he added with a nod in Clara's direction. "The Lorelei are only after men."

Jacob was just wondering whether Fox would be back in time when the vixen came down the landing pier. She licked a few feathers from her fur before jumping aboard the shallow boat. The horses were nervous when they were led onto the ferry. Jacob could barely calm them when the ferryman untied the ropes and the boat drifted out onto the river. Behind them, the houses of Blenheim dissolved into the twilight, and the only sound was the lapping of water against the metal-clad hull. Jacob could make out a dirt road on the other shore, leading further inland. The ferryman gave him another comforting wink, but the horses were still restless, and the vixen was standing behind the rails with pricked ears.

A voice wafted across the water.

At first it sounded like a bird singing, but then it resembled more and more a woman's voice. It came from a rock that protruded from the water to their left, its surface as grey as the twilight. Something slid into the water, fish-tailed, with a woman's breasts. A second nymph followed. And then they were everywhere.

Valiant uttered a curse. "What did I tell you?" he hissed at Jacob. "Faster!" he shouted at the ferryman. "Come on!"

But the man seemed to hear neither the Dwarf nor the voices that drifted ever more enticingly across the water. It was only when Jacob put a hand on his shoulder that he spun around.

"He can't hear!" Valiant screamed, hastily stuffing the wax into his ears. "That cunning dog is as deaf as a dead fish!"

The ferryman just shrugged and clutched his oar more tightly. Jacob wondered how often the ferryman had come back without his passengers while he pushed the grimy earplugs into his ears.

The horses shied. Jacob and Clara could barely control them. The last daylight was fading, and the shore inched toward

194

them so painfully slowly, as if the water was dragging them back again. Clara stepped close to Jacob's side, and Fox posted herself protectively in front of them, determined to guard him from what was stirring in the approaching night. The voices grew so loud that Jacob could hear them through the earplugs. They were luring him toward the water. Clara pulled him back from the rails, but the singing seeped through his skin like sweet venom. Heads emerged from the waves, hair drifting on the water like reeds, and when Clara let go of him for one second to press her hands over her own aching ears, Jacob felt his fingers reaching for the protective wax and throwing it overboard.

The singing cut through his brain like honey-coated knives. Clara tried once again to hold him back as he staggered toward the edge of the ferry, but Jacob shoved her away so hard that she stumbled against the ferryman.

Where were they? He leaned over the water. At first he saw only his own reflection, but then it melted into a face. It looked like a woman's, but it was nose-less, with huge silvery eyes, and fangs pushing over the pale green lips. Arms reached out of the river and fingers closed around Jacob's wrist. Another hand grabbed his hair. Water lapped into the ferry. There were so many of them reaching out for him, their scaly bodies pushed halfway out of the water, their teeth bared. Lorelei. Much worse than the song his grandfather had hummed so often. Reality was most times much worse.

The vixen dug her teeth into the scaly arms that had grabbed Jacob, but another Lorelei was already pulling him over the rails. He lost his footing, although he fought them with all his strength, but just when he felt himself sliding into the water he heard a shot, and the nymph sank back into the river, a gaping hole in her

195

forehead. Clara was kneeling behind him, holding the pistol he had given her in her trembling hands. Fox shot another two who tried to pull Valiant into the river. The ferryman forgot to hold on to his oar when she shapeshifted, and Fox had to shoot another three Lorelei to prevent them from pulling him over the rails. They tried to grab her too — obviously they showed no mercy for women who shot at them — but the fighting had brought Jacob back to his senses, and he killed the two who tried to pull Fox into the water. As the dead bodies drifted away from the ferry, the other Lorelei backed off and set about devouring their dead sisters.

The sight made Clara drop the pistol and throw up over the rails while Fox and Valiant caught the panicked horses, and Jacob helped the ferryman steer the wildly pitching boat toward the landing pier. The Lorelei screamed after them, but now their voices merely sounded like a swarm of shrieking gulls.

They were still howling as Jacob led the horses ashore. When the ferryman stepped in his way and held out his hand, Valiant nearly shoved him into the river.

"Oh, so you did hear the bit about the second coin?" he hissed at him. "Do you often earn your living by delivering dinner to the Lorelei?"

"I earned it!" the ferryman retorted. "You're on the other shore, aren't you? The Dark Fairy put them in the river. Everyone says so. Am I supposed to let her ruin my business?"

"Your business!" Valiant's face was still unusually pale. "I suggest you give back the other coin too, you lying sack of horse manure!"

"No, let him keep it. Maybe there is more he didn't tell us about." Jacob pulled the second gold coin from his pocket. "Any other man-eaters we should be on the lookout for?"

The ferryman hastily grabbed the coin and stuffed it into one of his grimy pockets.

"Oh yes. There are those Dragons! They come from the Fortress, as red as the flames they spit, setting the mountains on fire, the trees, the grass. Sometimes it burns for days and my boat is covered in ashes."

"Dragons? Sure." Valiant gave Jacob a knowing look. "Don't you also tell your children that there are Giants on this side of the river?" He lowered his voice, signaling the ferryman to lean down to him. "Shall I tell you where to find real Dragons?"

"Where?" The ferryman frowned with the effort to understand the Dwarf.

"Saw them with my own eyes!" Valiant shouted into his deaf ear. "Sitting on their nest of bones, just two miles upriver from here. But they were green, and one had a leg as scrawny as yours dangling from its ugly mouth. 'By the Devil and all his golden hairs,' I said to myself, 'I wouldn't like to be in Blenheim the day those beasts decide to fly downstream.'"

The ferryman's eyes grew bigger than Jacob's gold coins. "Two miles?"

He cast a worried glance up the river.

"Maybe even a little less." Valiant shouted, dropping the grimy earplugs into his hands. "Good luck on your way home!"

The ferryman kept staring down the river while he walked back to his boat, as if he were searching the night sky for the silhouettes of two Dragons.

"Not a bad story!" Jacob complimented Valiant when he swung himself onto his donkey. "But what would you say if I told you that I met a man in Parsia who claimed he saw a living Dragon just a few years ago, in a valley in Zhonghua?"

197

"I'd say that either you are a liar," Valiant replied, "Or that he was."

❊ ❊ ❊

Behind them the Lorelei were still screaming, and Clara looked once again at the river before she mounted her horse. Fox turned into the vixen again and raised her muzzle into the wind.

"What do you smell?" Jacob asked.

"Goyl," she replied. "Nothing but Goyl. As if both soil and air were made of them."

33
So Tired

Will wanted to sleep. Just sleep and forget the blood, all that blood on Jacob's chest. His dead brother. That was the only image that found its way into his dreams. And the sound of a woman's voice. She sounded like water—dark, deep water.

Will had to sleep. Sleep. And forget all the blood pouring out of his brother's chest.

"Why don't you wake up? Are you afraid of me?"

A hand caressed his face. Six fingers, soft and cool.

"I don't think so. That's your red sister's doing."

The voice of the murderer.

Will longed to kill him. He wanted to beat him to death with his bare hands...just to see him lying there, as motionless as Jacob. But sleep held him prisoner, paralyzing his limbs and his mind.

"My sister? When did he meet my sister? Why didn't you stop him?"

199

"We tried, but they had a Dwarf with them, who got them past the Unicorns. You didn't tell me how to manage that. I lost most of my men in that accursed valley!"

His brother's murderer. And he couldn't move. Will felt as if he was drifting in black water, sinking deeper with every breath he took.

"You are more powerful than all your sisters. Just reverse whatever she did to him."

"This is a thorn spell. Nobody can reverse it. He had a girl with him. I saw her. Where is she?"

"I had no orders to bring her here."

Thorn spell. Black water...the voices slowly receded, or was he just sinking deeper?

"Bring me the girl! Your King's life depends on it."

Will once again felt the six fingers on his face. They caressed his cheeks, the lids of his eyes, so firmly closed, his forehead...

"The Jade Goyl. Born from the flesh of his enemies." Even her voice caressed his skin. "My dreams never lie."

34

LARKS' WATER

For a while, Valiant led them quite purposefully through the
night. However, as the slopes around them became more rugged
and the road they'd followed from the river ended in gravel and a
thicket of thorny bushes, the Dwarf brought his donkey to a halt
and eyed his surroundings with a clearly baffled look on his face.

"What?" Jacob rode to his side. "Don't tell me you're already
lost. Or did you just remember that you saw that secret entrance
only in your dreams?"

It had sounded too good to be true from the beginning: an
entrance to their Royal Fortress that the Goyl didn't know of...
Jacob cursed himself for trusting the Dwarf once again, after he
had twice almost cost him his life. *Almost, Jacob? Last time you did die.*

"Nonsense, I used that entrance many times!" the Dwarf
snapped. "But never at night. How am I supposed to find a hidden

entrance when it's darker than up a Giant's backside? We're very close, I am sure!"

He climbed off his donkey and looked around with a fiercely determined frown creasing his forehead until Jacob dismounted and handed him the flashlight. The Dwarf let the beam of the light swipe over trees and shrubs with an incredulous smile.

"What's this? Some kind of Fairy magic?"

"Something like that," replied Jacob.

"That's fantastic! Where can I get such a thing?" Valiant pointed the flashlight down the shrubby slope. "I'd bet my hat it's down there somewhere."

"I'll get you a thing like that," Jacob said, "If you find that entrance."

Fox didn't take her eyes off the Dwarf when he stomped off down the hill.

You let him go all by himself?" she asked. "Don't you think there's a good chance he'll come back with a Goyl patrol?"

She followed Valiant into the night before Jacob could admit that she was, of course, right. His only excuse was that he still felt as if part of him had never left the Fairies' valley or the moss-covered bed on the island. Maybe that was Miranda's prize for giving him back his life...that she had kept half his soul...*Nonsense*, he told himself. He had barely slept for days, the Goyl had his brother, and he wanted his old life back. To go treasure hunting with Fox, without a thought about yesterday or tomorrow, or Fairies and Goyl...

Clara tied her horse and Valiant's donkey to a nearby tree — but not without making sure that there was no Bird-tree nearby. She had learned her lesson. Although Jacob was sure that she still didn't like this world. How could she? The golden threads in her skirt caught the moonlight. Jacob plucked a few leaves from an oak tree and handed them to her.

"Here. Rub these between your hands and then brush them over the embroidery."

The threads faded under her fingers as if she'd wiped the gold off the fabric.

"Elven thread," Jacob said. "Very beautiful, but at night worse than a swarm of will-o'-the-wisps landing on your dress."

Clara brushed her hand over her conspicuously fair hair as if she hoped to dull its shine, too. "I guess you plan to have the Dwarf take only you into the fortress?"

"Of course. It will be difficult enough for just the two of us to stay unnoticed." And yes, Valiant would probably desert him at the first glimpse of danger, but he would once again have to risk trusting him.

"No, wait." Clara grabbed his arm when he turned to check on the horses. "We only came so far because we could help each other. If you'd been alone on the river, you'd be dead by now! Stop thinking you have to do things without anybody's help. You only make an exception for Fox because she doesn't allow you to send her away. Let us come with you. Please."

"No." Jacob shook his head. "The only humans allowed in the Fortress are male and prisoners of war! The Dwarf won't arouse any suspicion because they trade with the Goyl, but a human woman and a vixen are clearly intruders, and I don't want you both to end up cast in amber."

How she looked at him. He was such a fool. Why did he tell her all that? To make her realize how suicidal a mission this was? Yes, Jacob saw in her eyes that his words had finally made her lose any illusion about how this would probably end. Maybe he kept on talking for that reason. Because she looked so desperate. And because he was a fool.

"You have to stay here for another reason." *Jacob!* But he couldn't lie to her anymore.

"What reason?"

"If I really find Will, he'll need you much more than me." *Fool.*

"Why?"

"You'll have to wake him."

"Wake him?"

It took her a few moments to understand.

She looked at her finger as if the thorn had pierced her skin. "The rose," she murmured.

'And the prince bent over her and woke her with a kiss...'

Above them, the crescents of the two moons looked like they had been starved by the night.

"What makes you think my kiss can wake him?" She tried so hard to hide the pain in her voice. "It is about true love, isn't it? But your brother doesn't love me anymore!"

Jacob took off the coat that made him look like a rich merchant. The only humans in the fortress were slaves, who definitely didn't wear fur-lined collars, and that's what he would have to pretend he was: a slave, caught by the Goyl troops, dragged underground.

"But you still love him," he said. "Don't you? We can only hope that's enough."

Clara was just standing there. She was probably back in the silent courtyard, with all the dead bodies sleeping under the wilted leaves. *Distract her, Jacob.*

204

"How long did it take Will to ask you out?" he asked, slipping back into his old coat.

"Two weeks." For a moment the memory did wipe the despair off her face. "I thought he would never ask. Although we ran into each other each time he visited your mother."

"Two weeks? That was quick for Will!" Something rustled in the bushes. Jacob reached for his pistol, but it was just a badger making its way through the bushes. "Where did he take you?"

"To the hospital cafeteria. Not the most romantic of places." Clara smiled, far away, in another world. "He told me about this stray dog he'd found. He brought it to our next date."

For a moment Jacob caught himself envying his brother. He was not sure anyone had ever smiled like that thinking of him.

"We should water the horses," he said. "You want to come?"

They soon found a small pond. The horses greedily lapped at the clear water, and Valiant's donkey waded in to its knees. When Clara knelt down to drink, however, Jacob pulled her back.

"In this world, you should never walk into a pond like that. Do you see the cart?" The wheels had sunk into the muddy bank, and a heron had built its nest on it. "It probably belonged to a farm girl. Watermen love to catch themselves human brides."

Jacob thought he could hear the Waterman sigh when Clara hastily backed away from the pond. They were dangerous creatures but, in contrast to the Lorelei, they didn't eat their victims. Watermen dragged the girls they caught into their caves, where they fed them and brought them presents. Shells, pearls, jewelry from people who had drowned...Jacob had worked for the desperate parents of such abductees for a while. He'd brought three girls back to the surface—poor deranged creatures who'd never quite returned from the dark caves where, surrounded by fish bones and pearls, they'd had to endure the kisses of an infatuated Waterman. In one case, the parents had refused to pay him because they no longer recognized their daughter.

Jacob left the horses to drink and went to search for the brook that fed the pond. He soon found it, a thin trickle that emerged from a crack in the nearby rocks. Jacob fished the wilted leaves off the surface, and Clara filled her cupped hand with the icy water. It tasted earthy and fresh. Jacob only noticed the birds after he had drunken from it as well: two dead larks, pressed against each other among the wet pebbles.

He spat out the water and hastily pulled Clara to her feet.

"What's the matter?" she asked, alarmed.

She was more beautiful than the Fairies. More beautiful than any woman he had ever seen. *Don't, Jacob.* But it was too late. Clara didn't flinch as he pulled her close. He caressed her hair and felt her heart beating as fast as his own. She kissed his mouth, his eyes, and whispered his name. A lark's tiny heart burst from the madness, hence the name: Larks' Water. Innocent, cool, and clear, but just one sip and you were lost. *Let her go, Jacob.* But he kept on kissing her, unbuttoning her dress while she pushed her hands under his shirt.

"Jacob!"

Woman or vixen. For one moment, Jacob thought he saw Fox in both shapes at the same time. But it was the vixen who bit him so hard that he let go of Clara. They both stumbled back, each one's shame mirrored on the face of the other. Clara brushed her sleeve over her lips as though she could wipe away his kisses.

"Will you look at that!" Valiant pointed the flashlight at them and gave Jacob a lecherous smile. "Does this mean we can forget about saving your brother?"

206

Jacob didn't answer. He only had eyes for Fox. She looked at him as if he'd kicked her. She wore her human skin, but she shifted shape as soon as he made a step in her direction. And she was all fox when she approached the brook and eyed the dead larks.

"Since when are you dumb enough to drink Larks' Water?" She bared her teeth.

"Dammit, Fox, it was dark!" His heart was still beating wildly.

"Larks' Water?" Clara's hands were shaking as she straightened her dress. She did not look at Jacob.

"Yes. Awful." Valiant gave her a theatrical smile of sympathy. "Once you've drunk from it, you go for the next living thing you see. One sip of Larks' Water and even the oldest hag looks like a Fairy. At least that's what I hear. It doesn't really work on Dwarfs. Bad luck it was he, not I, you shared the drink with."

"How long does it last?" Clara's voice was barely audible.

"Some say it wears off after one attack. But there are those who believe it lasts for months." Valiant gave them both a salacious smile.

"You seem to know a lot about Larks' Water," Jacob snapped. "I'm sure you bottle the stuff and sell it."

Valiant shrugged regretfully. "It doesn't keep. And the effect is too unpredictable. Shame. Can you imagine what a fantastic business that would be?"

Jacob felt Clara's eyes on him, but she turned her head away when he looked at her. He still felt her skin under his fingers. *But there are those who believe it lasts for months.* No. He only felt shame. And anger at himself for being so careless. He could just hope Will would never hear about it. It was already bad enough that he had tricked him with the rose. Magic. There were times

207

when he wished it would disappear from this world as well. *No, you don't, Jacob.*

"Did you find the entrance?" he asked.

"Yes." The vixen eyed him as if he was a stranger. "It reeks of death, if you want to know."

"Nonsense." Valiant waved his hand dismissively. "It's a natural tunnel that leads to one of their underground roads. Completely safe."

"Sure…" Jacob could feel the scars on his back. "Remind me how you know about it?"

Valiant rolled his eyes, despairing of such distrust. "Every Dwarf who trades in precious stones knows about it, but it's a well-guarded secret. Not even the Goyl we trade with know how we get the stones out of the fortress. We have to do it secretly because Kami'en has banned the export of quite a few popular stones. The Goyl traders are as upset about it as we are."

"I'm telling you, the tunnel smells of death." Fox repeated.

"You're welcome to try the main entrance!" Valiant sneered. "Maybe Jacob Reckless will be the first human to stroll into the Goyl's Royal Fortress without ending up in amber."

Jacob avoided looking at Clara when he walked over to his horse. Larks' Water. Fox was right. Every fool in this world would have been more careful. But it wasn't his world. He had come back from death and he was losing hope that he still had a chance to find his brother. Certainly not the right time to steal into the Goyl's main fortress, but he had to find Will. He had found him before. Once, Will had disappeared when Jacob left him outside a tobacco shop. He had run for hours through the streets, breathless with fear and guilt until he had found Will crouching on a doorstep, shaking with fear, his eyes red with tears. He had carried him all the way back to the apartment, just to not lose him again.

He reloaded his pistol and fetched a few things from his saddlebags: the snuffbox, the small green bottle he had refilled just a few months ago, and Chanute's knife. Then he filled his pockets with ammunition and went in search of Fox. It took a while until he spotted her under the trees. The wilted leaves covering the ground around her almost made her invisible.

"Keep a lookout for Goyl patrols," he said. "Valiant says they make their rounds every three hours. If I'm not back by tomorrow evening, don't wait for me."

She didn't look at him.

"It's madness to go into that fortress," she said, brushing a spider off her fur. "And you're a fool to once again trust the Dwarf. You can't think straight when it comes to your brother. Or maybe it's just your stupid pride."

She walked away as silently as if the vixen's body weighed less than the wilted leaves she stepped on. And Jacob wished she had once again bitten him before they parted. The vixen's bites always communicated love. *Why was she so angry with him? Because he had been careless enough to drink Larks' Water?* No. Because he once again left her behind after they had been to so many dangerous places together? Or was she just tired of chasing after his brother and watching over Clara?

Jacob was just going to follow her when Valiant stepped in his way.

"What are we waiting for? I thought you were in a hurry."

Yes, they were.

Clara was still standing by the brook. She turned away as Jacob walked towards her.

209

"Look at me."

She obeyed. But she blushed when their eyes met, and Jacob felt his own blood rush to his face. Anger, shame…he had to forget about it, or he would be dead a few steps into that tunnel.

"It meant nothing, Clara," he said. "Nothing, do you hear me? You love Will. If you forget that, we can't help him. Nobody can. Neither in this nor in the other world. You understand?"

She nodded, but her eyes were dark with shame. What could he say to make her trust herself again? And him. *Try the truth, Jacob.*

"You wanted to know what I'm planning to do."

How to say it without making it sound as hopeless as it was?

"I need to find the Dark Fairy. There is a way to force her to give Will his skin back. Her sister told me how. But I need to get close to her."

He put his finger warningly on Clara's lips when he saw her eyes widen with fear. "Please! Fox can't know about this. She'll just try to follow me! But I swear to you, I will find the Fairy, and Will. Your kiss will wake him, and all will end well."

All will end well, and they'll live happily ever after…

Jacob looked once again for Fox before he followed the Dwarf into the night. But he couldn't find her.

35

Into the Womb of the Earth

Fox hadn't exaggerated: the tunnel the Dwarfs used for their illegal trades with the Goyl did indeed smell of death. Death, decay, despair. The cave one had to enter to get to the tunnel had been an Ogre's cave.

There were many Ogre species behind the mirror and, contrary to popular belief, they did not only hunt humans, but Dwarfs and Goyl as well. The cave's ground was covered with bones, as all Ogres loved to surround themselves with their leftovers. Some even built music instruments or sculptures from their victims' remains; others recited poetry while they cooked them. This Ogre, though, seemed to just leave things where they fell during hunt and meal. Jacob spotted a pocket watch while his boots stepped on finger and leg bones; the torn sleeve of a woman's dress; a child's shoe, heart-wrenchingly small; and a notebook, the writing rendered illegible by dried blood. He had been to Ogre caves before, and he still felt a terror in them that no enchanted castle or Waterman's den could arouse. His first instinct was to turn back to warn Clara and Fox—until he remembered that the vixen had seen the cave.

"Did you ever meet this Ogre?" he asked Valiant while they made their way through the bones.

"No, the Goyl killed him and his wife years ago." Valiant kicked a withered belt out of the way. "Luckily they didn't find the tunnel when they raided the cave."

The crack through which he disappeared was wide enough for a Dwarf, but Jacob could barely squeeze through it. The tunnel behind it was so low that he had to get down on his knees at times (a sight Valiant enjoyed immensely), with a descent so treacherously steep that Jacob was grateful for every step and corner. He soon found it hard to breathe, and was very relieved when the tunnel finally opened onto one of the roads the Goyl built underground to connect their fortresses and above ground conquests. The road was wide enough to allow coaches and carts to pass each other, and paved with fluorescent stones, which glowed when Valiant shone the flashlight on them. Jacob thought he could hear machines in the distance and a constant hum, like the sound of wasps swarming above windfalls.

"What is that noise?" he asked the Dwarf in a lowered voice.

"Insects. They clean the Goyl's sewage. Their cities smell much better than ours. Bend down!" Valiant pulled a pen from his pocket. "It's time for your slave mark. P for Prussan—remember that name!" He pressed the pen so firmly onto Jacob's skin, as if he intended to carve the Goyl letter into his forehead. "Prussan's a merchant I do business with, and now he is your owner. Come to think of it, his slaves are much cleaner than you, though, and

212

they definitely don't wear weapons belts, so you'd better give that to me."

"No, thanks," Jacob whispered, straightening up and buttoning his coat over the belt. "I don't want to rely on your help, if the Goyl stop us."

Valiant responded to such mistrust with a shrug and simply waved him along.

The road they followed soon led them into a tunnel as wide as the grand boulevards of Vena, Lutis, or Londra. This underground avenue, however, was not lined with trees. When Valiant pointed the flashlight at the walls of solid rock rising at least twenty feet high on both sides to support a vaulted crystal ceiling, Jacob saw faces emerging from the darkness. He had always believed it to be a myth that the Goyl honored their heroes by lining the roads of their fortresses with their heads. But, as happened so often in this world, the stories told the truth. The heads of thousands of fallen Goyl warriors were staring down at them, set side by side like flagstones, their stone-skinned faces unchanged by death. Only the eyes had been replaced with golden topaz.

Valiant didn't stay on the Avenues of the Dead for long. He mostly led Jacob through tunnels as narrow as mountain roads, all of them leading deeper and deeper underground. More and more often, Jacob saw dim lights at the end of some passage or felt the activity of machinery like a subtle vibration on his skin. A few times, they heard the sound of hooves or wheels approaching, but every tunnel was flanked by countless caves where one could hide in thickets of stalagmites or behind curtains of dripstone.

The sound of dripping water was everywhere, constant and inescapable, and the flashlight revealed the miracles it had formed over thousands of years: chalk-white cascades of petrified

213

froth, forests of sandstone needles hanging above them from the ceilings, and crystal flowers blossoming in the dark. For the Goyl, all this was visible without illuminating their world. Their eyes were meant for the darkness, and Jacob wondered whether Will had seen all this, or whether he had already been sleeping when Hentzau had taken him to the Fairy, wrapped in Miranda's spell.

※ ※ ※

In many caves, the Goyl had barely left a trace, except for a straight path leading through the thickets of stone, or a few perfectly square tunnel openings. Other caves were lined with stone façades and mosaics that seemed to originate from earlier times, ruins among the columns the water had grown from the rock. The Goyl claimed to have settled underground far longer than humans had built their settlements on the surface.

It felt as if they had been wandering for days through the labyrinth of tunnels when one led them into a vast cave that rose like a cathedral's nave around a lake, its dark waters shimmering with the light of thousands of phosphorescent dragonflies swarming above its surface. The cave walls were covered with blackish green plants, and across the water spanned an endless bridge that was barely more than a stone arch reinforced with steel. Their steps echoed treacherously on its worn flagstones, stirring up clouds of bats, and the vast emptiness around them felt so threatening that Jacob caught himself looking over his shoulder more than once. They had crossed the bridge halfway when Valiant came to an abrupt halt and stared at something blocking his path. It was a corpse, not Goyl but human. The dead man wore the sign of his owner tattooed on his forehead, and his throat and chest were covered in gaping wounds.

Valiant cast a hasty glance at the cave ceiling.

"What killed him?" Jacob drew his pistol.

The Dwarf let the beam of the flashlight wander over the stalactites above. "The Guardians," he whispered. "The Goyl breed them as watchdogs to defend the outer tunnels and roads. They only come out when they scent something that isn't Goyl. But I never had any trouble with them on this route before...wait!"

Valiant muttered a curse when the flashlight found a row of worryingly large holes between the stalactites.

A chirping sound cut through the silence, and the Dwarf leapt over the body and ran, as fast as the narrow bridge allowed.

Above them, the cave filled with the flutter of leathery wings. The Goyl's Guardians dove out from the stalactites like birds of prey, their faces pale and almost human, their bat-like wings ending in sharp talons. Their huge eyes were so milky that Jacob suspected they were blind, but clearly their ears guided them quite reliably. He shot two in midflight while he ran after the Dwarf, but three more were already crawling out of the holes. One tried to swipe the pistol from his hand, but he managed to slam his elbow into the pale face and hack off one of its wings with his saber. The creature screamed so loudly that he was sure it would alert dozens more of its brethren, but fortunately not all of the holes seemed to be inhabited.

The Guardians were clumsy attackers, but one of them took Valiant down before he reached the end of the bridge. The bared fangs were already at the Dwarf's throat when Jacob thrust his saber between the wings. The face slackening in death resembled a human embryo. Even the body was childlike and Jacob threw up over the slaughtered body, feeling nauseated, as though he'd never killed before.

215

They escaped into a tunnel they hoped would be too narrow for their attackers with arms and shoulders torn, but fortunately none of the wounds were deep enough to worry. Jacob quickly dripped some iodine onto his bleeding hand while Valiant inspected his own wounds, cursing himself for ever having agreed to this endeavor.

"That gold tree —" he hissed. "—it had better shower me with treasure! Why did I ever allow you back into my life? It always ends like this. I should have known!"

Jacob was tempted to remind him of the damages he had suffered during their last two encounters, but he was too exhausted from the fight. In the cave, two Guardians were still circling the bridge but, as they had hoped, they weren't followed into the tunnel. Both Jacob and Valiant didn't find it easy to get back onto their feet, but they stumbled on, through the maze of dark roads and tunnels that seemed to have no end. Jacob was just beginning to wonder whether the Dwarf was playing another dirty trick on him when the tunnel suddenly took a sharp bend, and everything seemed to dissolve into light.

"And here it is!" Valiant whispered. "The lair of the beasts, or the lions' den, depending on whose side you happen to be on."

The tunnel had ended high up in a cave that was so vast Jacob couldn't see where it ended. It was sparsely lit, as the Goyl preferred it, but Jacob was amazed to see that the lamps seemed to run on electricity instead of gas. The city they illuminated looked as if the rock itself had grown it. Houses, towers, and palaces rose from the bottom of the cave, covering its walls like a wasps' nest, and dozens of bridges arched over the expanse of houses, as if there was nothing simpler than stretching iron through thin air. Their pillars soared like metal trees from between the roofs. Some of the bridges were lined with buildings, like the medieval bridges of Jacob's world and, high above the houses and the web of bridges that looked as if a steel-spinning spider had woven it, three huge funnel-shaped stalactites grew from the cave's ceiling. They were lined with windows, and the largest one gave off a glow as if its walls had been saturated with the moonlight of the world above. At its pointed end was a crown of shimmering thorns pointed at the city below, resembling a circle of crystal spears.

"Is that the King's palace?" whispered Jacob to Valiant. "No wonder the Goyl don't think highly of human architecture. And since when can they build such iron bridges?"

"How would I know?" Valiant replied. "They don't teach Goyl history at Dwarf schools. The palace is more than seven hundred years old, but there are rumors that Kami'en is planning a more modern version, as it's too old-fashioned for his tastes. The stalactite to the left is their armies' headquarters, and the one on the right is a prison." The Dwarf gave Jacob a devious smile. "You want me to find out whether they keep your brother in one of those cells? I'm sure your gold coins will loosen even Goyl tongues."

When Jacob reached into his coat pocket and produced three gold coins, Valiant couldn't help himself. He reached up and pushed his short fingers into the pocket as well.

"How is this possible?!" he muttered. "Nothing! Nothing at all. Is it the coat? No, it also worked with that leather jacket of yours. Do those coins grow from the palms of your hands?"

"Exactly," Jacob gave back, relieved that the Dwarf hadn't closed his fingers around the handkerchief.

"I'll figure it out one of these days!" the Dwarf grumbled while he tucked the coins into his velvet waistcoat. "And now: head bowed, eyes on the ground. Remember! You're a slave."

217

The alleyways leading through the maze of houses that covered the cave walls were almost as impassable for a human as the streets of Terpevas. Some of the alleys were so steep that Jacob had to clutch at doorframes and window ledges to prevent his feet from slipping, while Valiant moved as effortlessly as a Goyl. The humans they encountered were as pale as the corpse they had found on the bridge, wearing the initials of their owners branded or etched into their foreheads. Most of them probably hadn't seen the sun for years, and they rarely lifted their heads when Jacob passed them in the dimly lit labyrinth of houses. Nobody paid attention to them, neither human nor Goyl. A Dwarf with a human slave by his side seemed to be a common sight, and Valiant relished loading Jacob with all the things he purchased from the various shops he entered to make inquiries about Will's whereabouts.

"Bingo!" he finally whispered, after Jacob had been waiting for more than half an hour in front of a jeweler's workshop. "Good news and bad news. The good news is, I found out where your brother is. The King's most trusted man — I guess that's our milk-eyed jasper friend — brought a prisoner to the fortress, someone the Dark Fairy apparently sent him to find. There is a rumor that his skin resembles the Goyl's most sacred stone."

"And what's the bad news?"

"They didn't bring your brother to the prison stalactite. He's in the palace. In the Dark Fairy's quarters, to make the news even worse And he's fallen into a deep sleep from which not even she has managed to wake him. I assume you know what that's about?"

"Yes." Jacob looked up at the huge stalactite.

"Forget it!" Valiant hissed. "Your brother might as well have dissolved into thin air. The Fairy's chambers are in one of those crystal thorns. You'd have to fight your way through the entire palace. Not even you can be crazy enough to try that."

Jacob eyed the shimmering façade.

"Can you get an appointment with the officer you do business with?"

"And then what?" Valiant shook his head and sneered. "The slaves in the palace all have the king's mark burnt into their foreheads. Even if your brotherly love extends to doing that to yourself, none of them is allowed to leave the upper parts of the palace."

"What about the bridges?"

"What about them?"

Two of them were directly linked to the palace. One was a railway bridge that vanished into a tunnel in the upper part of the cave. The second was one of the bridges lined with houses. It connected to the stalactite halfway down. There were no buildings near where it entered the palace, and Jacob got a clear view of an onyx-black gate and a double line of sentries.

"That expression on your face!" Valiant muttered. "I don't like it at all."

Jacob ignored him. The metal trusses that held up the bridge looked from a distance as if they had been added later to support an older stone structure. That might be the way. Jacob hid in a doorway and pointed his spyglass at the stalactite. The trusses clung to the side of the Hanging Palace like iron claws. *In one of those crystal thorns…* there were six of them, but only one had windows made from malachite. Green. The Dark Fairy's favorite color, if one could trust what the newspapers wrote.

"The windows…" he murmured. "None of them are barred."

"Why would they be?" Valiant whispered back. "Only birds and bats can get anywhere near them. But obviously you consider yourself to be one of those."

A group of children pushed past the alley. Jacob had never seen a Goyl child before. For a crazy moment, he thought he recognized Will in one of the boys.

"Hold on!" Valiant hissed. "I think I know what you're planning to do! You've lost your mind. Probably not surprising, as you were dead just a few days ago!"

Jacob pushed the spyglass back into his coat. "If you want my sapling of the gold tree, you'd better get me on that bridge!"

36
THE WRONG NAME

"Fox?" Clara had been calling her for a while.

Fox was surprised that the Waterman hadn't dragged her into his pond by now. She knew nothing about this world. But everything about the world Jacob came from. Maybe that was the reason why she couldn't stop picturing him in Clara's arms. The Red Fairy hadn't made her that jealous. Nor had the Witch into whose hut Jacob had vanished almost every night for a year, nor the Empress's maid whose sickly sweet perfume she had smelled for weeks on his clothes. Yes, maybe she couldn't forgive Clara that one kiss because she came from his world. It would always be her greatest fear that Jacob would return to it one day. To never come back. Fox had tried to hide that fear from him, but he knew her far too well. Not even the vixen's fur could shield her secrets from him, except for one. She was quite good at hiding how much she loved him.

"Fox? Please!"

The vixen didn't move. It almost felt as if she had tasted the enchanted water herself. She had even caught herself cursing the fur, because it made Jacob forget that she also had lips he could kiss and skin he could caress.

"Fox?"

She had found her after all. Clara knelt down on the damp moss and pushed the branches aside. She looked quite desperate. But her hair was like pale gold. *Did he like that better?* Her own hair was red, like the fur of the vixen. She couldn't remember whether it had ever been different.

She shifted shape and rose to her feet. She didn't want Clara to look down on her. Even though she felt stronger wearing the fur.

Clara reached for her arm, but Fox walked past her, evading her touch. And her eyes. It wasn't just jealousy. Clara had discovered her secret, Fox could see it on her face. *You love him,* her eyes said. *You love him, Fox.*

So? she was tempted to reply. *Even if that is true, is it any of your business? You don't even belong in this world.*

"I still don't know your name," Clara said. "Your real name, I mean."

Real...what was real about it? And what gave Clara the idea that she would tell her? Not even Jacob knew her human name. *'Celeste, wash your hands. Celeste, comb your hair.'*

"Do you still feel it?" Fox turned and stared into her blue eyes.

Jacob could look you in the eye and lie. He was very good at it, but not even he could fool the vixen.

Clara lowered her gaze, but Fox could smell what she was feeling, all the fear and shame.

"Have you ever drunk Larks' Water?"

"Of course not. No vixen would ever be so stupid."

It was not her fault, Fox. Stop acting like a child. A child? Love had been so much easier as a child. The innocence—whatever that meant. She had been a child when she had first met Jacob, and he had been still a boy. Well, almost. And had it really been easier? With all the shadows that followed both of them. *Remember, Fox.* Love was never easy.

Clara stared at the brook where the dead larks were still caught between the stones. *Clara.* Her name sounded like glass and cool water, and Fox had liked her so much—until she had kissed Jacob.

Fox turned her back on her. The vixen could hide her feelings so effortlessly under her fur. It wasn't that easy with a human face. Fox was not even sure what that face looked like by now. She didn't like mirrors. They only reminded her of the one through which Jacob disappeared far too often. From time to time she caught a glance at herself in the surface of a lake or in the glass of a windowpane. She never looked at her reflection for long. She despised vanity. Was she beautiful? Probably. Her mother had been beautiful, but her father had beaten her anyway.

Don't call him your father, Fox.

"You prefer being the vixen, don't you?" The night tinted Clara's blue eyes black. "Does the fur make it easier to understand this world?"

She touched her arms as if she could still feel Jacob's hands on them. And was ashamed of it.

"The vixen doesn't try to understand the world." Fox replied, and realized that Clara wished for a fur of her own.

That took away all her anger.

223

37

AT THE DARK FAIRY'S WINDOWS

Butchers, tailors, bakers, jewelers...the bridge leading to the Hanging Palace was a shopping arcade with dizzying views of the city far below. Its windows displayed gems and minerals next to lizard meat and the black-leaved cabbage that grew without sunlight. Bread and fruits from the Goyl's above ground provinces lay next to the dried bugs and spiders that were considered a delicacy. But Jacob only had eyes for the palace whose onyx-black gates could be seen behind the storefronts. Its dimensions were even more impressive there than from below.

Jacob leaned over the balustrade between two shops to get a closer look. The six crystal thorns ended dozens of meters below the bridge. They resembled pointed towers standing on their heads, each containing several floors.

"I guess the Dark Fairy's chambers are behind the malachite windows?"

"Would you believe me if I said 'No'?" Valiant sighed and cast a nervous look at a group of Goyl soldiers strolling past the shops. There were lots of them on the bridge — not to mention the sentries by the palace gate. Jacob looked once again at the Fairy's windows. Green eyes gaped out from the crystal walls. The bridge's metal joists were bolted to the palace about sixty feet above them but, in contrast to the rest of the façade, the crystal surface was so smooth that it offered as much foothold as a mirror's glass.

Nevertheless. He had to try.

Valiant was muttering something about the limitations of the human mind when Jacob pulled the snuffbox from his pocket. It contained one of the most useful magical items he'd ever found: a single, very long golden hair. The Dwarf fell silent as Jacob began to rub the hair between his fingers. It started to sprout fibers, each as fine as the silk of a spider, and soon they formed a rope whose firmness could compete with ropes three times its diameter. It had other, even more wondrous properties. The rope could grow to any length needed, and it attached itself to the exact spot you looked at when you threw it.

"A Rapunzel-hair. Seems you're not as mad as I thought!" Valiant murmured. "But not even that rope will help you with the guards. They'll see you as clearly as they'd see a bug crawling over their faces!"

In reply, Jacob produced the green glass bottle from his pocket. The slime it contained granted invisibility for a few hours. It was produced by carnivorous snails that used it as camouflage to sneak up on any prey they fancied. Stilts and Thumblings bred the snails for the slime, which enabled them to go on their forays similarly undetected. Jacob had last refilled the bottle from the provisions the Stilt in the tower kept. One had to smear the slime under one's nose—quite an unsavory procedure, even though it didn't smell—and the effect was immediate. The only problems were the side effects, including hours of debilitating nausea as well as, after repeated use, temporary paralysis.

"Rapunzel-hair and waneslime." Jacob detected a trace of admiration in Valiant's voice. "I must admit, you're well equipped. All the same, I want to hear where your gold tree is before you climb over there."

Jacob was already smearing the slime under his nose.

"Oh no," he said. "What if you've once again forgotten to tell me about something that will make me end up with a broken neck, or in a cell of that prison stalactite over there? The rope carries only one, so you get to stay up here. In case the guards spot me, I suggest you try your best to distract them, as otherwise all memory of your gold tree will fade with me."

Jacob swung himself over the balustrade before the Dwarf could protest. The slime already made his body disappear and, as he climbed down to the bridge's iron girders, he could no longer see his own hands. Holding onto one of the struts, he threw the rope. The golden cord wound through the air like a snake until it attached itself to a ledge between the malachite windows.

And what will you do if you actually find Will and the Fairy behind those windows, Jacob? Even if he could break the spell, Will would still be asleep. How was he supposed to get him out of the fortress and back to Clara? That question had come to his mind before, but Jacob still didn't know the answer.

Climbing a Rapunzel-rope is easy. The rope adhered to the hands and Jacob tried to ignore the abyss beneath him. *All will end well.* The palace loomed above him, the cities' lights reflecting in its countless windows, and he could already feel the nausea brought on by the waneslime. *A few more yards, Jacob. Don't look down.*

He tightened his grip on the taut rope and climbed until his invisible hands finally reached the crystal. His feet found the ledge, and he took a moment to recover his breath while he leaned against the polished surface. To his left and right, the malachite windows shimmered like the frozen water of a distant ocean. He pulled Chanute's knife from his belt and set the blade against the window to his left. The hole with the moonstone rim was right above him, but he only noticed it when the snake shot out. Moonstone as pale as its scales, as pale as its mistress's skin. He tried to thrust the knife into its body, but it wrapped itself around his neck so relentlessly that his fingers let go of the haft to loosen the terrible noose the snake's body formed. But the snake was too strong, and soon his feet slipped from the ledge, and he hung helplessly above the abyss like a snared bird. Another two snakes slithered out of a hole underneath the windows and wrapped themselves around his chest and legs. Jacob gasped for air, but he couldn't breathe, and the last thing he saw was the golden rope coming away from the ledge with a jolt and disappearing into the darkness above him.

38
Found and Lost

Sandstone walls and iron bars, a lizard-skin boot kicking him
in the ribs, gray uniforms in the red fog that filled his head…the
Dwarf had sold him out once again. When had he done it? *In one
of the stores, while you were waiting in front of the door like an obedient
dog, Jacob?*

He managed to sit up, although they had bound his hands
and feet.

"So her red sister can indeed bring back the dead." The jasper
Goyl stepped out of the dark. "I'll admit I first didn't believe it
when the Dark Fairy told me you were still alive. I am a very good
shot." His Austrish was fluid, but he spoke it with a heavy accent.
"You went for her net like a fly; it was her idea to spread the word
your brother was with her. But, well, how could you know that
her snakes aren't fooled by waneslime? You did much better than

the two onyx Goyl who tried to break into Kami'en's chambers. We had to scrape their remains from the roofs of the city."

Onyx—the Goyl's former ruling class fought Kami'en even more passionately than his human enemies. Jacob usually tried to stay away from this world's political schemes, though that wasn't always easy while working for kings and empresses but, if the Goyl really thought his brother to be the Jade Goyl of their legends, there would be no more staying away.

"Where's my brother?" The snakes had strangled him so fiercely that Jacob barely recognized the hoarse croak as his own voice.

The Goyl ignored the question.

"Where did you leave the girl?" he asked instead.

He surely didn't mean Fox, did he? But why should they be interested in Clara? *What do you think, Jacob? Your brother is sleeping, and they can't wake him.* That was good news. And Valiant obviously did have a weak spot for Clara or he would have told them where she was.

So...just play dumb, Jacob.

"What girl?"

That answer earned him another kick. The soldier who drove her boot into his stomach was a woman. She looked familiar. Of course. He'd shot her out of her saddle in the valley of the Unicorns. No wonder she enjoyed kicking him.

"Leave him, Nesser," the Jasper Goyl said. "It will take hours to get any answers from him that way. Get the scorpions."

Jacob had heard about the scorpions of the Goyl.

Nesser let the first one crawl over her hand almost affectionately before she placed it on his chest. The creature was barely longer than his thumb and seemed to be made from breathing, moving crystal, including its pincers and stinger.

"There's not much they can do to our skin," said the jasper Goyl as the scorpion crawled under Jacob's shirt, "But yours is so much softer. So...once again, where's the girl?"

The scorpion dug its pincers into Jacob's chest. It felt as if it were cutting through his skin with shards of glass. He still managed to suppress a scream, but then the scorpion thrust its sting into his flesh. The venom poured fire under his skin and made him gasp with pain.

"Where's the girl?"

Nesser placed another scorpion on his shoulder.

Where is the girl? The same question, over and over again. But Will would sleep as long as they didn't find Clara, and Jacob wished for his brother's jade skin while he groaned and screamed.

✳ ✳ ✳

He had no memory of what he'd told them when he woke in another cell, its narrow window filled with a view of the Hanging Palace. The window was barred—obviously the Goyl didn't trust the height to hold their prisoners as much as they trusted it to protect their King. Maybe too many of their captives had thrown themselves into the abyss below after they met the scorpions. Jacob managed to get to his knees. His whole body was aflame, as if someone had scalded his skin. His weapons belt was gone and so were all the magical tools he'd had with him. They had only missed the handkerchief, but it wouldn't help him much. Goyl soldiers were infamous for their incorruptibility.

His cell was separated from the neighboring one by nothing but iron bars. Jacob pressed his shoulder against the wall and hauled himself to his feet. The prisoner in the other cell was his brother.

Will didn't move, but he was breathing, and there were still a few slight traces of human skin on his forehead. Miranda had kept her promise. She had stopped time and the completion of her sister's spell.

Jacob backed away from the bars that kept him separated from his brother when he heard footsteps on the corridor leading past the cells. The jasper Goyl was followed by two guards. Hentzau—by now Jacob knew his name. When he saw who the Goyl dragged with them, he wanted to smash his head against the bars.

He had told them what they wanted to know.

Clara had a bloody gash on her forehead and her eyes were wide with fear. *Where's Fox?* Jacob wanted to ask her, but Clara didn't even notice him. All she saw was Will.

Hentzau pushed her into his brother's cell. Clara took a step toward the bed Will was lying on and stopped, as if remembering that only a few hours earlier she'd kissed the other brother.

"Clara."

She turned, her face a torrent of emotions—horror, anxiety, despair—and still shame. She was shaking when she approached the bars.

"We tried to escape," she whispered, "But they were too many."

You told them, Jacob. How could he ever forgive himself for that?

"Where is Fox?" That was all he wanted to know. Had they killed her? Did she escape? The vixen was fast. But Clara took that hope from him.

"They caught her, too. But I don't know where they took her."

The Goyl who had brought her stood to attention. Even Hentzau straightened his shoulders, though his reluctance clearly showed. It wasn't hard to guess who the woman was coming down the corridor.

The Dark Fairy was indeed even more beautiful than her red sister. Her hair was, despite the name she was called by, much lighter than Miranda's. It resembled dark amber and polished copper, and the luster of her skin put the Empress's most precious pearl necklaces to shame.

Clara shrank away as the Fairy stepped into Will's cell, but Jacob clasped his fingers around the metal bars. *'You need to touch her and, while you do, say her name!'* Her red sister had made him repeat it twice. *'But you have to be fast, or she will kill you before you even stretch out your hand.'*

Touch her. *How?* Jacob wished for one of those magical nuts that shrank a human to the size of a Thumbling. The bars put the Dark Fairy as far out of his reach as if she were lying in Kami'en's bed.

She eyed Clara with the same disdain all her kind had for human women. *Because they can't give birth,* people said. Maybe.

The Dark Fairy stepped to Will's side and caressed his sleeping face.

"You love him?"

Clara took another step back, but her own shadow came alive and pulled her to the Fairy's side.

"Answer her, Clara! " Jacob said.

"Yes," she murmured. "Yes. I love him."

The shadow let go of her and was once again nothing but a shadow, while the Dark Fairy smiled.

"Good. Then you surely want him to wake up, don't you? Kiss him! He is waiting for that kiss, don't you see?"

233

Clara cast a pleading glance at Jacob. *No!* he wanted to say. *Don't do it, Clara.* But his lips were as numb as if someone had sealed them. He could not even shake his head. Magic. The stale air seemed to smell of it. Of evergreen leaves, of water and wet soil.

The Dark Fairy took Clara's arm and gently pulled her to Will's side.

"Look at him!" she said. "If you don't wake him, he'll just sleep like that forever, until all the love in his heart has turned to dust."

Clara tried to turn away, but the Fairy grabbed her arm once again.

"Is that love?" Jacob heard her whisper. "To sentence him to death, just because his skin is no longer as soft as yours? Look at him! My magic only made him strong. And so beautiful."

Clara looked down at Will.

"Touch him," the Fairy said. "Don't you see he longs for it?"

Clara hesitated, but then she lifted her hand and caressed Will's jade face.

The Dark Fairy stepped back with a smile.

"Make him feel that love when you kiss him!" she said. "You will see. It doesn't die as easily as you think."

Clara wiped a tear from her eyes. Then she bent over Will and kissed him.

39

AWOKEN

For a moment, Jacob had the faint hope that Clara's kiss would not only wake Will, but also remind him of the boy he had been before he had stepped through the mirror, of the love he had felt for Clara…

Who knew? Maybe it would have been that way if Clara had been the first thing Will saw when he opened his eyes. But the Fairy made sure it was her. She caught him with a smile, like a fly entangled in her amber hair, and Jacob watched the jade erase the last traces of human skin while Will rose from the bed, his golden eyes on the Fairy as if only she made him live and breathe.

Clara called his name, but what could a human voice do against the magic of a Fairy? Will could hear neither Clara's nor Jacob's voice. He only noticed what the Dark Fairy allowed him to see or hear, and all he felt was the skin she had given him. This wonderful skin of jade that made him so strong and so happy.

Jacob kept his eyes on Will as he followed the Fairy out into the corridor. He knew far too well what his brother felt. Hadn't he fallen under the same spell once? There was only her, nothing else. The pain Jacob felt was also far too familiar. It cut as deep as the pain he had felt the day their father had disappeared. The same void opened in his heart, so wide and dark and empty that no word could describe the feeling. It was so much more than pain. It was a black ocean swallowing everything—who he was, what he cared and lived for—Will followed the Dark Fairy, and Jacob felt as lost as he had felt at the age of twelve, lost and helplessly angry, at himself and at the world...and at his brother for bringing back that pain.

Where was Fox? That was all he still cared about. The vixen... he needed her by his side. She was the only one who could fill the abyss. The only one who never forgot who he was, even when he himself couldn't remember. But she was gone, like his brother.

Clara turned around and looked at Jacob. *What have I done?* her eyes asked him. *And why didn't you stop me?* But maybe he was just reading his own thoughts in her glance.

"What about this one? Shall we shoot him?" one of Hentzau's guards asked, pointing his rifle at Jacob.

"No, not yet."

The pistol Hentzau drew from his belt was Jacob's. The Goyl opened the chamber and scrutinized it like the core of a foreign fruit.

"This is an interesting weapon," he said. "Where did you get it?"

Jacob turned his back on him. *Just shoot me*, he thought. The cell, the Goyl, the Hanging Palace. Everything around him seemed so unreal. The Fairies, and the enchanted forests, even the vixen—all nothing but the feverish dreams of a twelve-year-old.

236

Jacob saw himself standing in the doorway of his father's study, Will inquisitively staring past him at the dusty model planes, the antique revolvers. And the mirror.

"Turn around." Hentzau's voice was impatient. Their rage was so easily stirred, constantly burning just beneath their stone skin. Will had been one of them for quite a while. One day Clara would realize that it hadn't been her who had made his brother a Goyl.

Jacob still didn't move.

He heard the Goyl laugh behind him.

"The same arrogance, but your father's can be shaken so much easier, and he isn't half as good at hiding his fear. Your brother doesn't look like him at all; that's why I didn't realize right away whose sons you are, although your face seemed so familiar."

Oh, he was such an idiot. 'The Goyl have better engineers.' How often had Jacob heard that sentence behind the mirror—be it in Schwanstein or from the lips of a despairing imperial officer—but never thought twice about it?

He turned around.

"Where did you meet him? Is he here?"

Hentzau twisted his narrow lips into a mocking smile. "Here? No. Not anymore. I'd hoped you'd tell me where he is. John Reckless…we caught him five years ago in Blenheim. As far as I remember, he'd been hired to build a bridge because the townspeople had grown tired of being eaten by the Lorelei. The river has always been teeming with them, although the Doughskins in Blenheim claim that the Dark Fairy put them in there. Funny. Your father always carried a photo of his sons, but I never looked at it. Kami'en had him build a camera, when he saw it, long before the Empress's engineers came up with a similar device. John

Reckless taught us many things. But who would've thought that a son of his would one day grow a skin of jade!"

The Goyl ran his fingers along the pistol's barrel. "As I said. He wasn't half as stubborn as you when it came to answering our questions. What he taught us turned out to be very useful in the war. And then he escaped. We searched for him for months. We still do, but no trace of him. What does it matter? Now we caught his sons."

He turned to the guards. "Keep him alive until I get back from the wedding. There are still a lot of questions I want to ask him."

"And the girl?" The guard who was pointing at Clara had carnelian skin like his King.

"Keep her alive as well," Hentzau replied. "And the fox girl, too. They will loosen his tongue much faster than the scorpions."

The fox girl, too...Jacob felt nauseous with relief. She was alive.

Hentzau's steps died away on the corridor, and through the barred windows came the sounds of the underground city.

Fox was alive.

And his brother was gone.

40

THE STRENGTH OF DWARFS

Jacob heard Clara sobbing in the darkness, but his tears wouldn't come. The Larks' Water madness, the Fairy island, the bullet that had shattered his heart...none of it mattered anymore. His brother had a skin of jade.

Jacob wondered whether the Fairy lake had shown Miranda how miserably he had failed his brother. And that her dark sister had won.

Clara leaned her head against the wall. And started crying once again. Jacob wished he could have comforted her, but the Larks' Water had made even an embrace suspicious. Would they ever manage to just be friends again? Even that seemed so unimportant now. They hadn't been able to save Will.

Jacob stared at the barred window and the Hanging Palace behind it. *Was Will in there, with the Dark Fairy?*

From outside the window came a dull scraping sound, as if something was climbing up the wall. Jacob raised himself to his feet. A hairy face appeared outside the bars. It took Jacob a moment to realize whose face it was. Valiant's beard was sprouting almost as luxuriantly as in the old days, when he'd still worn it with pride.

"You're lucky the Goyl haven't had many Dwarf prisoners yet!" he whispered while his short fingers bent the iron apart as effortlessly as if he were bending pipe cleaners. "The Empress has silver added to all bars in her cells."

He squeezed through the warped iron and dropped down from the window as nimbly as a weasel.

"What are you looking at?" He grinned at Jacob. "It was too funny when the snakes grabbed you. Absolutely priceless."

"I'm sure the Goyl paid you well for that show." Jacob glanced down the corridor, but there were no guards in sight. "Where did you sell me out? While I spent hours waiting in front of the jeweler's shop? Or was it at the tailor you had to see for the tear in your vest?"

Valiant just shook his head while he opened Clara's handcuffs as easily as he'd bent the window bars. "Will you listen to that!" he whispered to her. "He has such a tough time trusting anybody. I told him it was an imbecilic idea to climb over to the Fairy's window like a roach. But did he listen to me? No."

Valiant bent the bars between the two cells until he could step through. "I suppose it was also my fault that they found the girls?" he said, looking up at Jacob. "May I remind you that it wasn't my idea to leave them in the wilderness? And it was definitely not Evenaugh Valiant who told the Goyl where to find them." He

240

winked at Jacob. "They put the scorpions on you, didn't they? Oh, I wish I had seen that."

Somebody shouted insults at the Goyl in one of the other cells. A guard yelled back, but no one came their way.

"I saw your brother," Valiant whispered as he forced open Jacob's handcuffs. "If you can still call him that. Every inch of his skin is now Goyl, and he follows the Dark Fairy like a dog. She took him with her to the wedding of her beloved. Half the garrison went. That's why I could risk coming here."

Clara stared at the stone bench where Will had lain. Valiant grabbed her hand and pulled her toward the window.

"Up with you, Snow White!" he whispered while he helped her up to the window as effortlessly as if she didn't weigh any more than a child. "There a rope out there that does almost all the climbing for you, and luckily this building isn't guarded by snakes."

"What about Fox?" Jacob hissed. "We can't leave without her! Do you know where she is?"

Valiant pointed to the ceiling. "Right above us. And yes, I know you wouldn't leave without her. But one step after the other."

In contrast to the palace, the prison stalactite's façade was as fissured as dripstone and offered plenty of footholds, but Clara's hands trembled when she pushed herself through the window. She held on tight to the balustrade while her feet sought purchase between the stones. Valiant, however, clung to the wall like an insect.

"Just don't look down!" he whispered to Clara while he grabbed her arm. "It's easier than you think."

Clara cast a doubtful glance at the rope. The Dwarf hadn't climbed down from the main bridge like Jacob, but from a narrow

241

bridge barely wider than a footpath. The Rapunzel-rope stretched up ten steep yards to the bridge's girders.

"Valiant's right!" Jacob said, closing Clara's hands around the rope. "Just look straight up. And stay under the bridge until we get back with Fox."

The golden rope seemed little more than a spider's thread in the huge cavern, and Clara climbed painfully slow. Jacob followed her with his eyes until she finally pulled herself onto one of the metal struts of the bridge and hid in its shadow. Then he followed Valiant up the prison walls. Dwarfs and Goyl were well known for their climbing skills. Jacob, however, didn't even like hiking up a mountain, let alone free climbing on the inwardly tapering façade of a building hanging hundreds of feet above a hostile city. Luckily they didn't have to climb far. Valiant had told the truth. Fox was imprisoned in the cell right above theirs.

She was in her human form, and badly scratched and bruised. She clearly hadn't made it easy for the Goyl to catch her. Her arms and ankles were bleeding when Valiant freed them from the chains and, when Jacob knelt down beside her, she wrapped her arms around him and sobbed like a child.

"I thought they had killed you."

"You know they tried that before." He pushed her hair back from her bruised forehead. He was so relieved to see her. And that she wasn't angry with him anymore. Holding her felt as if he had lost and found part of himself. For that's what she was, after all these years: a part of him. The better part.

"They said they'd make you pay if I change shape." She wiped the tears from her face with her dirty sleeve, embarrassed that Jacob had caught her crying. The vixen didn't cry. She bit and fought. Jacob had seen Fox cry only once, when she had thought

242

he wouldn't come back from the other world and had shown him her human shape for the very first time.

Of course she read the despair on his face once she cleared her eyes of the tears.

"You didn't find Will."

"No, I did. But he is one of them now." The words felt wrong, so wrong. "The Fairy took him with her. He is under her spell."

A door slammed farther down the corridor. Valiant cocked his rifle. But the guards were dragging another prisoner out into the corridor.

Fox climbed as swiftly as the Dwarf, and Clara looked very relieved when she and Jacob pulled themselves up onto the iron beam next to her. Valiant swung himself onto the bridge while Jacob rubbed the Rapunzel-rope between his hands until it was once again nothing more than a golden hair.

A platoon of Goyl was marching across one of the iron passageways above them, and below a freight train belched black smoke into the huge cavern as it crossed the abyss. The wait seemed to last for hours, but finally Valiant waved them up to the bridge. There was no indication of how the Goyl dealt with their exhaust fumes, except for two shafts through which a hint of daylight entered the cave. Maybe his father had taught them that as well.

"What about horses?" Jacob asked Valiant as they ducked into one of the archways that lined the cave's wall.

"Forget it! The stables are right by the main gate. Too many guards."

"So you want to cross the mountains on foot?"

"You've got a better plan?"

No, he didn't. They would count themselves lucky if they ever saw the sun again. All they had to defend themselves were Valiant's rifle and a knife the Dwarf had brought for Jacob—in exchange for another gold coin, of course.

While Fox shifted into the vixen, Clara stepped behind one of the pillars and stared down at the Goyl's underground city. Jacob was sure that she saw neither the houses nor the Goyl between them. She looked as if she was back behind the mirror, in the shabby hospital cafeteria with Will, or kissing in front of the room where their mother lay dying. It would be a long journey back to the ruin, and every mile would remind her that they were leaving Will behind.

Windows and doors behind curtains of sandstone, houses like swallows' nests, golden eyes everywhere…to make themselves less conspicuous, Valiant first took only Clara with him while Jacob hid with Fox among the houses. Then the Dwarf fetched them while Clara hid somewhere in the shadows. Valiant had refreshed the letter on Jacob's forehead and still very much enjoyed treating him like his slave while he kept Clara by his side, as if he were presenting his new bride to the Goyl. Going down the steep stairs and alleyways was even more difficult than going up, and each time Jacob pushed past a Goyl uniform he expected a barked order or a stone hand on his shoulder. But nobody stopped them and, after seemingly endless hours, they finally reached the tunnel through which they first arrived at the palace cave.

An hour later, though, their luck ran out.

They were so exhausted by then that they'd stayed together. A foolish mistake. The first Goyl they encountered were returning from a hunt. There were six of them, and they had a pack of the tame wolves that followed them even into the deepest caves. Two horses were packed with their quarry: three of the huge lizards whose spines the Goyl cavalry wore on their helmets, and a dozen albino bats, whose hearts were said to be Kami'en's favorite delicacy. The hunters cast them only a cursory glance as they passed by, but the Goyl patrol that emerged from one of the dark side tunnels only a few minutes later was much less careless. There were three soldiers. Two jasper, one moonstone — the color of most of their spies because it came closest to the skin tone of their human enemies.

When Valiant named the merchant whose slave Jacob supposedly was, they exchanged a quick glance and the moonstone reached for his pistol, calmly informing the Dwarf that his business partner had been arrested for illegal mineral dealings. Valiant shot him before the Goyl could pull the trigger, and Jacob threw his knife into the chest of the second soldier. Valiant had bought the knife in one of the shops on the palace bridge, and its blade cut through the stone skin like butter. It sickened Jacob how much he wanted to kill them all. At the same time, he felt like killing his own brother. The vixen tried to frighten the third soldier's horse into throwing him off, but the Goyl regained control and galloped off before Jacob could pull a gun from one of his dead comrades' belts.

Valiant spat out curses that Jacob had never heard before. While the hoof-beats were still dying off in the distance, the tunnel they were standing in filled with a noise that resembled the chirping of thousands of crickets and, before they could take another step, the stone around them sprang to life. Hundreds of bugs crawled from the fissures and holes: millipedes, spiders, cockroaches. Moths fluttered into their faces; mosquitoes and dragonflies covered their hair and crawled into their clothes. The alarm of the Goyl made the earth breathe out life—crawling, biting, fluttering life.

They stumbled on, half-blind in the dark tunnels, crushing insects with their hands and feet. Not even Fox remembered which direction they had come from while she was snapping at the bugs in her fur, or in which direction they could find the tunnel that would lead them back to the Ogre's cave. The walls were chittering louder and louder, and the flashlight was nothing but a helplessly probing finger in the darkness. Jacob thought he could hear hooves in the distance. Voices…it would surely not take long until the Goyl chased them down. They were trapped, caught in an endlessly branching labyrinth. But suddenly the vixen barked and Jacob saw her disappear into a side passage. The hint of a breeze brushed his face as he pulled Clara with him. Light fell through the entrance of a huge cave, and there they were: the red Dragons the ferryman had warned them about. But they were made of metal and wood, and were the grown-up brothers of the model airplanes hanging above his father's desk.

41

Wings

The alarm could be heard in the plane-cave as well, but nothing was crawling out of its walls. The rock had been straightened and sealed and, through a wide tunnel, bright daylight poured in. The two Goyl working on one of the planes were mechanics, not soldiers, and unarmed.

They clenched their fists when Valiant pointed his rifle at them, but then lifted their arms. Jacob bound them with cables Clara found between the planes. When the younger one tore himself free, Jacob already imagined claws at his neck and his brother's fate for himself, but the Goyl stumbled back the moment Valiant cocked his rifle. Although Jacob reminded himself that his brother had been attacked by one of their soldiers, not by an unarmed mechanic, he longed to drive the knife into the Goyl's chest. He'd never enjoyed killing, but the void he felt since Will had followed the Fairy made him afraid of his own hands.

Fox took human shape, as though she sensed that fear. The Goyl barely reacted when the vixen turned into a young woman—they weren't scared of shapeshifters like most humans—and Fox just stepped to Jacob's side. She didn't say a word, just reached for his hand as if to make sure it wouldn't reach for the knife. Nothing bound them together more firmly than this—the knowledge of each other's darkness.

Valiant was still pointing his rifle at the Goyl, but his eyes wandered over to the planes. Outside, they could hear voices approaching through the tunnels, louder and louder, closer and closer, but the Dwarf was lost in admiration for the flying machines.

"Oh, this is fabulous!" he mumbled. "So much better than any stinking Dragon! But what makes them fly? And what do the Goyl use them for?"

"To spit fire," Jacob said. "As all Dragons do."

They were biplanes, similar to the ones built in his world in the early twentieth century. A huge leap into the future, much further than anything the engineers of the Empress or the Crookback were working on. Two of the machines were solo planes, like the ones flown by fighter pilots in World War I; the third one was a replica of a two-seater Junkers J4, a bomber and reconnaissance plane from the same period. Jacob had once built a model of that very plane with his father.

Fox looked clearly worried when he climbed into the tight cockpit.

"What are you doing?" she called. "Let's try the tunnel. We just have to follow the light."

Jacob ran his fingers over the plane's controls and checked the gauges. The Junkers was relatively easy to fly, but difficult to maneuver on the ground. *You know this from a book, Jacob, and from*

248

playing with model airplanes. You don't seriously think you can fly this thing? He'd flown a few times with his father, when John Reckless had still escaped his world in a single-engine plane instead of through a mirror. But that was such a long time ago that it seemed as unreal as the fact that he'd once actually had a father.

The alarm was still shrilling through the cave like crickets roused from a freshly mown meadow.

Jacob pumped up the fuel pressure. *Where was the ignition?* Valiant was watching him, his forehead one incredulous frown.

"Hold on! You think you can fly this thing?"

"Sure!" Jacob managed to sound so confident that he almost convinced himself.

"Nonsense! We have to go!" Fox pointed to the cave's entrance. "They're coming!"

She was right. The voices from the tunnels sounded worryingly close, but Jacob was tired of the endless tunnels, and they would never escape the Goyl on foot.

"I promise, I can fly this!" he called down to the others. "So get up here! All of you!"

Valiant was the first to forget his doubts and pull himself onto one of the wings. But there was only one more seat, and Fox still eyed the plane very skeptically. Finally, she shifted shape and jumped up to the wing to squeeze into the narrow space next to the pilot seat, while Clara shared the back seat with Valiant. Jacob sent a quick prayer to the god of pilots and planes that the four passengers wouldn't crash the Junkers while his fingers found the ignition switch.

The engine sputtered to life. The propeller began to turn, and, as Jacob made his final checks, he remembered his father's

249

hands going through the same motions — in another world, another life — memories he hadn't recalled for at least a dozen years.

'Look at this, Jacob! Aluminum body on a steel frame. Only the rudder is still made of wood.' John Reckless had never sounded more passionate than when he spoke about old airplanes. Or weapons.

Jacob felt the vixen shiver behind his legs. Machines. Engineered motion, mechanical magic for those who had neither fur nor wings. Jacob steered the plane toward the large tunnel. Yes, it certainly was hard to navigate on the ground. He could only hope flying it would be easier.

Shots rang out behind them as the plane rolled into the tunnel. The roar of the engine reverberated between the walls. Oil splattered onto Jacob's face, and one of the wings nearly grazed the rock. He accelerated, although that made it even harder to keep the wings clear of the tunnel walls, and held his breath, exhaling with relief when the heavy plane shot out of the tunnel and onto a gravel runway. Above them, a pale sun was drifting among gray rainclouds. A flock of crows rose from the nearby trees when he pulled the plane up but, luckily they stayed clear of the propeller.

Fox had her fur, his brother had a skin of jade, and now he had a pair of wings.

Engineered magic. John Reckless had brought metal Dragons through the mirror, and Jacob caught himself having the same irrational thought he had had that night the sheet of paper slipped out of the book to reveal the mirror's secret — that maybe his father had left some things behind for him after all.

The plane rose higher and higher, revealing roads and railways below them, which disappeared through massive gates inside a mountain. Gone were the times when the Goyl had hidden from the world. The gates were made from silver, and high above them Kami'en's coat of arms was inserted into the mountain's flank: the silhouette of a black moth on a carnelian moon, so huge that it could be seen for miles. The sun drew the plane's silhouette onto the carnelian when Jacob flew past it.

He was robbing the Goyl King of one of his Dragons.

A pitiful revenge against him for stealing his brother.

42

WHAT NOW?

Back. Over the river where the Lorelei had almost devoured them, the mountains where Jacob had died, the plundered lands where the princess was still sleeping between the roses and where Will had almost joined the Goyl for the first time. Kami'en's airplane covered the miles it had taken them more than a week to travel in just a few hours, but Jacob could have sworn that they were in the air for months.

'*Jacob, where's Will?*'

When they were children, he'd most times lost Will because he'd felt embarrassed to hold his little brother's hand, and Will would be off stalking a squirrel, a stray dog, or a crow as soon as one let go of his fingers. Their mother never heard about those adventures. They had never given each other away, although Jacob had at times been very tempted to just lose Will in the park or in the ever so busy streets of their childhood. Each time

253

he got away, Will seemed incredibly relieved when Jacob finally found him—as if something in him got so lost at times that only his brother could bring it back. What had happened when he'd stayed behind the mirror more and more often, leaving Will alone? Maybe Will had lost himself in those years without another world to escape to like his older brother.

None of them talked much on that flight in the Goyl King's plane. The noise of the propellers trapped them all in their own thoughts. Fox was the only one who closed her eyes and slept away the exhaustion of the past few days. It was bitterly cold in the open cockpit, though Jacob kept the plane quite close to the ground, and they were all glad when they spotted the familiar roofs and towers of Schwanstein in the distance. Jacob landed the plane on a barren field, not far away from the railway tracks that made it so much easier by now to get to Vena. It still took the train more than eight hours to reach the Empress's capital, but the journey was much more comfortable than on horseback or in one of the coaches Jacob had travelled on, whenever the Empress summoned him.

It wasn't a coincidence that he landed the plane so close to the rails. Fox was aware of that. The vixen didn't take her eyes off him while she was stretching her furry limbs to make her body forget the ride in the plane.

Valiant, in contrast, had of course only one thought on his mind.

"Where is it?" he asked, scanning the fields and meadows.

"What?"

"My gold tree! Don't play the fool, Jacob Reckless! I took you to the fortress—that was the deal, not to bring your brother back! And I'll be generous and won't charge extra for saving your neck."

254

A column of smoke was rising into the sky. A train was approaching. Jacob had seen it from above.

"Fox will show you the tree," he said.

The vixen stared at the upcoming train. The wind stirred her fur.

Jacob knelt down by her side. "Will you bring Clara back to the ruin?"

She didn't ask where he was going.

"Your brother is gone," she said. "As you were, when you stayed with her red sister. He belongs to the Dark Fairy now, and he likes the skin she gave him." *Even though you don't want to admit that*, her eyes added.

Clara was standing a few steps away. Jacob couldn't read what she wished for from her face. All he saw was exhaustion. And the void he felt himself.

"You know I was never good at letting go," he whispered into the vixen's pointed ear. "I simply don't know how to do it, Fox. I cannot even give up on a glass shoe or a magical ring. How am I supposed to give up on my brother?"

"And I guess you once again don't want me to come with you."

"You hate the city!" They both knew that was not the reason why he wouldn't take her. He would look for the Fairy, and he couldn't bear the thought of losing Fox as well.

The vixen looked at Clara.

"What if she doesn't want to go back?"

She was right. Clara would want to stay. He was not the only one who hadn't given up on Will yet.

"For now, just don't tell her where I'm going. And ask Chanute to let her stay in my room. Until…"

Until what? *You don't seriously believe you'll come back, Jacob?*

255

"Chanute?" The vixen uttered an amused purr. "That will be interesting."

The train grew toward them, cloaking the fields and meadows with its smoke. Eight hours to Vena.

Jacob rose to his feet. *And then what, Jacob?* He didn't even know when the wedding was supposed to take place.

Valiant shouted something after him when he headed for the rails, but Jacob didn't look back. The air filled with the smoke and the noise of the train. He broke into a run and pulled himself onto one of the wagons.

43

Dog and Wolf

Trams, carriages, carts, and riders on horseback...Jacob had never seen Vena so crowded. It seemed as if all of Austry had come for the wedding, rich and poor, young and old. There were guests from Lotheraine, Albion, and Lombardia, visitors in the traditional costumes of Varangia, Parsia, even Zhonghua. Some of them had surely been invited by the Empress, but Kami'en had been weaving his diplomatic net far and wide as well, and his allies were not just human. Dwarfs were being carried through the busy streets by their human servants, Giantlings and Trolls towered above the crowds, and, of course, every color of Goyl could be found amongst the visitors.

It took Jacob nearly an hour to get from the station to the Grand Hotel where he usually stayed when he came to Vena. Its magnificent rooms were worlds apart from the modest lodgings at Chanute's tavern, but from time to time Jacob enjoyed sleeping

257

between the gold embroidered curtains of a four-poster bed. He paid one of the chambermaids to keep a few clothes ready for him to wear at the palace. The girl didn't turn a hair when he handed her his torn and bloody shirts with the request to wash and mend them. She was used to finding such stains on his clothes, and repaired his torn sleeves and pants as naturally as if all guests of the Grand Hotel in Vena arrived with such damaged clothes.

The countless bells of the city were chiming midday when Jacob made his way to the palace. On many walls, the official photographs of the wedding couple were smeared with anti-Goyl graffiti. The slogans competed with the pompous headlines the newspaper boys were yelling at every corner: ETERNAL PEACE... HISTORIC EVENT...TWO POWERFUL EMPIRES...OUR GREAT PEOPLES...the same fondness for big words on both sides of the mirror.

Jacob himself had posed just a year ago for Robert Fenton, the court photographer, who had portrayed the bride and groom. Fenton was a master of his trade, but Amalie of Austry didn't make it easy for him. The beauty the Fairy lily had granted her was as cold as porcelain, and her face was as blank in real life as it was on the posters. Her groom, in contrast, photographed like a sculpture chiseled from petrified fire.

The crowd in front of the palace was so dense that Jacob was at some points tempted to use his sword to clear a path to the gates. The imperial guards pointed their bayonets at him when he called for entrance through the wrought-iron bars, but one of them was an old acquaintance. Justus Kronsberg was the youngest son of a nobleman who owed his wealth to the fact that his meadows were swarming with Grass Elves, whose threads and glass adorned so many dresses at the Empress's court. Therese of Austry required all her guardsmen to be at least six and a half feet tall, and the youngest Kronsberg was no exception. Justus was almost a head taller than Jacob, not counting the plumed helmet, but his thin mustache couldn't hide the fact that he still had the face of a boy.

Years ago, Jacob had saved one of Justus's brothers from the wrath of a Witch whose daughter he'd rejected. Since then Jacob never ran out of elven glass buttons for his clothes, but the rumor that the glass protected against Stilts and Thumblings had sadly not proved to be true.

"Jacob Reckless!" The youngest Kronsberg spoke with the soft dialect one could hear in the south of Austry. "Just yesterday someone told me you were killed by a Goyl."

"Really?" Jacob wondered what Justus would have thought of the imprint he wore above his heart. The moth hadn't faded since the Red Fairy had brought him back to life. "I guess you see a lot of Goyl at the palace these days. Where did the Empress put the groom? In the North Wing?"

The other guards eyed Jacob warily when Justus Kronsberg let him in through one of the gates.

"Where else?" Kronsberg lowered his voice. "Are you back from an assignment? I hear the Empress has been offering thirty gold coins for a Wishing Sack after the Crookback made two of her spies disappear in the one he owns."

A Wishing Sack. Chanute claimed to own one, but not even he was ruthless enough to put such an item into the Empress's hands. You just had to name an enemy, and the sack made your foe disappear without a trace. The Crookback was rumored to have dealt with hundreds of his enemies—and friends—this way.

259

"No, I'm not here about a Wishing Sack." Jacob looked up at the balcony from which the Empress would present the bride and groom to her subjects the next day. "It's a private matter. Please give my best to your father and your brother."

Justus Kronsberg was clearly disappointed not to learn more about the purpose of Jacob's visit, but he still unlocked the gate to the First Inner Courtyard for him. After all, it was Jacob's doing that his brother hadn't ended up as a toad at the bottom of a well or, as Witches tended to prefer these days, as a doormat or a tray for their china.

Jacob had been to the palace only three months earlier, when he'd been called to authenticate a magic nut in the Empress's Chambers of Miracles. The wide courtyards seemed almost modest compared to what he had seen in the Goyl fortress, and the buildings surrounding them looked quite conventional, despite their gilded gutters and crystal balconies, compared to Kami'en's Hanging Palace. The splendor within, however, was still impressive.

Especially in the North Wing, the Emperors of Austry had spared no expense, as its main purpose was to lodge official guests, both allies and foes, and to humble them with the wealth and power of the Empire. In the entrance hall, golden fruits and flowers climbed the columns. The floor was plain white marble, maybe because the builders had been all too aware of the fact that no human mosaic could compete with the stone artistry of the Goyl, while the walls were painted with frescoes of Austry's most famous sights: the highest mountains, the oldest towns, and the most spectacular castles. The hunting lodge whose ruin housed the mirror was depicted in all its lost glory, with Schwanstein as a fairy-tale idyll at its feet. No roads or railway tracks scarred the painted hills; instead, they teemed with all the creatures Her

Majesty's family had been hunting with great vigor for generations: Giants, Dragons, Witches, Watermen, Lorelei, and Ogres.

The stairs leading to the upper floors were lined with less peaceful images, most of them commissioned by the Empress's grandfather; they showed sea-, land-, summer-, and winter campaigns, battles against his brother in Lotharaine and his cousin in Albion, against rebellious Dwarfs and the Wolf- and Bear Lords in the east. Every visitor was sure to find a painting depicting the army of his own nation in battle with the Empire—and of course they were always portrayed in defeat. The Goyl were the only ones to climb these stairs without witnessing their ancestors' annihilation in battle. Ever since their King had declared war on his human neighbors, Kami'en had been the victor.

The two guards Jacob met on the stairs didn't stop him, although he was armed, and the servants who scurried past him just gave Jacob a deferential nod. Everyone in the North Wing knew Jacob Reckless, for Therese of Austry often called on his services to give important guests a tour of her Chambers of Miracles, and tell them true and untrue stories about the treasures on display.

The quarters the Empress had allocated to the Goyl were on the second floor, the most sumptuous part of the North Wing. Jacob saw their sentries as soon as he peered down the first corridor. They noticed him, but Jacob pretended not to see them as he turned left from the staircase into a hall where the rulers of Austry demonstrated their knowledge of the wider world by displaying souvenirs brought back from their travels.

The hall was deserted, just as Jacob had hoped. The Goyl weren't interested in the Troll-fur hat her Majesty's father had brought back from Yurtland, or in the Leprechaun boots from

Albion, and whatever was written about their people in the books that lined the walls was most likely far from flattering.

The North Wing was far from the Empress's chambers, thus giving her guests the illusion of being unobserved. But the walls hid a network of secret passages from which every room could be spied on and, in some cases, even entered. Jacob had used these passageways before, to pay nightly visits to an ambassador's daughter. The network was entered through hidden doors. The one Jacob had come for was hidden behind a curtain embroidered with the pearls found in the stomachs of Thumblings, a royal souvenir from Lotharaine. The door itself looked like part of the paneling. It opened easily, suggesting it was used quite regularly. Jacob nearly stumbled over a dead rat when he stepped through it. The Empress had her secret alleyways fumigated regularly, but the rodents loved the dark corridors. Every three yards there were peepholes in the walls, each approximately the size of a thumbnail, camouflaged on the other side by ornamental stucco or two-way mirrors. In the first room, a bored maid was dusting the gilded furniture, but the second and third rooms had been turned into temporary offices for the Goyl, and Jacob instinctively held his breath when he saw Hentzau sitting behind one of the desks. Surely he had heard about their escape by now, and the stolen plane. But it wasn't for the jasper Goyl that Jacob had come.

He heard a maid softly humming to herself behind the thin walls, the clanking of porcelain, and then, worryingly close by, a cough. Jacob quickly switched off his flashlight. Of course. Therese of Austry had all her guests watched; why should her greatest enemy be treated any differently, even if he was her future son-in-law?

A gas lantern appeared around a corner up ahead, illuminating a pale man who looked as if he spent his entire life in these corridors. Jacob squeezed into an alcove, holding his breath until the spy had shuffled past him and out through the hidden door. He would be back soon, either he or someone to relieve him. There wouldn't be much time.

The spy had been watching the very room Jacob was looking for. He recognized the Dark Fairy's voice even before he saw her through the tiny hole. The room was only lit by a few candles. The curtains were all drawn, but a trickle of sunlight seeped underneath the pale yellow brocade. The Fairy was standing by one of the curtains, as though she was shielding her lover from the light. Her skin shimmered in the darkness as if it were made from moonlight. *Don't look at her, Jacob!*

Kami'en was standing by the door, fire in the dark. Jacob sensed his impatience even through the wall.

"You're asking me to put my faith in a fairy tale."

Every word filled the room. One could hear his strength in his voice—and the ability to control it. "I admit it amuses me that all those who want us to crawl back into the earth seem to believe in it. But don't expect me to be that naïve. No man's skin can guarantee what more than a hundred thousand soldiers have fought for. I am not invincible, and no Jade Goyl will change that. Even this wedding will only buy me peace for a while."

The Dark Fairy tried to reply, but Kami'en cut her off.

"We have uprisings in the north; the east is only quiet because they're more interested in slaughtering each other; in the west, the Crookback takes my bribes and arms his troops behind my back, not to mention his cousin on the island. The onyx Goyl despise the color of my skin; my munitions factories can't keep up

263

with the demands of my fighting soldiers; the field hospitals are overflowing, and the resistance has just blown up two of our most vital railroads. As far as I remember, none of that was mentioned in the fairy tale my mother told me. Let the people believe in sacred stones and the Jade Goyl. But the world is made of iron."

He put his hand on the door handle "They do make beautiful things," he murmured, touching the gold fittings above it. "I just wonder why they're so obsessed with gold. I always preferred silver."

"Promise me he'll be by your side. Even when you exchange your vows with her. Promise!" The Fairy raised her hand, and all the gold in the dim room turned to silver.

"He is a Man-Goyl! As far as my officers are concerned, not even the jade can make up for that. And he's less experienced than any of my bodyguards."

"And he still outfought every one of them! Promise me!"

He loved her. Jacob saw it on Kami'en's face. He loved her so much it scared him.

"I have to go." He turned around, but the door wouldn't open.

"Promise me!" the Fairy repeated.

The door sprang open when she dropped her hand. But her lover left without an answer, and she was alone.

Now, Jacob!

His fingers searched for a hidden door, but they found only wooden panels, and the Fairy was walking toward the door through which Kami'en had left. *Come on, Jacob! She's still alone! There'll be guards outside that door.* Maybe he could kick in the wall. And then what? The noise would immediately summon dozens of Goyl. He was still in the dark passage, unsure what to do, when the Fairy waved one of the guards into the room.

264

Jade.

It was the first time he saw his brother in the Goyl's gray uniform. Will wore it as though he'd never known anything else. He still looked like his brother, but everything about him was Goyl. His lips might have been a little fuller, his hair a little finer, but his body spoke their language. And he looked at the Dark Fairy as if she was all he knew and all he cared for.

There is nothing but her, Jacob. Remember. A full year and he hadn't thought once about Fox, waiting at the shore of the lake. Or about Will. Or his mother. He hadn't even remembered his own name. Fairy magic. There was nothing more powerful in this world.

"I hear you disarmed Kami'en's best bodyguard." The Dark Fairy caressed Will's face, the face her spell had turned to jade.

"He isn't as good as he claims."

Did that sound like his brother? No. Will had never been keen to measure his strength against others. He fought only for one reason: to protect something or someone he considered vulnerable or in need of help. Like a stray dog. Or their mother. *'You made her cry!'* Yes, there had been times when Will had picked a fight with him. And Jacob hadn't let him win those…

The Dark Fairy smiled when Will closed his fingers almost tenderly around the hilt of his saber. Jade fingers.

You will give him back! Jacob thought while he felt his heart drowning in helpless rage. *And your sister will get her revenge!*

He'd completely forgotten about the spy. The man's eyes widened as the light of his lantern brought Jacob into view. Jacob smashed his flashlight into the spy's temple and quickly caught the slumping body, but one of his scrawny shoulders brushed against the wall, and the lantern crashed onto the wooden floor before Jacob could catch it.

265

"What was that?" he heard the Dark Fairy ask.

Jacob extinguished the lantern and held his breath.

Steps.

He reached for his pistol. Until he realized who was coming toward the wall.

Will kicked it in, and Jacob didn't wait for his brother to push through the splintered wood. He was already stumbling back along the dark passageway when the Dark Fairy called the guards. *Stop, Jacob!* But nothing had ever frightened him as much as the sound of the footsteps behind him. What if the Fairy had made him even forget his face? His face, Clara's, everything he had been before...

Jacob tore down the curtain as he pushed through the hidden door. The sudden light blinded Will, and Jacob managed to strike the drawn saber from his hand as he raised his other arm to shield his eyes.

Will didn't remember him. Jacob saw it in his eyes.

It felt so wrong to point his pistol at him.

"Leave the sword where it is, Will!"

Why call him by his name? Surely the Dark Fairy had given him another one. One to fit his new skin.

Of course he went for the saber. Jacob tried to kick it away, but Will was faster and he still had the same face, although it was cast in jade. Jacob dropped the pistol. He knew the magic all too well that made his brother attack him like a stranger.

He barely managed to deflect Will's sabre with his own. The next stroke cut into his arm. The Fairy was right: he fought very well. His brother was fighting like a Goyl, cold and precise, without any fear.

'I hear you disarmed the King's best bodyguard.'

266

'He isn't as good as he claims.'

Another strike. It almost sliced his chest. *Fight back, Jacob!*

Blade struck against blade, sharpened metal instead of the toy swords they had fought each other with as children. So long ago. Above them the sunlight caught in the crystal blossoms of a chandelier, and the carpet beneath their feet bore the symbols on which the Witches danced to summon spring. Will was panting. Both of them were breathing so heavily that they noticed the imperial guards only when they cocked their rifles. Will backed away from the white uniforms, and Jacob instinctively stood in front of him, protecting his younger brother as he'd always done. But that brother no longer needed his help. The Goyl had also caught up with them. They were coming through the hidden door, an officer and three soldiers. Will lowered his sword and stepped back to join them.

"That man tried to enter the King's chambers!" The officer was a malachite Goyl. He spoke Austrish with barely an accent.

Jacob tried to catch his brother's eyes. Will returned his glance. *Strangers.* Oh yes, the Fairy had made sure he was hers, and hers alone. *And maybe he doesn't want to remember, Jacob.*

He offered his saber to the palace guards. "Jacob Reckless. I need to speak with the Empress."

The guard who took the saber whispered something to his officer. Jacob's portrait was still hanging in one of the palace's halls. The Empress had ordered it after he brought her the Glass Slipper.

Will turned and followed the Goyl as the guards led Jacob away. He didn't look back.

267

44

Too Late

It had been quite a while since Jacob had last stood in Therese of Austry's audience chamber. It was usually Auberon, her favorite court Dwarf, who'd negotiate the reward or give the next assignment. The Empress only granted personal audiences when an item had been particularly dangerous to acquire, as had been the case with the Glass Slipper and Wishing Table, or when the story of its acquisition had sufficient blood and death in it. Therese of Austry would have made a great treasure hunter if she hadn't been born the daughter of an Emperor.

She was sitting behind her desk when the guards brought Jacob to her. The silk of her dress was embroidered with elven glass and as saffron yellow as the roses on her desk. Her beauty was legendary, but war and defeat had left their mark. The lines around her brows were more defined, the shadows under her eyes darker, and her gaze had grown even colder.

A general and three of her most powerful ministers were standing by the windows, behind them the roofs and towers of Vena—and a view of the distant mountains the Goyl had already conquered. Jacob only recognized the adjutant talking to them when he turned and faced him. Leo von Donnersmarck. He had accompanied Jacob on three of his expeditions for the Empress. Two of them had been so successful that they had earned Jacob a lot of money, and Donnersmarck a medal. They had been friends for a long time, but the look Donnersmarck gave Jacob didn't show it. There were a few more medals on his white uniform, and when he stepped to the general's side, he dragged his left leg. Compared to war, treasure hunting was a harmless trade.

"Unauthorized entry to the palace. Threatening my guests. One of my spies knocked unconscious?" The Empress put down her quill and waved Auberon to her side. The Dwarf kept his eyes firmly on Jacob while he pulled back his mistress's chair. The court Dwarfs of Austry had thwarted more than a dozen assassination attempts since they served its dynasty, and Therese always had at least three of them by her side. Rumor had it they could even take on Giantlings.

Therese waited for Auberon to smooth her dress before she stepped out from behind her desk. She was still as slender as a young girl.

"I thought you were finding me an Hourglass. As far as I remember, you promised to deliver it for my birthday. Instead you are fighting a duel in my palace, with my future son-in-law's bodyguard!"

Jacob bowed his head. Therese didn't like it when you looked her in the eyes. "I had no choice, Your Highness. Kami'en's bodyguard attacked me. I only defended myself."

Kami'en's bodyguard. The Empress could never know that he talked about his brother. She would immediately wonder how she could use Will to her advantage.

"You have to surrender him, Your Majesty." The minister who made the suggestion despised Therese's passion for treasure hunts.

"I suggest you have him shot yourself, Your Majesty." That was the general. "To prove your desire for peace."

"Nonsense," the Empress replied testily. "As if this war hasn't cost me enough already. He's the best treasure hunter I had for years—even better than his teacher, Albert Chanute."

She stepped so close to Jacob that he could smell her perfume. One of its ingredients supposedly was the aromatic oil of Sorcerer Poppy, which made whomever inhaled the scent far more impressionable to orders and royal demands.

"Did someone pay you who doesn't like this peace? If so, tell them Therese of Austry doesn't like it, either."

"Your Majesty!" All three ministers glanced at the door as if the Goyl were listening on the other side.

"Oh, be quiet!" the Empress snapped. "I'm the one who is paying for this peace with my daughter."

Jacob looked at Donnersmarck, but his glance was not returned.

"Nobody paid me, Your Highness," he replied. "And this fight had nothing to do with your peace. They caught me spying on the Dark Fairy."

The Empress's face went almost as blank as her daughter's.

"The Fairy?" Therese tried valiantly to sound unconcerned, but her voice gave her away. Hatred and disgust—Jacob heard them both. And anger. Therese of Austry was proud of her fearlessness, and the Dark Fairy frightened her.

271

"Why would you spy on her?"

"I would like to do more than that. Grant me five minutes alone with her. I promise you won't regret it. Or does it please your daughter that her groom brought his mistress to the wedding?"

Careful, Jacob. But he was too desperate to be careful.

The Empress exchanged a glance with the general.

"He's as disrespectful as the man who taught him," she said. "Chanute used that same impertinent tone with my father."

"Five minutes!" Jacob repeated. "Tell Kami'en I have to meet the Fairy to discuss a surprise you plan for him. Tell him anything!"

Therese of Austry was a brilliant liar.

"Her magic cost you the war and ten of thousands of your subjects. It will cost you your daughter! Don't you want to take revenge for that? Use me! Nobody will ever know I also acted on your behalf."

Revenge. A dangerous word. Therese surely wished for nothing more, but she also wanted peace. She needed this peace.

"Your Majesty…" The general fell silent when Therese shot him a warning look.

"You're too late, Jacob," she said. "I wish you had come earlier, but I've already signed the treaty."

She turned and walked back to her desk.

"Tell the Goyl he inhaled elven dust," she ordered while one of the guards grabbed Jacob's arm. "Take him to the gate and give orders not to let him in again."

Jacob opened his mouth to protest, but the guards already pushed him through the doors.

"Oh yes, Jacob!" Therese called after him. "Forget about the Hourglass! I want a Wishing Sack!"

45

PAST TIMES

Jacob had no idea how he found his way back to the hotel. In every shop window, he saw his brother's face of jade, and every woman he passed turned into the Dark Fairy. It couldn't be over. He would break her spell. At the wedding, at the station, when she'd board the Goyl train with the freshly married couple. He would follow her back to the Hanging Palace, if he had to. Yes, he would, although he had to admit that he could no longer tell what was driving him: the hope of somehow getting his brother back, the hunger for revenge, or simply his injured pride.

At the hotel, a group of newly arrived guests waited at the reception desk surrounded by stacks of luggage and a flock of harried bellboys. Wedding guests. A Goyl family attracted more looks and whispers than the Empress's younger sister, who had arrived without the Wolf Lord her father had married her to. She wore a coat tailored from black bear fur, which made her look as though she was in mourning over her niece's wedding.

The ceremony would take place the next day—that much Jacob had found out—in the cathedral where Therese of Austry had also been wed, just like her mother and her grandmother before her.

Jacob nearly dropped the clothes the chambermaid had washed and mended when he came up to his room to find a man standing by the window. Donnersmarck was in uniform. "You have to admit it," Albert Chanute liked to mock the imperial white. "No other uniform makes a better show of the bloodstains."

Jacob put his clothes on a chair and closed the door behind him.

"Is there any room the adjutant to the Empress does not have access to?"

"An Ogre's cave, a Bluebeard's red chamber. That's where your talents are still more useful."

Leo von Donnersmarck had lost his sister to a Bluebeard. They had tried to save her together, but they had come too late.

"What's your business with the Dark Fairy?"

They hadn't seen each other for nearly a year, but hunting a Bluebeard forges a bond not easily broken, and they had faced even more than that together. They'd never found the Devil's hair the Empress had wished for, but Jacob had brought her a Wishing Table because Donnersmarck had distracted the Brown Wolf guarding it, and he surely still remembered how Jacob had saved him in a shabby inn from being clubbed to death by a Cudgel-in-the-Sack.

"What happened to your leg?"

"What do you think?" Donnersmarck walked haltingly toward him. "There was a war on."

From outside the window came the din of carriages and cursing coachmen. Not so different from the other world. But next to the bed, two Grass Elves were swirling above a small bouquet of sweet pea flowers. Many hotels released them in the rooms because their dust gave most guests enchanted dreams. It could be quite addictive, though. The crown prince of Lotharaine was said to consume vast amounts.

"I am here to ask you a question. You can probably guess on whose behalf." Donnersmarck brushed a fly off his flawlessly white tunic. "If you were to get your five minutes, would Kami'en's Fairy mistress still attend his wedding?"

It took Jacob a few minutes to absorb the meaning of Donnersmarck's words. So Therese would grant him the five minutes. What if he had to get past his brother again? He would have to take that risk—hoping that Kami'en had given in to his lover's wish and kept Will by his side.

"No, she won't," he answered. "I promise, the Empress's daughter won't have to compete with an immortal lover in the future. I can't change the fact, though, that Kami'en has at least two Goyl wives."

Donnersmarck eyed him intently, trying to read from his face what Jacob wasn't telling him. "You're no longer wearing that medallion." He pointed at Jacob's neck. "Have you made peace with her red sister?"

They had learned a lot about each other hunting for magical treasure.

"I have. It is too dangerous to not live in peace with her."

"Dangerous…since when do you care?" Donnersmarck gave him a mocking smile. He adjusted his saber. He had brought it back from the ruined castle where they had found the Wishing

Table. Leo von Donnersmarck was quite a swordsman, but his leg injury had probably changed that.

"You make peace with one sister only to declare war on the other. It's always like that with peace, isn't it? Always to someone's detriment, already sowing the seed for the next war."

He sat down on the edge of the bed. "Sorry, standing for hours at audiences and receptions doesn't make this leg any better. I guess the Empress didn't consider that when she made me her adjutant."

He rubbed his knee and shooed one of the Grass Elves away when she sat down on his sleeve. There was still something he wished to say, but Leo Donnersmarck was careful with words. He didn't really trust them. Living at court, with all its well-phrased flatteries and eloquent lies, hadn't changed that.

"I know I shouldn't ask," he finally said. "But I have to. As your friend. Why, Jacob? Why the Dark Fairy?"

Of course he should have just lied. But he hadn't been able to talk to anyone since his haunting encounter with his brother. Fox. He should have asked Fox to come. *No, you shouldn't have, Jacob.*

"Did you see the Jade Goyl?" he said. "He is one of Kami'en's bodyguards."

"Of course. Everybody is talking about him. They say he was one of us. Now he's the legendary Goyl who'll make Kami'en invincible. Maybe you and I should team up one more time, to kill him instead of the Fairy. Together we may have a chance."

"I can't sign up for that, Leo. He is my brother."

Donnersmarck looked at Jacob as incredulously as if he had told him that the Dark Fairy was his sister.

"Your brother? I didn't know you had a brother. Come to think of it, there's probably a lot I don't know about you."

276

Yes. A lot indeed. Jacob wondered whether Donnersmarck would have believed him if he had told him about the other world. Maybe. He was staring out of the window as absently as if he were back on the battlefields where the Goyl had beaten his Empress.

"If it hadn't been for the Fairy, we would have won this war."

No, you wouldn't, Jacob thought. *Because Kami'en is the better general, because my father showed them how to build better rifles and planes, because they made the Dwarfs their allies. And because you've been stoking their rage for centuries.* Donnersmarck knew all that as well, but it was so much easier to blame the Fairy.

"She walks every evening in the palace gardens, just after sunset." Donnersmarck struggled to his feet. "Kami'en has them searched beforehand, but his men aren't very thorough. Even the Goyl are afraid of her. And they know what you should know as well: that there's no one who can harm her."

"There is a way."

Why don't you tell him, Jacob? So he can try in case you fail? No. If the Dark Fairy killed him, she would kill Donnersmarck as well, and Jacob wanted him to live.

"I am not a fool, Leo," he replied. "You can be sure of that. And I didn't lose my mind. I just want my brother back."

Donnersmarck nodded. He had wanted his sister back. He would have faced the Dark Fairy to save her, but the Bluebeard hadn't given them a chance.

"What if you kill the Fairy and your brother is still a Goyl?"

"Well…their King will soon be married to your Empress's daughter. It may soon be tougher to be human than to be Goyl in this world."

Donnersmarck didn't reply to that.

277

Someone walked down the corridor. They both listened until the steps died away.

"I will send you two men as soon as it gets dark." Donnersmarck limped to the door. "They will take you to the gardens."

He turned once again.

"Did I ever show you this?" He pointed at one of the medals on his chest, a gilded star with the Empress's crest in the center. "They gave me this after we found the Wishing Table. After *you* found it."

He reached for the door knob.

"You will die, Jacob," he said. "You know, I would have given my life for my sister, and I understand why you have to try. After all, you're the only mortal man who survived being the lover of her red sister. But this Fairy is different. The Dark Fairy is more dangerous than anything you or I have ever encountered, and your brother is gone. I have seen him. He is a Goyl. Nothing will change that. Go and look for the Wishing Sack the Empress envies the Crookback so much for, the Tree of Life, or the Dragon's egg you've always have been dreaming about. Anything. But please! Send me back to the palace with the message that you've changed your mind. Make peace with the Dark Fairy. As we all will make peace with the Goyl, even though it's the last thing we want to do."

Of course he knew what Jacob's answer would be.

"I'll be here at dusk."

"Of course you will," Donnersmarck replied. And closed the door behind him.

46
THE DARK SISTER

An hour had passed since sunset, and Jacob was still waiting for the men Donnersmarck had promised to send. He was just beginning to suspect that his old friend had decided to protect him from himself, when he heard a knock on his door. But it was a woman standing in the hotel corridor.

Jacob recognized Fox only when she pushed back the veil she was wearing over her red hair.

"Don't look at me like this," she snapped. "It wasn't my idea to come here. Clara wants to see your brother one last time."

Jacob pulled her into the room and closed the door.

"Why didn't you talk her out of it?"

Fox eyed the room, the Grass Elves, the bed. "Talk her out of it? Did that ever work with you? And I understand that she wants to see him."

279

She touched the fabric of the bed curtains and ran her fingers over the embroidered flowers. "I told her how the Fairy's magic works. That Will has probably forgotten everything. That I've seen it with you. She says it doesn't matter. And the Dwarf has promised to take her to the wedding."

Great.

Fox eyed his arm. Jacob flinched when she touched it exactly where Will's saber had cut into his flesh.

"What happened? Jacob!" She took his face between her hands. They were much stronger than their slender form suggested. "You're here to find the Fairy, right? Did you already try? No, you probably would be dead."

She read him so easily. And she always knew when he was lying, but this time she couldn't know or she would follow him. And if the Fairy killed her, he would never forgive himself. Although he was usually so good at it.

"I saw Will. That's what I came for," he said. The best lies stay close to the truth. "We fought and he almost killed me. He is one of them. You were right. And there is no return."

Believe me, Fox. Please.

Another knock.

"Jacob Reckless? Lieutenant Donnersmarck sends us." The two soldiers standing in the doorway were barely older than Will.

"I am coming." Jacob pulled Fox with him out into the corridor.

"I'm getting drunk with Donnersmarck," he whispered into her ear. "There's nothing else left to do, so whatever...I'll see you tomorrow at the wedding. I guess you're right. Clara should see Will one more time. Maybe it will make her realize as well that it's over."

Her eyes went from him to the two soldiers.

She didn't believe him. Of course she didn't. She knew him better than he knew himself.

She didn't say a word as she followed him and the soldiers to the elevator. She would be so angry, even angrier than at the brook with the Larks' Water.

"I wish you hadn't come," he said when they reached the elevator. It was a terrible thought that they would part like this and that he might never see her again. But she would be alive. "She cannot follow me," he said, turning to the soldiers. "I need one of you to stay with her to make sure of that."

She tried to shift shape, but Jacob quickly grabbed her arm. Skin on skin, that mostly kept the fur at bay. She tried desperately to free herself, but he wouldn't let go.

"Make sure she doesn't leave the room before the morning." The soldier Jacob handed his room key was as broad as a wardrobe, despite his boyish face. "But be careful. She's a shape-shifter."

The soldier didn't look too happy about his task, but he nodded and took Fox's arm. It hurt so much to see the anger in her eyes, but the mere thought of losing her hurt more.

"I knew it! You are going to see the Fairy!" She fought like the vixen when the soldier dragged her back to the room. "Don't! Jacob! Don't!"

He could still hear her voice when the elevator opened into the lobby. For one moment, he actually wanted to go back up, just to wipe the anger from her face. But the Dark Fairy was surely already walking in the Palace Gardens.

※ ※ ※

The other soldier was clearly relieved that Jacob hadn't picked him to look after Fox. On their way to the palace, Jacob learned that he came from a village in the south, that he still thought his life as a soldier was exciting, and that he obviously had no idea whom Jacob was hoping to meet this night.

The large gate on the rear side of the palace was open to the public only once a year. His guide took forever opening the lock, and Jacob once again missed his magic key and all the other items he had lost in the fortress of the Goyl. The soldier chained the gate again as soon as Jacob had slipped past him. He would stay at his position, back to the gate. Donnersmarck would want to know whether Jacob had come back from his night walk.

The sounds of the city could be heard in the distance—the horses and carriages, the drunkards, the street vendors, and the calls of the night watchmen—but, behind the walls of the Empress's garden, fountains gurgled peacefully, and from the trees came the songs of the artificial nightingales Therese had gotten for her last birthday from one of her sisters. There was still light behind some of the palace windows, but it seemed eerily quiet for the eve of an imperial wedding, and Jacob tried not to wonder whether Will was standing behind one of those windows. As long as he was not with the Fairy...

It was a cold night, and his boots left dark prints on the frost-glazed lawn, but the grass absorbed the sound of his steps far better than the gravel-covered paths winding past hedges and frozen flower beds. Jacob didn't have to look for the Dark Fairy's footprints. He knew where she'd gone. The centerpiece of the Palace Gardens was a pond, almost as densely covered with water lilies as the Fairy lake and surrounded by willow trees.

The Fairy was standing between them, the light of the stars on her amber hair. The two moons caressed her skin, and Jacob felt his anger drown in her beauty. He had to touch his wounded arm to remember what he had come for.

She spun around as she heard his steps behind her, but he wore black over his white shirt as her sister had instructed him. *'White as snow. Red as blood. Black as ebony.'* Only one color was missing.

Her moths swarmed out to attack him, but Jacob had already drawn the knife through his skin, opening the wound his brother's sword had cut. He smeared the blood onto his white shirt and the moths tumbled down as if he'd singed their wings.

"White, red, black. Snow-White colors," he said, wiping the blade clean on his sleeve. "That's what my brother used to call them. It was one of his favorite fairy tales. But who would've thought these colors had such power?"

The Dark Fairy took a step back.

"And how do you know about the Three Colors?"

"Your sister told me."

She smiled. *Don't look at her, Jacob.*

"Yes. That sounds like my red sister. She rewards her lover for abandoning her by telling him all our secrets. She is so weak."

She slipped off her shoes and stepped closer to the water.

Jacob felt her magic as clearly as the cold night air. "It seems what you did is even harder to forgive."

She laughed quietly.

"Yes, they are still offended because I left them." The moths slid back into her hair. "Still, what did she think she'd gain by telling you about the Three Colors? It's not that I need my moths to kill you."

She stepped back, until the water closed over her naked feet. The night began to whir, as if she were turning the air itself into black water.

Jacob could barely breathe. "Give me my brother back."

"Why? He is what he was meant to be." She brushed back her shimmering hair. "Do you want to know what I think? My red sister is still too much in love with you to kill you herself. So she sent you to me."

Jacob felt how her magic made him forget everything. Will, Fox, the anger that had brought him to this garden, even himself.

Do not look at her, Jacob! He once again clutched his injured arm so the pain would remind him. The wound caused by his brother's sword. He dug his fingers into the cut until the blood ran over his hand.

The Dark Fairy stepped out of the water. She approached him slowly, like a hunter approaching her prey.

Yes. Closer. Come closer.

"Are you really so arrogant as to believe that you could come here and make demands of me?" she said, stopping right in front of him. "Do you believe that just because one Fairy couldn't resist you, we're all doomed to fall for you?"

So close.

"No, it's not that," Jacob replied.

She realized her mistake the moment he reached for her white arm. Her eyes widened and the night wove itself around his mouth like spiderwebs spun from darkness, but Jacob said her name before her magic could silence his tongue.

She raised her hands as though she could still fend off the fatal syllables. But her fingers were already transforming into twigs, and her feet were pushing roots into the soil. Her hair turned to leaves, her skin to bark, and her scream sounded like the wind rushing through the branches of a willow.

"It is such a beautiful name," Jacob said, stepping under the hanging branches. "Did you ever tell it to your lover?"

284

The willow sighed and its trunk bent over the pond, weeping over its own reflection.

"You gave my brother a skin of jade. I give you a skin of bark." Jacob buttoned his black jacket over the bloody shirt. "Sounds like a fair trade, don't you think? Now I'm going to go and look for Will. And if I find that his skin is still made of jade, I'll come back and set a fire to your roots."

Jacob couldn't tell where her voice was coming from. Maybe it was just in his head, but he heard it as clearly as if she were whispering the words into his ear. "You can't break my spell. You have to let me go, if you want your brother to get back his human skin."

"Your sister told me that you would make promises," Jacob said. "And that I shouldn't believe you."

"Bring him to me," the willow's branches whispered, "And I will prove it!"

"No." Jacob reached into the branches. "Your sister also told me to do this."

The willow sighed when he plucked a handful of the silvery-green leaves and wrapped them in his handkerchief.

"I'm supposed to take these leaves to your sister," Jacob said. "But I think I'll keep them, in case you speak the truth and I need them to trade for my brother's skin."

A shudder ran through the willow. The pond at its feet was a silver mirror.

"Please!" its leaves whispered. "The Jade Goyl must be at Kami'en's side until the wedding is over."

"Why?"

"I saw it."

"What did you see?" Jacob still felt her magic. It was all around him. But it couldn't free her, thanks to her sister's betrayal. For a moment, he caught himself lost in her pain and her fear for her lover. *Enchantment, Jacob. Leave!*

"Whatever you saw," he said stepping away from the sighing willow, "My brother won't be part of it. I'll bring him to you and you'll lift your spell." He closed his fingers around the handkerchief he had wrapped the leaves in. It felt as if he was once again touching her arm. *Go!*

"Promise!"

※ ※ ※

He could still hear her voice after the pond had long vanished behind the hedges.

"Please! He needs to be by his side!"

Even the stars seemed to whisper the words.

But his brother had not even been born in this world. Why should he be the savior of its carnelian king?

Her pain followed him nevertheless. As if the night felt it too.

47
The Chambers of Miracles

'I'll bring him to you.' How? For at least an hour, Jacob stood behind the stables that lay between the gardens and the palace, searching for an answer. In the North Wing light seeped from one of the windows into the night, flickering and muted candlelight, as the Goyl preferred it. From time to time a silhouette appeared behind the window. The King of the Goyl was searching the night for his immortal lover. Was he worried she had left him because he intended to marry another woman once the sun would rise?

'I'll bring him to you.'

How, Jacob?

A children's toy gave him the answer. A dirty ball, lying between the buckets the grooms used to water the horses. *Of course.* The Golden Ball. He himself had sold it to the Empress three years earlier. It was one of Therese's most treasured possessions. He had been with her when she had brought it to her Chambers of

287

Miracles in person. But no guard would let him back into the palace, and the Goyl had taken his waneslime.

It took him another hour to find one of the snails that produced the slime. The Empress's gardeners killed any they could find, because they bit them when they weeded the flower beds. But Jacob finally spotted two under a fountain's moss-covered ledge. They had been hunting, but their shells were already visible again, and their slime worked as soon as Jacob rubbed it under his nose. It wasn't much, but it was enough to last for one, maybe two hours.

There was only one sleepy guard by the servants' entrance. He was leaning against the wall, and Jacob snuck past him without disturbing his snooze.

The palace's kitchens and laundries were busy even at night. An overtired maid gave a start when Jacob's invisible elbow brushed her side, but soon he reached the stairs that led away from the servants and up to the nobility. He felt his skin already go numb, as he had used the slime only a few days ago, but fortunately there was no paralysis yet.

The Chambers of Miracles were situated in the South Wing, the newest part of the palace. They occupied six halls, their walls clad in lapis lazuli, as it was presumed to weaken the magical potency of the artifacts on display. The Emperors of Austry always had a penchant for magical objects. They shared that passion with most nobles of this world, and over six generations they had built a substantial collection. It was the Empress's father who had finally decreed that all objects, plants, and creatures with magical powers had to be reported to the authorities. After all, it was difficult to rule a world where a pauper could be turned into a lord by a gold tree, or where talking animals whispered seditious ideas into the ears of forest laborers.

There were no guards by the Chambers' gilded doors. The smith who'd made them had learned his trade from a Witch. Branches of Witch birch had been encased within the golden trees that spread their boughs across the doors. They impaled whoever attempted to break into the Chambers without knowing the doors' secret. The branches would shoot out like lances as soon as someone touched the handles and, like the birches in the Hungry Forest, they aimed straight for the eyes. But as a regular guest of the Chambers of Miracles, Jacob knew how to get past them unharmed.

One had to step very close to the doors to find the woodpecker the smith had hidden among the gilded leaves. The moment Jacob breathed on the golden bird, its plumage became as colorful as the feathers of a living bird, and the heavy doors swung open without a sound, as if caught by a sudden gust of wind.

Austry's Chambers of Miracles. Only the Tsars of Varangia were supposed to have an even more impressive collection.

The first hall was filled with magical animals that had fallen prey to various members of the imperial family. Their glass eyes seemed to follow Jacob as he walked past the cabinets that protected their preserved bodies from dust and moths. A Unicorn. Winged rabbits. A Brown Wolf. Swan-men. Magic crows. Talking horses. There was also a vixen, of course. Jacob couldn't bear to look at her.

The second chamber contained Witches' artifacts. The Chambers of Miracles made no distinction between the healers and the child-eaters. Knives that had separated human flesh from bone lay right next to needles that could heal a wound with a single stitch, and owl feathers that restored the powers of sight. There were also two of the brooms on which the healing Witches were able to fly as fast and as high as birds, as well as some gingerbread from the deadly houses of their child-eating sisters.

The cabinets of the third chamber displayed scales from Nymphs and Watermen. These scales enabled whoever put them under the tongue to dive very deep and stay underwater for a long time. There were also Dragon scales in all sizes and colors. Every part of this world had its own stories about surviving Dragons, but Jacob had only once seen a shadow in the sky that looked like the mummified body on display in the fourth chamber. The tail alone took up half a wall, and the gigantic teeth and claws probably made some visitors grateful that the imperial family had eradicated its kind. Jacob, though, hadn't given up hope that one day he would meet a living Dragon behind the mirror, or at least find an egg that still had a spark of life in it.

The Golden Ball he had come for lay on a cushion of black velvet in the fifth chamber. Jacob had found it in the cave of a Waterman, next to the abducted daughter of a baker. The Golden Ball was barely bigger than a chicken's egg, and the inscription attached to the black velvet sounded almost like a quote from the fairy tale he had heard so often in the other world:

ORIGINALLY THE FAVORITE TOY OF THE YOUNGEST DAUGHTER OF LEOPOLD THE BENIGN, WITH WHICH SHE FOUND HER BRIDEGROOM (LATER TO BECOME WENZELSLAUS THE SECOND) AND FREED HIM FROM THE FROG-CURSE

That was not the entire truth. The ball was a trap. Anyone who made the mistake of catching it was sucked inside, and the victims could only regain their freedom if someone polished the ball's golden surface.

Jacob broke the lock of the cabinet with his knife. For a moment, he was tempted to take another few objects to replenish his chest in Chanute's tavern, but the Empress would be angry enough about the ball. Jacob had just tucked it into his coat pocket when the gaslights in the first chamber suddenly lit up. As his body was already becoming visible again, he quickly hid behind a cabinet displaying a well-worn Seven Miles Boot. Chanute had sold the boot to the Empress's father. The matching one was, much to Therese's disdain, in the possession of Wilfred the Walrus, King of Albion.

The footsteps echoing through the rooms came closer, and finally Jacob heard someone getting to work on the cabinets. He couldn't see who it was but he didn't dare to find out, for fear that his steps would give him away. Whoever the late visitor was, he didn't stay long; the lights were extinguished, the heavy doors fell shut, and Jacob was once again alone with the treasures of Austry.

The waneslime made him sick with nausea by now, but he couldn't resist walking past the cabinets once again to check what the other nocturnal visitor had taken. One of the healing Witch needles was gone, as were two Dragon claws that supposedly protected from injury, and a piece of Waterman skin that was said to have similar properties. Jacob couldn't make any sense of it. In the end, he came up with the explanation that the objects were intended to be wedding presents to Kami'en, to make sure he wouldn't be replaced by a Goyl less interested in bargaining for peace.

The golden doors shut behind Jacob as silently as they had allowed him in. He was by now so sick that he nearly vomited. His limbs were cramping — the first sign of the paralysis caused by the slime — and the palace corridors seemed endless. Jacob followed them back to the gardens. The walls surrounding them were quite high, but he had forced Valiant to give back the Rapunzel-rope — at least one useful thing he'd brought back from the Goyl Fortress — and it once again didn't let him down.

Donnersmarck's man was still standing by the gate, as Jacob had expected, but he managed to sneak past him unnoticed. His body became more visible with every step, but it was still as vague as a ghost's. A night watchman doing his rounds dropped his lantern in fright when Jacob crossed his path.

Fortunately, he was a lot more visible by the time he reached the hotel. Every step was a struggle, and he could no longer move his fingers. He barely managed to reach the elevator.

The soldier only opened the door after Jacob had knocked so often that several guests poked their heads out of their rooms. Jacob stumbled past him to throw up in the bathroom sink.

"Where is she?" he asked when he came back into the bedroom. He had to lean against the wall to prevent his knees from giving out.

Fox was nowhere to be seen.

"I locked her in the wardrobe!" The soldier held up a hand wrapped in a bloody handkerchief like a piece of incriminating evidence. "She shifted shape and bit me!"

Jacob pushed him out into the corridor.

"Tell Donnersmarck that what I promised has been done."

The soldier's boyish face betrayed how much he longed to hear more, but he was used to following orders without asking questions. Jacob barely had the strength to close the door behind him, When he leaned against it to catch his breath, one of the Elves that were still fluttering around the room dropped her silvery dust on his shoulder. *Sweet dreams, Jacob.* But he still had to bring his brother to the sighing willow.

The vixen bared her teeth when Jacob opened the wardrobe. If she felt any relief to see him alive, she did hide it very well.

"I guess that's the Fairy's doing?" she asked, eyeing his bloodstained shirt, watching him impassively as he made a vain attempt to take it off. His fingers were as stiff as if they'd been carved from wood.

"I smell waneslime," Fox purred, licking her fur.

Jacob sat down on the bed while he still could. His knees were also getting stiff. "You need to bite me. Please. I am running out of time and I can barely move."

She looked at him for such a long time that Jacob wondered whether she'd forgotten how to speak.

"Yes, a good bite might help," she said finally. "And I admit I am very much in the mood for it. I've been longing to dig my teeth into you since you left. But first I want to hear what you're up to. And don't try any lies."

293

48
WEDDING PLANS

The first red of dawn showed above the roofs, but Therese of Austry had not slept. She had been waiting, hour after hour, for the one message she yearned to hear, but when Auberon finally led Donnersmarck into her audience chamber, she hid all the waiting and hoping behind a mask of powder.

Her adjutant delivered the news reluctantly, although it was exactly what Therese had wished for:

"It's done, Your Majesty. Kami'en has called a search for her, but Jacob swears they won't be able to find her."

Yes. Her defeat was not final yet. For the first time in months, Therese felt her old confidence.

"Tell Jacob I am glad I didn't have him shot." She touched her tightly coiffed hair. It was turning gray, but she had it dyed. Golden, like her daughter's. She would get to keep Amalie. And her throne. And her pride.

Donnersmarck hadn't moved.

"What are you waiting for? Give the orders."

He lowered his head, as was his habit whenever he disliked a command.

"What?"

"You can kill Kami'en, but his armies are still barely twenty miles away."

"They'll surrender once he is dead.."

"One of the onyx Goyl will replace him."

"And bargain for peace! The onyx just want to rule underground." She made sure Donnersmarck felt her impatience. She didn't want to think, she wanted to act. Before this opportunity passed.

"They'll want revenge, both his soldiers and his people. The Goyl worship their King. Whatever the onyx say."

Heavens, he was so obstinate. *Why had she made him her adjutant?* Because he was smarter than anyone else. And incorruptible. And because he dared to tell her the truth. That took a substantial amount of courage.

"I won't say it again: give the orders."

Auberon waved in the servant, who brought her breakfast. Good. She was hungry. For the first time in weeks.

Donnersmarck still hadn't moved.

"What about Jacob's brother?"

"What about him? He's Kami'en's bodyguard, so I expect that he will die with his King. Did you get what I asked you to bring for Amalie?"

He placed the items on the table where Therese had often sat as a child, watching her father put his seal on treaties and death warrants. Now it was she who wore the signet ring.

Yes, Donnersmarck had brought everything: a healing Witch needle, a Dragon's claw, and the skin of a Waterman. Therese stroked the pale green scales that had once covered the Waterman's hand.

"Have the claw and the skin sewn into my daughter's wedding dress," she instructed the maid waiting by the door. "And give the needle to the doctor who will be standing by the sacristy."

Donnersmarck handed her a second Dragon's claw.

"I brought this one for you, Your Majesty."

He saluted and turned to the door.

"What about Jacob? Did you have him arrested?"

Donnersmarck turned around, his face as expressionless as hers.

"The soldier I ordered to wait for him swears that he didn't return from the gardens. The palace guards haven't seen him, either."

"You're having his hotel watched, I presume?"

He returned her glance calmly.

"Of course. I will be informed as soon as he returns to his room or tries to check out."

The Empress closed her fingers around the Dragon's claw he had dropped into her hand.

"I want him found. You know what he's like. You can let him go again as soon as the wedding is over."

"It'll be too late for his brother by then."

"It is already too late. He is a Goyl. Since when do I have to explain to you what that means?"

Outside, a new day was breaking and the Dark Fairy was gone. Time for Therese of Austry to claim back what the crowned Goyl had stolen from her.

Who makes peace when you can have victory?

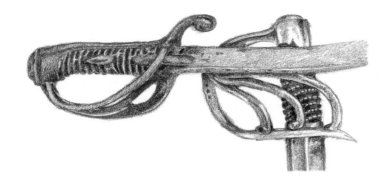

49

ONE OF THEM

Will tried not to listen. He was the King's shadow, just there to watch and to protect. But Hentzau was speaking so loudly that what he said was hard to ignore.

"You have to postpone the wedding! We expected to have the Fairy by your side. With her gone, I have to reorganize your protection and the additional troops won't get here any earlier than tomorrow."

Kami'en buttoned up his uniform. No tails for this groom. He had defeated them wearing the uniform, and he would marry one of them in it. The first Goyl to take a human wife.

"You know I never trusted her. I admitted it more than once, but this is not like her. To just vanish like that!" Hentzau's voice betrayed something Will had never heard in it before. Fear. Fear for his King.

"On the contrary. It is very much like her." Kami'en signaled Will to hand him his saber. "She hates our custom of having several wives, although I've told her often enough that it also gives her the right to have other husbands."

He fastened the saber to his silver-studded belt and stepped up to the mirror. Hentzau had had it inspected after they'd found one of them to be a device for the Empress's spies. The shimmering glass reminded Will of something. But what was it?

"She probably planned this from the start," Kami'en said. "That's why she was so eager to find the Jade Goyl before the wedding. Because she knew she wouldn't be here. And there he is —" he looked at Will, "— You see, I am completely safe. As long as we both believe in fairy tales."

Kami'en didn't believe in them. And neither did Hentzau. Will knew that by now. But the Dark Fairy believed in them, and she knew more about the world than the King of the Goyl, and far more than his jasper dog. She knew everything, because she was everything the world was made of. She was life. And death.

'Never leave Kami'en's side. Never.' She had told him that so often that Will heard the words in his dreams. *'Even if he sends you away, do not obey him.'*

She was so beautiful, more beautiful than anything he had ever seen. The Goyl didn't dare to look at her, except for their King. Kami'en looked at what he feared. He took danger as a challenge and loved to put his own strength to the test. Maybe he loved the Fairy because of that more than any other woman. After all, there was nothing more dangerous in this world than her. Hentzau, on the other hand, despised her. A shadow could see and understand all that, and Will loved to be a shadow. Watching, silent, serving and protecting. Had he ever done something else? He couldn't remember.

Hentzau had trained him hard, sometimes so hard that Will had been sure he intended to kill him. Fortunately, the jade skin healed fast, and just yesterday he had for the first time managed to strike the saber from Hentzau's hand. "What did I tell you?" the Fairy had whispered in his ear. "You were born to be a guardian angel. Maybe one day I'll grow you a pair of wings."

A guardian angel. Yes. He liked the sound of that. He had almost failed her, though, with the one who'd been hiding in her walls. He couldn't forget his face: the gray eyes, the dark hair as fine as cobwebs, and the soft skin that betrayed his frailty.

"The truth is, you don't want this peace." Kami'en's voice gave away his irritation. "You'd rather slaughter them all. Every single one of them. Men, women, children."

"Yes," Hentzau replied hoarsely "Because they want to do the same to us. My King! I urge you once again. Postpone the wedding, until the reinforcements get here."

Kami'en pulled the gloves over his fingers. Most Goyl wore gloves when amongst humans, to hide their claws. Kami'en was no exception, although he kept them almost as short as human fingernails. His gloves were tailored from the leather of a snake that dwelled deep underground, where the heat melted even Goyl skin. The Fairy had told Will about the snakes. She had described it all to him—the Avenues of the Dead, the sandstone waterfalls, the underground lakes and amethyst meadows. He couldn't wait to see all those wonders with his own eyes. The fortress...that was all he remembered. And then the train that had brought them here.

"You know exactly what they'd say." Kami'en turned away from the mirror. "'The Goyl postponed the wedding because he can no longer hide behind his lover's skirt. He only won the war because she helped him with her magic.'"

Hentzau handed him his helmet. It was adorned with lizard spikes. Feathers for the humans, spikes for the Goyl.

"You know I'm right." Kami'en turned his back on Hentzau, and Will quickly lowered his head when the King stepped up to him.

Kami'en eyed him as if he was still surprised to see him. The Jade Goyl. The other soldiers called him by another name: the Fairy-Tale Goyl. It was intended as mockery, but Will could hear their fear—of what couldn't be, although this world was filled with magic. A trace of that fear nestled in Kami'en's eyes as well, but it was outmatched by his curiosity. Kami'en's curiosity was insatiable, and it never gave in to fear. Will was glad that the Fairy had made him Kami'en's shadow. He wouldn't have wanted to serve any other king.

"I was with her when she dreamed of you, did you know that?" Will saw his own reflection in Kami'en's eyes. "How can one dream of something that has not yet happened and see a man one has never met? Or did she dream you into existence? Did she sow all that Petrified Flesh only to reap you?"

Will bowed his head. "I am here to be at your side, my King. I will live and die for you." For that's what she wanted, and there was nothing else.

Kami'en smiled.

"You heard him," he said to Hentzau. "It seems the fairy tale continues. The King of the Goyl lost his lover, but she left him a present that will keep him safe, made from breathing sacred stone."

He once again turned to Will.

302

"What were the exact orders you received from her? Do you have to stay by my side, even during the vows?"

Will felt Hentzau's milky gaze like hoarfrost on his skin.

He nodded.

"Then that's how it shall be." Kami'en turned back to Hentzau. "Have the horses readied. The King of the Goyl is taking a human wife."

50

Beauty and the Beast

A wedding. A daughter in payment, and a white dress to hide all the blood-soaked battlefields under its train. The cathedral windows were dyeing the morning light blue, green, red, and yellow. Jacob stood behind one of the garlanded columns, watching as the pews filled with guests. He was wearing the uniform of an imperial guard, whose owner he had left tied up in an alley behind the cathedral. The guards were posted all over the massive church, so nobody noticed the unfamiliar face. Their uniforms bleached flecks of white into the sea of color that was filling the nave. The Goyl's grey, in contrast, made them look as if they had all stepped out of the walls. They shuddered in the cold, humid air trapped between the church's columns. The twilight, gilded by countless dripping candles, was much more to their liking.

Jacob felt for the Golden Ball in his pocket. He still cursed the waneslime that had made him as helpless as a newborn during

305

the precious hours of the night. He was only on his feet thanks to the sharp teeth of the vixen, but now he would have to steal his brother from Kami'en's side, witnessed by hundreds of wedding guests. And hope that the willow leaves in his pocket would indeed force the Dark Fairy to send the Jade Goyl back into the fairy tales he came from.

The Jade Goyl must be at Kami'en's side until the wedding is over.

Yes. Maybe it would be better to wait for that. After the wedding, all eyes would be on the bride and groom, and the Dark Fairy would be much more willing to lift her spell. But what made her fear this wedding so much? Surely it was not the vows. What was Will supposed to protect her lover from? *What?* *'Who' is probably the right question, Jacob.*

He saw Valiant walk down the center aisle, followed by Clara and Fox. The Dwarf had shaved, and not even the imperial ministers sitting in the front row were better dressed. Fox and Clara caught many admiring glances as well. The attire Valiant had bought for them must have cost a fortune, but what did he care, as he soon would be the proud owner of a gold tree? Fox clearly hadn't shown it to him yet. She frowned when she spotted Jacob between the columns. She didn't like his plan, of course. He didn't think much of it himself, but this was his last chance. Once Will followed Kami'en and his bride to the Royal Fortress, it would be even more impossible to get him to the Dark Fairy who, thanks to his brother, would still be residing in the Empress's gardens.

Outside, the huge crowd that had been gathering in the cathedral square since dawn began to cheer. Goyl, Dwarfs, and human guests turned in the pews to stare expectantly at the garlanded portal.

It was the groom who appeared among the white lilies and roses. Kami'en halted his step, and the church filled with murmurs when Will joined him. Carnelian and jade. They did look as if they were made for each other—even Jacob caught himself in that thought.

Including Will, there were six bodyguards flanking Kami'en. And Hentzau.

The organ on the balcony struck up a wedding march, and the Goyl began to walk toward the altar. They must have sensed the hatred coming from the pews filled with the human guests, but Kami'en radiated confidence, as if the cathedral had been built by his ancestors and not by Therese of Austry's great-great-grandfather.

When Will walked past the pew where Clara was sitting, he almost brushed her shoulder with his grey sleeve. Clara's face became rigid with pain while she followed him with her eyes and, for a moment, Jacob was worried that she would get up to run after his brother. Maybe Valiant had the same thought. He reached up to her shoulder and kept his hand on her arm until Will was a few pews ahead.

Kami'en had just reached the steps in front of the altar when the Empress arrived. Her ivory dress would have done credit even to the bride. The four Dwarfs carrying her train pointedly ignored the groom, but the Empress gave him a benevolent smile before proceeding up the steps. Therese of Austry had always been a magnificent actress. She sat down in the royal enclosure to the left of the altar, surrounded by her Dwarfs.

Now there was only one guest missing.

Once upon a time, there was an Empress who had lost a war. But the Empress had a daughter...

Not even the organ could drown out the roar drifting in from outside, announcing Amalie's arrival. Whatever the crowds thought about the groom, a royal wedding was still a good occasion to cheer and dream of better times.

The bride wore her beauty like a porcelain mask, but nevertheless Jacob thought he could detect something akin to happiness on those all-too-perfect features. Amalie's eyes fixed upon Kami'en as if she herself had chosen him to be her husband, not for his crown or to make peace, nor to support her mother's political ambitions. No. Jacob would have accepted any bet that Amalie of Austry was in love with the King of the Goyl.

Kami'en awaited his bride with a smile. Whether he was in love too…his carnelian face kept the secret. Will was still right by his side.

'The Jade Goyl must be at Kami'en's side until the wedding is over.'

Jacob scanned the crowds, but he could detect nothing to justify the Dark Fairy's worries. He just wanted it to be over. He had decided to catch Will when the couple was waiting for their coach, or when they stepped out of the cathedral. Yes, maybe already then. *Walk faster!* He was tempted to call out to the bride. *Get it over with.* But her mother's highest-ranking general was leading the bride to the altar, and he was in no rush.

Four additional guards had positioned themselves in front of the enclosure from which the Empress was watching, surrounded by her Dwarfs. Donnersmarck had joined her. He was whispering something into the Empress's ear. They both looked up at the balcony, but Jacob still didn't realize what was going on. Blind and dumb, he would tell himself later. He already imagined himself on his way back into the palace gardens with Will. And like many others, he was foolish enough to believe that even Therese of Austry was first a mother and then an Empress.

The first shot rang out when Amalie was barely a dozen steps down the aisle. It came from a sniper hidden next to the organ on the balcony and was obviously aimed at Kami'en, but Will pushed the King aside in time. The second shot missed Will's head by an inch. The third bullet hit Hentzau in the chest. He fell to his knees.

The Dark Fairy was trapped in a skin of willow bark and sighed with helpless rage in the Palace gardens.

Well done, Jacob. Therese of Austry had used him like a trained dog. Therese and Donnersmarck. *No, Jacob, he tried to warn you. In his very own way.*

The Empress had obviously kept her assassination plans not only from her daughter. Her ministers were desperately ducking behind the thin wood paneling of their pews. Amalie stood in the aisle and stared at her mother, her perfect face contorted by horror and disbelief. The general who had led her into the church was trying to pull her away with him, but they were swept along by the screaming guests as they stumbled out of the pews. They hadn't realized yet that there was nowhere to go. The great doors had been bolted. Clearly the Empress was hoping to rid herself of a few unwanted subjects as well, along with her future son-in-law.

Jacob tried desperately to spot Fox and Clara in the panicked crowd. He reminded himself that Fox was usually far better at keeping herself safe than he himself, and that neither Clara nor Valiant could wish for better protection, but he was nevertheless sick with worry when his eyes couldn't find her. Will was still shielding Kami'en. The bodyguards had formed a wall of gray uniforms around their King, while the other Goyl were trying to fight their way through the crowds to join them. Not many of them reached the altar steps. The imperials shot them down like farmers shooting rabbits.

Jacob was luckier. He managed to reach the steps unharmed. He had to help Will, whether his brother still knew him or not. One of the court Dwarfs jumped him on the stairs. Jacob drove his elbow into the bearded face just to slip in a puddle of blood when he took another step. It was everywhere, on silken dresses and marble tiles, but the Goyl stood their ground amid all the screaming and shooting. They supposedly prepared their skin for battle by eating a plant they bred especially for that purpose. Maybe they'd been wise enough to do the same for their King's wedding, but there were at least ten imperial guards for every Goyl. Will and Kami'en still appeared to be unharmed though, and even Hentzau was back on his feet.

Jacob closed his fingers around the Golden Ball, but it was impossible to get a clear throw. Will was surrounded by imperials, and Jacob could barely lift his arm without someone stumbling into him. Another Goyl fell. Hentzau was next. It took three bullets to bring him once again to his knees, and then Will was the last guard shielding the King. Kami'en was fighting off three imperials when another two attacked him from the side. Will killed them both, though one of them rammed his saber deep into his shoulder. The Fairy had been right. The Jade Goyl, her lover's shield. *Too bad Will was also his brother.*

Will and Kami'en were fighting back-to-back by now, surrounded by white uniforms. Soon not even their Goyl skins would save them.

Do something, Jacob. Anything!

But what? He had no ammunition left. For a moment, he caught a glimpse of red fur, and Valiant standing protectively in front of a crouched figure. Right next to them, a Goyl was stabbed down by four imperials. And Therese of Austry remained sitting among her Dwarfs, waiting for the death of the King who had defeated her.

Donnersmarck was still standing right next to her.

For a moment, their eyes met across men fighting and dying.

I warned you, his gaze said.

He did.

Will was fighting four imperials at once by now. Blood was running down his face. Pale Goyl blood. He wouldn't last much longer.

Jacob pushed his bloodstained hand into his pocket. One of the Empress's ministers stumbled against him, a gaping wound on his forehead, when he pulled out the handkerchief, and the dry willow leaves scattered over the many fallen bodies. Most of them were Goyl. Jacob gathered the leaves from the blood-soaked chests and limbs. Goyl and humans. *Whose side are you on, Jacob?* But he could no longer think of sides, just of his brother, and of Fox. And Clara. Even the Dwarf came to his mind.

He yelled the name of the Dark Fairy through the cathedral's nave. It drowned in the ocean of screams, shots, and moans that raged around him, but she did hear him nevertheless, far away, a willow's roots tying her to the wet soil of the Empress's garden.

The bark was still peeling from her arms when she appeared in front of the altar steps, her long hair covered in willow leaves. She lifted her six fingered hands, and glass tendrils grew up around Will and her lover, deflecting sword blades and bullets as if they were children's toys. Jacob saw his brother collapse, his eyes on

311

the Fairy, and Kami'en catching him in his arms. The Dark One, however, began to grow like a flame fanned by the wind, and the moths swarmed from her hair, thousands of them, covering the flesh of humans and Dwarfs wherever they could find it.

Therese tried to flee, her Dwarfs clearing a path for her, but they collapsed under the onslaught of the moths, as did her guards, and finally black wings covered the Empress's skin as well.

Human skin. Fox was hopefully wearing her fur, but where was Clara?

Jacob jumped down the altar steps and leapt over the dead and the wounded. His eyes found the vixen. Fox was standing in the center aisle, shielding two slumped bodies, desperately snapping the moths off their skin.

Jacob dropped to his knees next to her and searched in his pocket for more of the leaves, but he couldn't find them. Valiant was still moving, but Clara was as pale as death. And the Fairy was still blazing.

"Call them back!" he yelled at her, but without the leaves she didn't even hear him.

White, red, black. Jacob brushed the moths off Clara's skin and unbuttoned his white guardsman's tunic. There was enough blood on it, but where could he get something black? The moths were attacking him when he put his jacket over Clara. Fluttering wings and stings that pierced his skin like splinters. They sowed a numbness that tasted of death. Jacob barely had the strength to pull a black cravat from a dead man's neck. He wrapped it around Clara's arm. Then he collapsed next to the Dwarf.

"Fox!" He barely managed to utter her name.

She swiped the moths from his face, but they were too many. He was so glad the fur protected her from them. So glad.

312

"White…red…black," he muttered, but of course she didn't understand what he meant. The leaves…he felt around the floor for them, around the cold tiles, wet with blood, but his fingers were made from lead.

"Enough!!"

Kami'en's voice made the moths whirl up as if the wind had come to their victims' aid.

Even the venom in Jacob's veins seemed to dissolve, leaving only a deep weariness behind. The Dark Fairy shrank, like a fire slowly burning down, until she once again resembled a mortal woman. One could still feel her magic though, like a scent filling the vast nave, dark and heavy, tasting of anger and love. And sadness.

Valiant rolled over with a groan, but Clara still wasn't moving. She only opened her eyes when Jacob leaned over her. *Will is still one of them.* Jacob didn't have to say it. Clara's gaze found Will while she pulled herself up holding onto one of the pews.

He and Kami'en were back on their feet. The Fairy's magic was already healing their wounds, and the glass tendrils turned to water as soon as Kami'en took a step toward them. It washed the blood off the altar steps, while the moths landed on the fallen Goyl.

The Dark Fairy walked up the steps to meet her lover while many of his dead Goyl began to stir under the wings of her moths. She wiped the pale blood off both his face and Will's. Jacob saw her say something to his brother. Maybe she thanked him for her lover's life. One of Kami'en's surviving soldiers dragged the Empress to her feet. Auberon attacked him, but the moths' venom still weakened the Dwarf and the Goyl just pushed him aside, dragging Therese towards Kami'en. Some of the other Goyl were driving the survivors from the pews. Jacob spotted one of

313

the willow leaves between the dead but, before he could grab it, a ruby Goyl had his arm around his throat.

"Hide, Fox!" Jacob managed to gasp, but of course she ignored him and followed the Goyl as he pushed both Jacob and Clara toward the altar steps.

Another grabbed Valiant, who tried to hide between the corpses, but they all froze when a slender figure rose in the last pew.

White silk speckled with blood, and a face that, despite her fear, still looked like a mask. Amalie stepped unsteadily into the central aisle. Her veil was as torn as her dress. She gathered it up to climb over the body of the general who had led her into the church and made her way toward the altar like a sleepwalker, followed by her long, white train, heavy and wet with blood.

Kami'en watched her as if he were weighing whether to kill her himself or to leave that pleasure to the Dark Fairy. The rage of the Goyl. In their King, it had turned to cold fire.

"Get me a priest," he ordered Will. "Let's hope one of them is still alive."

Therese looked at him incredulously. She could barely stand, but Auberon, still shaken himself, supported her.

"Why the surprise?" Kami'en stepped toward her, his bloody saber in his hand. "You tried to have me killed. Did you hope that would also erase all the promises you and your daughter made?"

"No!" Amalie was standing at the bottom of the stairs. She had to clear her throat, and when she spoke again her voice was shaking, but there was no doubt that she meant what she said. "No, I will keep my promise to you. Despite what my mother did."

Therese stared at her daughter.

"Well. I will…" she straightening her back, as if that would make Kami'en forget that she was his prisoner, "…I will give my permission. As long as he — " she kept her eyes on her daughter, " —keeps his word, of course. Peace." She finally looked at Kami'en. "Peace is still the price for my daughter's — "

He silenced her with a gesture that came very close to slapping her face.

"Peace?" he repeated, his eyes on the Goyl whom the moths had not brought back to life. "I fear that's one of today's fatalities. I think I've actually forgotten what that word means. But — " he turned to Amalie, " —as it is our wedding, I will for now resist the temptation to kill your mother. Feel free to consider that either a gift or a punishment."

Will had found a priest, a scrawny old man who rushed so hastily to the groom's side that he stumbled over the corpses. The Dark Fairy's face was whiter than the bride's dress when Amalie walked up the steps to join Kami'en in front of the altar.

And so it happened that the King of the Goyl exchanged wedding vows with the daughter of Therese of Austry, in a church that was filled with death. And the sadness of his lover.

51

HOSTAGES

When Amalie of Austry stepped out of the cathedral, her wedding dress was covered in flowers. The Dark Fairy had turned the bloodstains into roses: white blossoms for the Goyl blood, red roses for the blood of men. On Kami'en's uniform, hiding the cuts and stains, rubies and moonstone spread so lushly that the waiting crowd forgot their hatred and greeted him and the bride with equally enthusiastic cheers. Some of the onlookers wondered why so few of the wedding guests followed the happy couple; a few even noticed the fear on the faces of those who did, but the street noise had drowned out the shots and screams from the cathedral. The dead were silent, and the King of the Goyl helped his human bride into the golden carriage that had taken many royal couples before them back to the palace.

The parade of coaches and carriages waiting in front of the cathedral was endless. The Dark Fairy remained on top of the stairs while the Goyl escorted the surviving wedding guests down the steps. Not one of them tried to escape. They all felt the Fairy's gaze following them from above, and none of the imperial soldiers managing the crowds realized that the Goyl were loading the waiting carriages with hostages right in front of their eyes, and that one of them was their Empress.

Therese almost stumbled when Donnersmarck helped her into the carriage. He'd survived the carnage, along with Auberon and two other Dwarfs. Auberon was known for his fearlessness. The Empress liked to tell visitors about the countless Watermen and Ogres he had killed, but his fighting skills hadn't protected him from the Fairies' moths. His bearded face was so swollen from their stings that he could barely see, and needed Donnersmarck's help to follow the Empress into the coach. Jacob knew only too well what a state the Dwarf was in. His skin was as numb from the stings as if he had stolen it from a dead man. Clara wasn't any better, and Valiant tripped over his own feet as they descended the cathedral steps. Jacob begged Fox with his eyes to steal away when the Goyl waved him into one of the coaches, but the vixen jumped in with Clara before the Goyl even noticed her. *Hostages...* Jacob was sure that the Goyl only kept them alive because they could use them as human shields for Kami'en, who had survived the Empress's assassination attempt thanks to his Fairy lover, to the Jade Goyl, *and thanks to you, Jacob.* It had taken two brothers to save the King of the Goyl. Jacob didn't dare to imagine how Kami'en would take revenge for Therese's betrayal, for it would be all on him. Every single death. He knew he would have done it again for his brother, for Fox and Clara. But that didn't make it easier to accept.

Will joined Kami'en in the golden carriage after he had one more time gazed up the stairs, as if to make sure he was doing what the Dark Fairy wanted him to do. Yes, he was still alive, and though it felt very strange to have ended up fighting on the Goyl's side, Jacob regretted only one thing: that he had lost the willow leaves and, with them, any hope of protecting them all from the Fairy, not to speak of breaking the spell she had cast on his brother.

The Dark Fairy had her eyes on the golden carriage when she finally walked down the cathedral stairs. She had won and lost, and Jacob was surprised to once again feel compassion for her. As hard as she tried, she couldn't hide the love she felt for Kami'en. In that, she proved to be as helpless as a mortal woman, like her red sister. All those thousands of men who had died in despair loving a Fairy...they obviously couldn't make them immune against the pain they so easily inflicted themselves.

The Fairy exchanged a glance with Jacob before she climbed into her coach. *I remember*, it said. *The bark and the leaves. And my sister's betrayal. Beware, Jacob Reckless.* He had made many enemies in these past few days: the Empress, the Goyl, and now the darkest of all Fairies. And Will still wore a skin of jade.

When the coaches finally set off, each coachman had been joined by a Goyl. The imperial guards probably assumed that to be a gesture to demonstrate the union of men and Goyl, but as soon as the carriages reached one of the bridges leading out of the city, the Goyl pushed the coachmen off their boxes. The few guards escorting the wedding couple tried to stop the carriages, but the Dark Fairy unleashed her moths once again, the Goyl steered the coaches across the bridge Amalie's ancestors had built, and soon all of them had disappeared into the streets on the other side of the river.

A dozen carriages, forty soldiers, a Fairy protecting her lover, a princess who had said *I do* amongst corpses, and a king who had trusted his enemy, only to be betrayed by her...

The sky was covered with dark clouds when the convoy passed through a gate, behind which a group of plain buildings surrounded the courtyard of an abandoned munitions factory. The river had flooded the area years earlier, leaving the buildings filled with water and foul-smelling mud. Since then, the factory had been deserted until it came into use again during the last cholera epidemic, when many of the infected had been brought to the deserted buildings. Vena's citizens had avoided the site since then, but the Goyl didn't worry about human diseases. They were immune to most of them.

"What are they going to do with us?" Clara whispered as the carriages came to a halt between the redbrick walls.

Valiant clambered onto the coach seat and peered out into the deserted yard. "Nothing pleasant, to be sure," he muttered. "But I think I know why we came here."

Will was the first to climb out of the golden carriage. He eyed the empty buildings while Kami'en followed with Amalie. The Goyl weren't too gentle with their hostages when they gathered them in the yard, which was not surprising after the events at the cathedral. They shoved the Empress back when she tried to get to her daughter. Donnersmarck drew her to his side while his eyes searched for Jacob. He had heard him call the Fairy, Jacob saw it in his face. He'd made another enemy, and this one hurt...

The Dark Fairy stood in the middle of the yard, her moths surrounding her like smoke. Some of them swarmed out toward

320

the empty buildings. Their mistress wouldn't allow Kami'en to walk into another ambush.

The Goyl had gathered around their king. Forty soldiers who had all narrowly escaped death and were now isolated in the heart of their enemies' territory. *What now?* their faces asked. They struggled to hide their fear under their helpless rage. Kami'en waved one of them to his side. He had the moonstone skin of the Goyl's spies. Kami'en didn't show any sign of fear. If he was afraid, he managed to hide it better than his soldiers.

"What did you mean when you said you may know why we're here?" Jacob whispered to Valiant when the moonstone vanished between the factory buildings.

"Three years ago," Valiant whispered back, "One of our most dimwitted ministers built two tunnels from Terpevas to Vena. The idiot didn't believe there was a future in trains. One of the tunnels was supposed to bring supplies to this factory. There are rumors that the Goyl connected the tunnel with their western fortress, and that their spies like to use it."

A tunnel. *Back underground, Jacob.* If the Goyl didn't decide to escape without their hostages and to just shoot them here. He bent down to the vixen. He had to convince her to run. She was the only one who might get away, but before he could talk to her one of the Goyl pulled him roughly out of the crowd. Jasper and amethyst. *Nesser.* Jacob thought he felt the scorpions once again under his shirt. Fox bared her teeth and wanted to come to his aid, but Nesser drew her pistol. When Clara stepped protectively in front of the vixen, the She-Goyl raised her hand to slap her, but something made her remember her orders and she aimed the pistol at Jacob.

321

"Get going!" she snapped, pushing him away from the others. "Hentzau's more dead than alive! Why are you still breathing?"

She shoved him across the courtyard past Kami'en, who had gathered his surviving officers around him. Will stood right next to the King. His shadow. Jacob lowered his head while he walked past him. Will didn't remember his brother, but he surely remembered the man he had fought at the Empress's palace. The Goyl did not have much time. By now, someone had surely found the dead in the cathedral.

The Dark Fairy was waiting at the bottom of a steep flight of steps leading down to the river. To her left, a landing pier reached out into the water. The refuse of the city covered it like a grimy skin, but the Fairy was looking at the shallow waves as if she could see the lilies among which she had been born.

"Leave me alone with him, Nesser," she said.

The She-Goyl hesitated, but one frown from the Fairy and she headed for the stairs.

The Dark Fairy touched her arm. Her white skin was still spotted with a few remnants of bark. "You gambled everything, and you lost."

"My brother is the one who lost." How was she going to kill him? With her moths? With another curse?

She looked up at Will. He was still standing by Kami'en's side. They reminded Jacob of the friends Will had loved as a child, often older, fiercely admired, and always loved with a faithfulness that easily compared to the devotion it required to serve a king. Once upon a time Will had even treated his older brother like that. *When he still remembered you, Jacob.*

"Look at him. Your brother is everything I hoped for." The Dark Fairy smiled. "All that Petrified Flesh, sown just for him, and it was all worth it."

She brushed her finger over a streak of bark marking her white skin until it disappeared.

"I will give him back to you," she said. "Under one condition: that you take him away from here, far, far away. So far that I won't be able to find him. For if I do, I'll kill him."

Jacob couldn't believe what he'd heard. He was dreaming. Yes, he must be. Some kind of fevered hallucination. He was probably still lying in the cathedral, her moths' venom pumping in his veins.

"Why?" *Why are you asking her, Jacob?*

The Fairy ignored his question anyway.

"Take him to the building by the gate. But hurry." She turned to the water. "And watch out for Kami'en. This day taught him to believe in fairy tales."

❅ ❅ ❅

She's trying to fool you. That was the only thought on Jacob's mind when he once again stood between the wedding coaches. His heart believed her, though; he couldn't say why, but it did. He longed to share the good news with Fox and Clara, but they were nowhere to be seen. Two Goyl were standing guard in front of a building on his left. They'd probably locked all the hostages in there. If only Fox had run. Jacob cursed the vixen's stubbornness while he crossed the yard. The Fairy had promised him his brother back, but she hadn't mentioned the others.

He kept his head low while he was walking past the Goyl. Certainly none of them were aware that they owed their escape to him, but fortunately they were busy receiving instructions

323

from their King or looking after their wounded. Kami'en was still discussing the situation with his officers. The moonstone was not back yet. Amalie approached her husband and tried to talk to him, until finally he grabbed her arm and pulled her away from his men. Will followed them with his eyes, but he stayed with the other Goyl.

Now, Jacob.

Will's hand went for his saber as soon as he saw him appear from between the carriages. Whatever the Dark Fairy had promised—his brother was still under her spell. Will eyed him like a stranger, but remembered him as the Fairy's enemy, the man he had chased through the Empress's palace.

He pushed a Goyl out of his way and began to run. *Time to play 'Catch and Seek,' Will.* As they had done so often as children, chasing each other through the apartment to fill the vast silent rooms with laughter and chase away their mother's sadness.

Will's wounds didn't seem to impede him. *Let him come closer, Jacob, just as you used to do when you were kids. Run.* Back behind the carriages, past the barracks where they'd locked up the hostages. The next building was the one closest to the gate. Jacob pushed open the rotten door. A dark hallway with boarded-up windows. The patches of light on the grimy floor looked like puddles of milk. The first room was still filled with rusty beds for the cholera victims. Jacob hid behind the open door. *Once upon a time...*

Will spun around the moment Jacob slammed the door shut behind him. For a moment, his face showed the same surprise Jacob had seen there so often, as when he jumped out from behind a tree in the park, despite the jade. He still didn't recognize him, but he did catch the Golden Ball. Hands have their own memory. *Will, catch!* The ball swallowed him faster than Jacob could blink and, outside, Kami'en looked in vain for the Jade Goyl who had stepped out of a fairy tale to save his life.

Jacob picked up the ball and sat on one of the beds. His reflection stared back at him from the gold, distorted, as he had seen it so often in his father's mirror.

"I knew the girl who once played with that golden toy." The Fairy appeared so suddenly in the door that Jacob almost dropped the ball. "She caught not only her husband with it, but also her older sister. She kept her as her prisoner for ten years."

Her dress brushed over the dusty floor when she walked towards Jacob. It was cut after the human fashion. Her sisters despised her for dressing like a mortal.

"I thought you might need my help to convince your brother to go with you. My magic doesn't let go easily, but the ball was surely the right tool to bring." She looked at the empty beds. "Once you let him out, my spell will wear off and he will remember. The jade will need more convincing."

She reached out for the ball. Jacob hesitated, but then he dropped it into her hands.

"Such a pity. Your brother is so beautiful in his skin of jade."

She lifted the ball to her lips and breathed on the gleaming surface until the gold misted over. Then she handed the ball back to Jacob.

"What?" She smiled when she noticed his doubtful look. "You mistrust the wrong Fairy."

She came so close that Jacob could feel her breath on his face. "Did my sister tell you that any man who speaks my name speaks his own death sentence? It won't be executed immediately — immortals don't rush these things, you may have a year — but you will die, for no one is allowed to know my name. She knows that very well. She even left the henchman on your chest."

Jacob felt a piercing pain when she pressed her hand against his shirt. Blood seeped through the fabric, and when she pushed it open he saw that the moth above his heart had come to life. It felt as if it were feeding on his heart but, when the Fairy touched its black wings, the fluttering insect turned once again into a mere imprint on his chest, a winged shadow as pale red as her lover's skin.

The Dark One stepped back.

"I am sorry," she said. "I despise playing the accomplice for my Red Sister. But she left me no choice, and she knew it."

She looked at the beds where death had harvested countless lives, as if she tried to understand how it felt to be mortal.

"Release your brother as soon as the ball's gold clears again," she said. "There's a carriage waiting by the gate. And remember what I told you. Take him as far away from me as you can."

Then she turned and walked away, leaving Jacob alone with the Golden Ball in his hands and her sister's death sentence written over his heart.

52

HAPPILY EVER AFTER

The tower and the scorched walls, the fresh wolf tracks — it felt as if they'd only just left. But the Fairy's carriage drew dark lines through freshly fallen snow when Jacob reined in the horses. He was not alone. Fox had been waiting in the carriage, along with Clara and Valiant, when he had stepped out of the factory's gates. The Dark Fairy had returned everything he loved to him, maybe to make up for the mark on his chest. *'Why did she let you go?'* That was all Fox had asked when he had climbed onto the coachman's bench. Jacob had evaded the answer by telling them all that they'd better leave before the Fairy changed her mind. Fox had watched him ever since. She had followed the coach most of the time as the vixen, showing up, casting him a glance, and disappearing again. *'Why did she let you go?'* Fox knew she wouldn't like the answer.

327

The massacre at the wedding was blamed on the Goyl. Of course. They had broken the truce and kidnapped the Empress and her daughter; that was the only story they had heard on their way back.

Jacob climbed off the coach. The vixen was already standing between the ruin's walls licking the snow from her paws. She lifted her head when he took the Golden Ball from his pocket. It hadn't escaped her how often he looked at it, and Jacob was sure that she knew whom he kept prisoner inside. The golden surface was almost clear by now, but he still hadn't told the others. How could he believe the Dark Fairy after her red sister had sentenced him to death while kissing him?

In the two days it had taken them to get back to the ruin, Clara had barely spoken a word, although Valiant had tried very hard to cheer her up. At times, Jacob had been so worried she'd jump out of the carriage to run back to the deserted factory that he had almost told her about the Fairy's promise, but to make her hope in vain felt even more cruel than letting her believe they had left his brother behind.

Clara walked slowly over to the tower and looked up to the room where the mirror was waiting. Her breath clung to her mouth in white clouds, and she was shivering in the dress Valiant had bought her for the wedding. The blue silk was torn and dirty, and no Fairy had turned the blood stains into flowers.

"A ruin?" Valiant jumped out of the carriage and eyed the scorched walls with dismay. "What is this?" he snapped at Jacob. "Where's my tree?"

His angry voice made a few shivering Heinzels drop the acorns they had been digging out of the snow.

"Fox, show him the tree," Jacob said.

328

She gave him a mischievous glance before she led Valiant toward the overgrown castle gardens. He marched after her so eagerly that he nearly fell over his own boots.

Clara was still lost in her own thoughts. "You want me to go back, don't you?" she asked when Jacob joined her. "'Forget Will, Clara. The way he forgot you...'"

Jacob took her hand and closed her fingers around the Golden Ball. The surface shimmered as if he had plucked it from the sun.

"Polish it," he said. "Until you can see yourself in the surface as clearly as in a mirror."

Then he left her alone. He wanted Will to see her face first. *If he remembers her, Jacob. If this Fairy didn't deceive you as well.* He stepped into the tower, his heart drowning in both fear and hope. Above him, the rope leading up to the mirror was silvery with elven dust. He had found it in his father's study. *Where else?* He felt the imprint of the moth like a brand under his shirt. The skin over his heart was still sore. Would he have tried to save Will had he known about the price? Maybe.

He heard Clara cry out, and then Will spoke her name. His brother's voice hadn't sounded so soft in a long time. Jacob heard them whisper. And laugh.

He leaned against the wall, black with soot, damp with the cold caught between its stones. The Dark Fairy had kept her promise; he knew it even before he pushed through the ivy. Will was holding Clara in his arms. The jade was gone and, when his brother's eyes looked at him, his eyes were blue.

Gone, the rage and the anger. Will let go of Clara, his face soft with love, as it always had been when Jacob had come back to see him. His steps, though, were still hesitant with disbelief when he walked up to him, to hug him as fiercely as he did when they were children.

"I thought you were dead." He stepped back and looked at Jacob as if to make sure he was truly unharmed. Then he looked at his own hands and, for a moment, Jacob saw a strange yearning on his brother's face.

"You were right," Clara said, stepping to Will's side. "Your brother always finds a way." Her eyes were bright with gratitude, but Jacob could see that she was still afraid that Will had changed.

He was inspecting his sleeve where a saber had cut the grey fabric. Did he recognize the uniform as Goyl? And the pale stains as his own blood? Jacob couldn't tell. There was something in Will's face, as if the jade had glazed his soft features with a firmness that was new.

Once upon a time, there was a boy who set out to learn the meaning of fear.

"Look at this! I'm richer than the Empress! What am I saying? Richer than Wilfred the Walrus and the Crookback throwing all their treasures on one pile!"

Gilded hair, gilded shoulders—even Jacob had trouble recognizing Valiant. The tree had covered the Dwarf more densely with gold than it had showered Jacob with its foul-smelling pollen.

The Dwarf pranced past Will without even noticing him.

"I was sure you would try to trick me!" he said, looking up at Jacob. "But for this I'd take you back to the Goyl fortress right away. Do you think it'll harm the tree if I dig it up?"

The vixen appeared from the ruin's walls, a few flakes of gold shimmering in her fur. She stopped dead when she saw Will. *What do you say, Fox? Does he still smell like a Goyl?*

Will picked up a small clump of gold that the Dwarf had brushed from his hair. Valiant still hadn't noticed him.

"No!" the Dwarf proclaimed. "No, I'll take the risk! You may shake all the gold out of it if I leave it here!"

He nearly stumbled over Fox when he ran off again, while Will was still just standing there, wiping the snow from the tiny nugget in his hand, as golden as his eyes had been.

Take him away from here. Far, far away.

Clara cast Jacob a worried look.

"Let's go home, Will," she said.

His brother looked at the tower. And then at the coach. Kami'en's coat of arms was on the door. The black moth on carnelian red.

"Clara's right. Let's go."

Jacob put his hand on Will's shoulder. No, that wasn't gold in his eyes. Just the sunlight.

Fox followed them to the tower, but she didn't go in. She rarely did. She shifted shape to embrace Clara and Will and kissed them both farewell. Then she stepped back, her eyes on Jacob. He saw the usual worry in them. *How long will you stay this time? Will you one day decide not to come back?*

"It won't be long," he said while Clara pulled Will through the ivy. "I promise. Make sure the Dwarf collects his gold before the ravens get here."

Enchanted gold attracted them in swarms, and even one Gold-Raven could drive you insane with its cawing.

331

"How am I supposed to do that?" Fox replied. "Not even a pack of Brown Wolves would get that Dwarf away from his gold."

She made Jacob smile. But her face remained serious.

"You saved him," she said. "You really did."

"Did I?"

She knew what he meant. She had seen Will at the wedding. And at Kami'en's side. *'Why? He is what he was meant to be,'* the Dark Fairy whispered in Jacob's head.

"Go," Fox said. "Make sure they really leave. I'll admit I am quite tired of watching them both."

Then she turned to find Valiant.

❀ ❀ ❀

In the tower room, a dead Heinzel was lying between the acorn shells. The Stilt liked to kill them. Jacob pushed the tiny body under a few leaves. Will and Clara had seen enough death.

The mirror caught them all in its glass. His brother gazed at himself as though he were seeing a stranger. Clara stepped to his side and reached for his hand, but Will turned away from her when he saw Jacob retreating.

"You're not coming with us?"

"No. I have to find something."

"Of course." Will smiled. "And it's always something you can't find on the other side...right?"

Jacob was not sure whether his brother was talking about himself or Jacob. He seemed far away. With the Fairy. Or with the King whose jade shadow he had been. *The things we find behind mirrors...*

"Well, don't stay too long," he finally said. "Promise?"

That's how he had always parted from him as a boy. And Jacob had always answered with *yes*, breaking the promise more

332

often than he had kept it. He was sure Will remembered that as well as the words.

"I promise," he answered. *Just go. Go Will!* he almost added. *'Take him away from here. Far, far away. So far that I won't be able to find him. For if I do, I will kill him.'*

Will still looked at him when he reached for Clara's hand and pressed his fingers onto the glass.

And then they were both gone.

❊ ❊ ❊

Fox had freed the coach horses of their harnesses and watched them graze among the ruin's walls. Jacob was surprised she still wore her human skin. Maybe she kept it because the vixen didn't like the snow, though the gown she was still wearing from the wedding could not warm her as well as the fur.

"They're gone?" she asked when Jacob stepped to her side.

"Yes."

"So?"

"So what?"

"Don't play the fool. Why did she let him go? Him, all of us…"

"Her red sister told me a secret of hers."

Jacob walked over to the horses. He would give one to Chanute, as compensation for the packhorse he'd lost.

"What secret?" She sensed that something was wrong. Of course. She knew him too well.

"I can't tell you. I had to promise." Another lie. To protect her. The truth would make her sick with worry, and the vixen would hate the Fairies even more, which meant she'd try to take revenge on them. No. She could never know.

Jacob looked at the sky. It had begun to snow again. "We should head south. What do you think? Find the Hourglass?"

"Maybe." She couldn't help but smile. Back to the old times. Just her and him. Hunting treasure. Without a worry in the world. *Well...*

Fox looked toward the stables. The garden was right behind them, overgrown, still filled with healing herbs, but none would help him.

"That Dwarf is still collecting his gold. Although I warned him of the ravens."

Jacob put his arm around her shoulder. "Another reason to leave. Let them get him."

'You may have a year.' A lot could be done in a year. In this world, there was a cure for everything.

They had only to find it.

335

CORNELIA FUNKE

RECKLESS

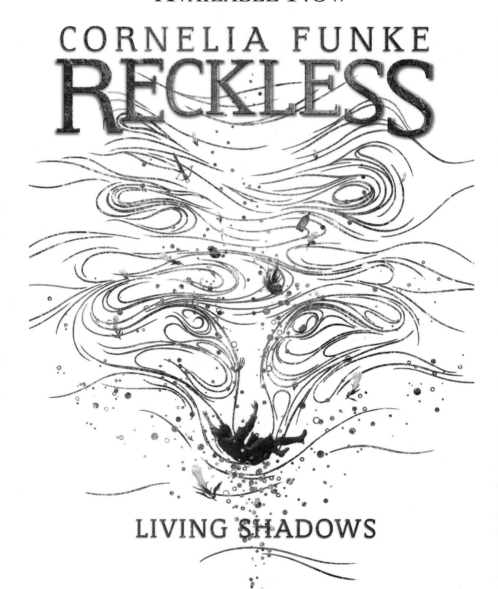

LIVING SHADOWS

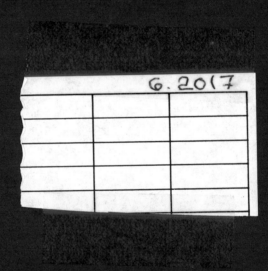

6.2017